EXPERIMENT AT PROTO

———

Within hours of joining the research unit of Proto (Animal Nutrition) Ltd, Mark Barrow is feeling slightly uneasy. The unit's object is to develop ways of communicating with apes: a perfectly respectable form of research. Its methods, however, appear somewhat quirky and have not been up to preventing at least one grave accident when an ape called Otto nearly killed Mark's predecessor, Ryman.

There are also other reasons for Mark's unease in his new job. His marriage is already under strain, and his wife Biddy doesn't take to Proto's self-contained social life; a situation not likely to be remedied by the sensuous Charlotte Bloom, with whom Mark collaborates when he continues Ryman's risky work with Otto.

But working with chimps is fascinating, and Dr Hoover, the unit's dedicated chief, is impressive. By the time the reasons for Mark's anxiety break on him in their full force, he has become too deeply involved to escape. A series of dramatic events, during which the students of animal behaviour have themselves provided some startling examples of it, comes to a terrifying climax, and he is at its centre.

Philip Oakes

EXPERIMENT AT PROTO

A Novel

ANDRE DEUTSCH

First published 1973 by
André Deutsch Limited
105 Great Russell Street London WC1

Copyright © 1973 by Philip Oakes

Printed in Great Britain by
Ebenezer Baylis and Son Ltd
The Trinity Press, Worcester, and London

ISBN 0 233 96435 5

At the Primate Research Centre in Georgia a chimpanzee was given a heap of photographs of apes and human beings, which it sorted into two piles, humans and apes.

The only thing was that it invariably put its own picture on the pile with the humans.

NEWS ITEM

Post coitum omne animal triste

ANON

ONE

'I'm sorry about the green coats,' said Dr Francis Hoover. 'They may look institutional, but they do have a function. For one thing they help you to spot members of staff. More to the point, they're a blessing when a chimp pees on you.'

'I imagine so.' Mark Barrow dug into the pockets of his overall, and wondered if he dared light a cigarette. He decided not. As a newcomer to the ranks of Proto (Animal Nutrition) Ltd, he was not yet sure of his ground.

'Does it happen often?' he asked. 'Chimps peeing on you?'

'Often enough. The minute they get excited . . .' Dr Hoover raised a warning finger. 'Always wear old clothes to the lab. You never know what you're likely to take home with you.'

A fragrant prospect, thought Mark; home is the hunter, reeking of ape's urine. It was not the conversation he had imagined three months ago when Biddy had passed the letter across the breakfast table. On that distant day the sentences had arranged themselves into a pardon, a time tunnel to speed them out of loathsome Los Angeles and home to England. They had clasped hands across the grapefruit, while blue jays braved the smog beyond the patio to drill more holes in the scabby palm trees fronting the apartment.

'The escape hatch,' he had told her, his fingers stroking the embossed letter heading. 'A job with Proto.'

'What's Proto?'

'They make animal foods. But I won't be doing that.'

She had gazed at him trustingly. 'Of course not, darling. What will you be doing?'

'Research. They have this special unit. I've been asked to join it.'

'What are they offering?'

'Three thousand a year, a company house, and air passage home.'

'Darling!' She had thrown the toast in the air, and kissed him as the crumbs rained down like wedding rice.

Possibly, thought Mark, he had been over-optimistic. But,

five hours off the plane with sleep gritting his eyes, the prospect was still pleasing. America the golden had served him basely. At the age of thirty-four – and still a promising young zoologist, he told himself – he had been forced to earn his living by conducting pregnancy tests. American females were amazingly fecund, he discovered, but he did not find the fact all-engrossing.

'You like chimpanzees, I trust,' said Dr Hoover.

'I love them,' said Mark.

Dr Hoover peered over his half-moon spectacles in a way which Mark instantly discerned was meant to be quizzical. 'Love is not necessary,' he said. 'There is a vital difference between love and like. Liking permits objectivity, loving destroys it.'

'Precisely.'

'Your phrasing was imprecise.'

'I apologize. A bad American habit.'

'We'll cure you of that.' Dr Hoover fished a huge silver snuff box from his pocket, tapped the lid, and proffered the contents.

'No, thank you.'

'I suppose you smoke.'

'Now and then.'

'Another bad habit. Don't you read the statistics?'

'I try to avoid them.'

'Indeed!' Dr Hoover piled two mounds of snuff on to the back of his left hand and lowered his nose towards the target area. He sniffed twice, and the mounds disappeared. 'The only way to imbibe tobacco,' he said. 'Death to germs. Invigorating for the sinus.'

'Really.'

Dr Hoover flourished a blue and red handkerchief. 'We'll have you taking it yet.'

Not if I can help it, thought Mark. He smiled politely. He was no stranger to the Hoovers of this world. The grey hair, tangled like steel shavings, the spectacles, the snuff box, the heavy brown brogues, the trout flies worn like a buttonhole were all affidavits to personality. Properly interpreted they could reveal the true identity buried beneath the baroque. 'I'm always willing to learn,' he said.

The point being, he reminded himself, that Hoover had plenty to teach. His credentials filled a column in *Who's Who*. He was, without doubt, the world authority on primates. At the age of twenty-three he had disappeared into the forests of the Cameroons and returned two years later, leading an adult female gorilla by the hand. For six months they had shared an estate in Bedfordshire until influenza put an end to the idyll. His subsequent thesis, *Domestic Patterns of Primate Behaviour Under Controlled Circumstances*, had established his reputation, and it had grown with the years. For four decades he had been a prophet in the field of animal behaviour studies. But, untypically, he had never been without honour, even in his own country. Hoover was one of the élite, up there with Lorenz and Tinbergen. The invitation to join his research unit was a compliment for which Mark had been wholly unprepared. Years before he had published a paper on the facial language of zebras, the most striking point of which was that the male zebra at the moment of orgasm furled back his upper lip like an over-dry pancake. It was not, he admitted privately, an observation which was likely to affect the fate of nations. But there had been something there to engage Hoover's attention. He had obeyed the summons, and he felt reasonably sure that life was not about to play him false.

It would have been a cruel trick if it was. Although it was only the first week in March, sunlight poured through the windows as though the trigger had been squeezed on a pressurized vat of brightness somewhere beyond the blue horizon. No dust hung in the air. The floor, yielding so springily to their heels, looked as sterile and healthy as scrubbed flesh. Stainless steel gleamed, and matt surfaces held the light. A whiff of pine disinfectant swept along the corridor, leaving in its wake a hygienic freeway. Mark filled his lungs and resolved to be happy despite the long flight, the interminable drive from the airport, and his growing fatigue. It was a day made for delight.

'I hope you will feel you belong here.'

'I'm sure I will.' Was Hoover a mind reader? he wondered.

'We are all colleagues, a band of brothers. All suggestions are valuable. We try to rid ourselves of personal ambition. We aspire towards a common end.'

'Which is?'

Dr Hoover smiled warmly. 'Knowledge.'

'Knowledge about what?'

Dr Hoover paused by a pale blue door and selected a key from his watch fob. 'The name of my particular unit is Contact,' he said. 'I think you should meet our principal subject for research.'

He unlocked the door and ushered Mark into a short gallery overlooking what appeared to be a child's playroom. In the middle of the floor sat a small chimpanzee. Its eyes were brown, and its face was naked, with big transparent ears like waxed paper cut-outs. Its body was covered in coarse black hair, long, but not dense. Its skin showed through, a pale lemon colour. On its legs the hair looked like puttees which ended abruptly over flat, pink feet. The palms of its hands were pink also, with stubby thumbs, and short black nails.

'Her name is Rosie,' said Dr Hoover.

'She's very nice,' said Mark uncertainly.

Dr Hoover stared at the chimpanzee, and hooked both thumbs into the lapels of his overall. 'She is eighteen months old, and quite possibly a genius.'

'How do you know that?'

'Yesterday she spoke her first intelligible word,' said Dr Hoover. 'She called me Pa-pa.'

Mark lay in bed watching his wife dress. It was six o'clock the same evening, and the last of the sunlight seeped through the blinds, striping walls and carpet, branding flesh with gold. Balanced on one foot, Biddy Barrow rolled a stocking up the other leg, sheathing its whiteness in pale bronze. 'I don't believe it,' she said.

'Please yourself.'

'Do *you* believe it?'

'I await the evidence.'

'Playing safe.'

'Following accepted procedure.' He lit another cigarette. The bathroom door was ajar, and the smell of bath essence wafted towards the bed as though it was being exhaled by some tame household giant who had gargled with the bath water and now stood hidden, his back to the turquoise tiles, his head jammed against the gently domed ceiling which dripped condensation, but harboured no dirt. Somewhere, an air conditioner hummed to itself, and sparrows hopped along the gutter.

'But what exactly is he trying to do?'

Mark blew a smoke ring towards the ceiling and impaled it with his index finger. 'Dr Hoover is seeking to communicate with chimpanzees. And vice versa.'

'You mean, talk with them?'

'Speech is only one form of communication.'

'But what are you supposed to do in all this?'

'I've no idea. Yet.' Mark stubbed out the cigarette and drew the sheet up to his chin.

'Get up,' said Biddy.

He shook his head, and burrowed voluptuously into the pillow.

'Come back to bed.'

'We're due at the party.'

'Forget the party.'

'It's in our honour. We can't be late.' She turned to the mirror and inspected her armpits.

'No five o'clock shadow,' said Mark. 'Let it grow and give us all a treat.'

'Not everyone has your little ways.' She crossed the room and prodded the bulge of his thigh. 'I said hurry up.'

Mark extended both arms. 'I can't. I'm in agony.'

'You're just horny.'

'Of course.'

She shook her head, and stepped back through a bar of sunlight. Where she had been talc hung suspended, like sand trapped in honey. 'We should be there now. They'll be knocking on the door soon.'

'Let them knock.' He crooked his little finger, and made soft clucking noises as though he were enticing a horse. 'Celebrate our homecoming,' he said. 'Consecrate the ground.'

'Not now.' The light and shadow patterned her body like a jigsaw; crisp red hair, soft mouth, clavicle made of chicken bones, sharp nipples on small breasts, shallow navel, trim pubic mound, thighs like long petals, the skin streaked with silvery stretch marks. It was amazing how they lasted, thought Mark. Months after the birth, long after the whole bloody business had fallen into perspective, the reminders were still there. He felt his flesh wilt, and he sat up promptly. 'You're right,' he said. 'It's time we were off.'

'That was very sudden.'

'I heard the voice of reason.'

'Honestly?'

'What else?'

He got out of bed and put his arms around her. 'Nothing,' he said. 'Nothing at all.' He kissed her shoulder, then sniffed the flesh, and dabbed it with his tongue.

'Nice?'

'Like icing sugar.' His tongue carved a track between her breasts, and darted towards her navel.

She struggled half-heartedly. 'You said it was time we were off.'

He shook his head, and she writhed against him, her limbs softening like wax passed over a fire. His hands caught at her buttocks wrenching her towards him. He felt himself grow huge, a giant, loving obliterator, and then, through the thunder of blood, he heard the cry. They both heard it.

'I must go,' said Biddy.

He nodded resignedly. 'I know. See what Thingy wants.'

'Don't call him that. Call him by his proper name.'

'All right. See what James wants.'

He walked slowly into the bathroom. He must remain calm, he decided. He had an intriguing new job, and a beautiful wife. It was no one's fault that he also had a son who was twelve months old and who had nearly destroyed his marriage.

'What premium would you place on loyalty?' demanded Dr Hoover, gripping Mark's left elbow, and steering him into the kitchen. 'Is it more valuable than ambition? What if it impeded your career?'

'Theoretically, of course.'

Dr Hoover nodded vigorously. 'I wasn't propounding an actual case.'

'Then I don't know,' said Mark. 'I'm not a philosopher. I never speculate in ethics.'

He made waves in the quarter inch of whisky in his glass, and wondered how long he had to make it last. In almost an hour it was the only drink he had been offered. Soon he would have to telephone the babysitter, and he prayed that the conversation with Dr Hoover was not going to develop into a debate, which in turn was a subterfuge for a lecture.

'You would describe yourself as a pragmatist?'

'God forbid. I'm a zoologist.'

'Of course. But none of us are single-celled creatures. We are various within ourselves. We show different faces to the world.'

Mark drank the whisky and set the empty glass noisily on the draining board. 'The hangman grows roses. The murderer loves children. They believe in doing one thing at a time.' He ran his finger round the rim of the glass, and a high-pitched keening filled the room.

Gently, Dr Hoover removed the glass. 'This is not an academic discussion,' he said. 'Have you observed your fellow guests?'

'There's hardly been time.'

'Observe them now. Tell me what you see.'

'Now?'

'This moment.' He waited until Mark was half-way through the door, then called him back. 'I mean, professionally,' he said. 'Make it a field study.'

It was turning out to be a hell of an evening, thought Mark. They had arrived late. The Hoovers' house, the largest in a circle facing inwards across a two-acre green, was blazing with light. A double row of coloured bulbs hemmed the drive. Chinese lanterns nodded to their reflections in a small garden pond. The house itself spilled radiance from artificial flambeaux jutting from either side of its neo-Georgian front door, and music stammered softly through half-open windows.

'It's straight out of *House and Garden*,' said Mark.

'In a bad month,' said Biddy.

Hand in hand they stood in the electric dusk and noted the details. Colonial shutters flanked each window like butterfly wings. The door knocker was an ape's head in polished brass. A crane, cast in lead, stared fixedly at the lily pads. A family of gnomes gambolled beneath what seemed by its twiggy silhouette to be an apple tree. There was an air of elegance gone awry, of cosiness from the catalogue. The house and its setting reminded Mark of a painting done by numbers. The tints were all according to the book, but the sequence had been scrambled.

Also, thought Mark, there was something strained about the Hoovers' greeting. They were cordial enough towards their guests, but they were formal to each other; distant almost, as though they had called a truce for a limited period, and that when the house was empty, hostilities of one kind or another would be renewed. 'My wife, Louise,' said Dr Hoover, pressing Biddy to his pleated shirt front. 'She enjoys these occasions.'

'They don't happen very often,' she said. 'We must make the most of them when they do.'

Mark shook her extended hand and then stepped back to take stock. She was a short, solid woman whose hair was brushed back over neat ears. Its blackness was etched with white. Swimmer's hair, he thought, which looked as though it had been moulded to her skull by a shallow dive. She wore a red velvet dress, pinned above one breast by a gold claw. Her skin was olive, and a vaccination mark stood out like a badge on her left shoulder. She touched it with the tips of her fingers and smiled. 'They're more considerate these days. I believe they do it on the thigh.'

'Science marches on,' said Mark.

She was much younger than Hoover, he thought. 'Are you part of the firm?' he asked. 'I mean, do you work for the company?'

She shook her head. 'Not any more. I used to.'

'Are you a zoologist?'

'Good Lord, no.' She signalled a passing waiter and took a glass of whisky from his tray. 'Drink this,' she said. 'Francis distils his own gin. Sometimes he tries to pass it off on his guests.'

'Thank you.'

'You do drink whisky, I hope. I should have asked.'

'Whisky is fine,' he said. 'What did you do for Proto?'

'This and that. I was a kind of go-between. Public relations really, before it became a profession.' She took his arm and steered him round to face the room. 'You must meet some of these people.'

'I'd like to.'

Lie number one, he told himself, or rather the first airing of that particular lie on this particular evening. In his repertoire of falsehoods it was perhaps the oldest standby. He had no objection to meeting people, but he preferred to meet them singly, as individuals, and not as members of a pack. He had difficulty in remembering names, occupations, relationships. More than once he had criticized husband to wife, mistress to lover. Charm had saved him on all but a few occasions. Women found him attractive, approving his height, his fresh complexion, his long fair hair, and his readiness to listen. Men, as a rule, were less welcoming.

But there would be no incidents tonight, he thought. There were no obvious drunks, no whisky picadors. He was there to be scrutinized, but manners would prevail. On Louise's arm he circled the room, occasionally catching sight of Biddy travelling the same circuit. He waved to her across a jumble of gossiping heads.

'And this is David Dempsey,' said Louise. 'He's our dietician.'

A slender man with cropped black hair thrust a bowl of vari-coloured biscuits towards him. 'Try one of these.'

'What are they?'

'Snacks. Something to soak up the booze.'

'Thank you.' He selected a pink lozenge shaped like a star.

Dempsey watched him intently as he chewed and swallowed it. 'How was it? How did it taste?'

Mark deliberated for a moment. 'Like shrimp.'

'Good. Now try a green one.'

Mark took another biscuit. The flavour was vaguely vegetable. 'What's special about them?' he asked. 'Are they homemade?'

Dempsey wheezed with private laughter. 'You could say that.' He shook the bowl and offered it again. 'Tell me what you think of the yellow ones?'

'Not just now.' Mark sipped his whisky. 'Tell me the worst. What's the secret ingredient?'

Dempsey set the bowl down on a table and laced his fingers. 'Our life blood,' he said. 'Or to put it another way, the staff of our company's life.'

'I don't follow.'

'Proto,' said Dempsey. 'Pure, nutritious protein. Plus a little vegetable dye, and a trace of artificial flavouring. Straight from Mother Dempsey's kitchen.' He dangled his hands like paws, and panted rapidly. 'Doggies beg for them.'

'What about people?'

'All in good time.' Dempsey lowered his voice. 'Actually I wanted to send a batch to Oxfam to try them out in field conditions.'

'No luck?'

'I was told I'd be exploiting hardship.' He nibbled a biscuit thoughtfully. 'I don't see it that way at all.'

'To the pure all things are pure.'

'Exactly. It's the results that matter.'

Mark felt a tug at his sleeve and obediently followed Louise across the room. There were a great many people, he thought. Where did they come from? What did they have to do with Proto? 'Do they all work with Dr Hoover?' he asked.

'Not all of them.'

'But which are his people?'

Louise smiled. 'I think he'd like to know that himself,' she said. Oh, Christ, thought Mark: politics. He recalled his earlier conversation. 'Make it a field study,' Hoover had told him. Very well, he would. He poached another whisky from a passing tray and tried to set his thoughts in order. Consider the habitat, then the species. First the habitat: a large, panelled room with curtains of rosy silk; several pictures, mostly prints of insects and birds; a log fire, with stereo speakers buried in the walls on either side; in one corner a bar manned by a single waiter; to his right, an open door leading into a small study. There were two deep settees upholstered in moss green velvet, facing each other across a plate glass table, and three armchairs, each with a chrome ash-stand on guard beside it. There was a small sideboard, and a long bookcase with a brass trellis front; an assortment of lamps; two bowls of spring flowers, and a number of potted plants. Mark's nostrils twitched and he remembered himself as a boy making the rounds with the local vet, an Irishman who bred springer spaniels. 'Jesus,' he had murmured with uncommon reverence, as they were shown into one house, 'there's money here.' He had been able to smell it, he claimed, and now Mark believed him. He could smell money in the Hoover household: not in excess, but in plenty. It announced itself in contradictions; in the garishness of the drive, and the discretion of the interior lighting; in the excellence of the furniture and the tawdriness of the ash-stands. It said: we have enough. We need not worry.

The species – his fellow guests – were less easy to pin down. There were between thirty and forty people in the room, the men in dark suits, the women, for the most part, in long dresses. They did not share any pronounced characteristic; they flaunted no marked difference. Their ages, he thought, ran from twenty to seventy. There were few beards. Hair styles ranged from short back and sides to bouffant. Some jackets had three buttons, others had four. Trousers were worn with cuffs, and without. There was not much jewellery in evidence. He counted ten wedding rings on the fingers of the women; a pair of star sapphire cuff links, three signet rings, and an enamelled dress watch which a short, balding man with a meaty face kept dropping into his fob pocket and hauling out again as if he was fishing for mackerel.

Mark folded his arms and rubbed the whisky glass on the side of his nose. In the chiselled grooves he saw the room washed in whisky, split into multiples of synchronized heads and jabbing hands, and he saw suddenly what Hoover wished him to see. The species was fundamentally divided. No badges were worn, no arm bands. But as Hoover entered the room from his study, Mark saw the company stir like an amoeba. One half flowed in Hoover's wake, the other remained in the environs of the man with the dress watch. There was no kind of confrontation, no shape-up. But as clearly as though a toe had been scuffed in the dirt, the middle of the room marked a boundary line, and everyone present knew on which side they belonged.

Dr Hoover came towards him, his broad palm cradling Biddy's elbow. 'Well?' he enquired.

'Point taken.'

'The point being?'

'There's more to Proto than making animal food.'

'But you already knew that.'

'I didn't realize it was between Us and Them.'

Dr Hoover clicked his tongue. 'It's really not as basic as that.'

'Isn't it?' Mark looked from one group to another. It was like a quiet evening in Dodge City, he thought, minutes before the bullets began to fly. 'Who's the man with the watch?' he asked.

'The watch?' Dr Hoover surveyed his guests. 'That's Alec Bell. He's another director of Proto. He looks after the food side of things.'

'While you look after research.'

'I wish it was so cut and dried. I'm the scientific director, so that in one sense we have joint responsibility for testing the product that's manufactured. But on the other hand Alec Bell has no say whatever in the doings of Contact. That's the name of my little group.'

'And he objects to that.'

Dr Hoover smiled forgivingly. 'You over-simplify. Alec Bell wouldn't be so crass. He doesn't object. He merely argues that one budget should not have to finance two programmes of research. And I must admit, he has a point.'

'Who decides on the budget?'

'The board decides. Influenced, of course, by the managing director. You may have heard of her. Mrs Monica Deeley.'

The name snagged in Mark's memory like a burr in wool. 'I think I read something once . . . '

'Possibly,' said Dr Hoover. 'What matters is that Mrs Deeley is one hundred per cent behind Contact. We have her support. She believes in what we are doing.'

'How convenient,' said Biddy.

Dr Hoover looked down at her and patted her arm as if rediscovering a trinket, temporarily mislaid. 'I think you should meet Dr Bell,' he said. 'A diplomatic move.' He turned back to Mark. 'We'll discuss it tomorrow. Go and look after my wife.'

He strode across the room, and behind him the amoeba reformed. No more biology, thought Mark, and looked for another drink.

TWO

Under the shower Mark turned the tap to cold, and gasped as the icy jets hammered his skull and shoulders. He stepped out shivering, his lips lilac, his penis clenched like a peony bud. The time, he heard on a remote radio, was eight o'clock precisely. Time to make haste, he thought.

They had got home at three-thirty, the babysitter long gone, the house chilly. He had been slightly drunk. The stairs had given him some trouble, but he had scaled them without actually falling on his face. Half-way up he had heard Biddy behind him, shushing vehemently, warning him not to wake the baby. 'The baby,' he had told her, enunciating clearly and well, 'is fine. You do not have to worry about the baby.' And that, he recalled, wincing, had been that. Right on cue, James had begun to bawl, and had continued to bawl for the next hour.

Mark put on a bath robe, and plugged in his razor. The vibrations hurt his head, but his hand was too shaky to risk cold steel. It was amazing, he thought, that in the old days there had not been more accidents. Hangovers and open razors anticipated all the arguments for spare-part surgery. It was probably worth looking into; a useful line of research.

He snapped off the razor, and put out his tongue. It looked like a strip of mustard-coloured suede. Resignedly, he spooned health salts into a glass of water, and gulped the mixture down. Considering his state of health, he thought, he was functioning well, especially in a bathroom where every personal possession fought for survival against a mounting tide of baby-ware. The washbasin was flanked by cans of talc, jars of cotton wool, small vats of soothing cream, ear drops, nail scissors, packs of disposable nappies, plastic pants, a box of rusks, and an especially loathsome bib. It was too much. 'Biddy,' he yelled.

'What?' Her voice was faint. She was in the kitchen, he thought, making breakfast which he could not possibly eat.

'This bathroom. It's a pig-sty.'

'Come again.'

'A pig-sty,' he bellowed.

'Can't hear you.'

'Turn the radio off.'

The gentlemanly murmur of the announcer ceased in mid-sentence, and a series of doors were flung violently open. 'Now,' said Biddy, from below. 'What was it?'

He faced her down the stairwell. 'I said that the bathroom was like a pig-sty. All that baby stuff. And a horrible bib.'

'The babysitter left it there.'

'I don't care who left it there. I want it out.'

'Bring it out, then.'

'I will.'

End of skirmish, thought Mark. But hostilities continue. Searching for fresh underclothes in his valise (they had not yet unpacked) he wondered how many acts of aggression constituted a war. He and Biddy had been married for five years. Their wedding had actually taken place on her twenty-first birthday, a piece of planning, he now realized, which was highly significant. For four years, or rather, two years and three months, they had lived in complete harmony. But James had put an end to that. The pregnancy had been difficult. The birth had been a bloody nightmare.

'I almost died,' she told him solemnly when they let him into her room, and he had held her hand while, outside, the sky darkened and rain smeared the windows. There was no need to worry, said the doctors. He would have to make allowances, he would have to give Biddy time, but everything would mend, everything would come right in the end.

Mark knotted his tie, and brushed his hair. What they had omitted to say was how much time. They had not warned him how devotedly Biddy would tend her son, as though any neglect, however slight, would remind her of her own mortality, of how close to death she had been. Of course, she tried. He reminded himself of that fact again and again. The surface of their life together was pleasant, predictable. They did what young people were supposed to do. They dined out, went to movies, drove into the country. Separately, and together, they made an effort, but it was no more successful than using scotch tape to bind a compound fracture.

Each day the sticking power lessened. Irritation masked fear. Biddy was afraid of becoming pregnant again, she was afraid of dying. Mark was afraid of fathering another child, of weakening their personal bond.

He loved James, he reminded himself, as he took his seat at the breakfast bar in the kitchen. But, as things were, he was a cuckoo in the nest. Unconsciously, he braced himself. He did not intend to be thrown out.

'Yogurt?' said Biddy. 'Scrambled eggs?'

'Just coffee.'

'Black or white?'

'Black. No sugar.'

He watched James finger painting with porridge on the tray of his high chair, and felt slightly sick. 'Do you think he enjoys doing that?'

'It's perfectly natural. All children do it.'

'How long does it go on?'

'For years.' Biddy rescued the spoon, and popped another helping of beige glue into James's mouth. Some of it overflowed and ran down his chin.

'I'm sorry about last night. I was a bit tight.'

'You're telling me.'

'I wasn't too bad, was I?'

'You were noisy.'

'I didn't insult anyone? I didn't pick an argument?'

She poured his coffee, and pushed the cup along the bar. 'You were perfectly charming. At one stage you became very profound about hierarchies and the peck order, and you tried to tell a dirty joke which nobody understood.'

Mark sipped his coffee, and burned his mouth. 'That doesn't sound too bad.'

'You also forgot to phone the babysitter, and you told Louise Hoover that she looked like a fertility goddess.'

'Christ!'

'She didn't seem to mind.' Biddy shovelled more porridge into James. 'I believe I have some of the wives calling on me today. This morning, in fact. I've got to move.'

'All right. Just let me drink my coffee.' Breathe deeply, he told himself. Find your centre of gravity. 'I'll give you a ring around lunch time,' he said. 'Let me know if you want anything.'

'Don't worry about me,' said Biddy. She tilted her cheek to receive his kiss, and made way for him to reach James.

Mark hesitated. 'He's covered in porridge.'

'Don't be so fussy.'

'I'll get it all over me.'

'It's an old suit, isn't it?'

'That's not the point.' He compromised, and planted a kiss on the top of James's head. 'It's still soft in the middle,' he said.

'That's the fontanel,' said Biddy. 'It's a gap which allows room for the brain to expand.'

'Isn't nature wonderful.'

She grimaced and fed the last of the porridge to their son who spat it out to add to the ullage on his tray.

'Goodbye then,' said Mark.

'Goodbye.'

She did not turn round and he tapped her on the shoulder. 'Was I really as pissed as all that?'

'Yes, you were.'

He felt his temples pound anew. 'I believe you,' he said.

The high winds of the previous night had died down, leaving the sky a pale and cloudless blue. Standing outside his house Mark felt the imminence of spring. He was not country born, but the smell of earth and the sight of new green moved him profoundly. It was just as well, he thought. There was a lot of it around.

The Hoovers' house faced him across an acre of roughly mown grass. Six other houses, three on each side, completed the circle. It was like a hamlet, idealized and conceived immaculately on a planner's drawing board. The Hoover's house was the largest and probably the oldest. Black timbers striped its façade, and the tiles on the north side were weathered and grey with lichen. The other houses, including Mark's, were scaled-down versions of the same model. It was almost as though a manor house had given birth to a brick and plaster litter. The family resemblance was striking.

Every house had a garden; every garden had a pond. Behind the back fences ploughed fields extended choppily to the horizon which was banded by the tops of trees. A white concrete road encircled the green, and to the left veered sharply towards the Proto plant, out of sight over the rise. Mark began to walk in that direction.

As he passed the last house he was joined by David Dempsey. 'How d'you feel today?' he enquired.

'Fine. And you?'

'I always feel fine. I don't fill myself up with poisons.'

'You mean you don't drink.'

'That's only part of it.' Dempsey quickened the pace, and Mark was forced to hurry to keep up with him. 'I follow a strict diet,' he said. 'Vegetarian, of course. Stone milled flour. Sun dried fruits. Nothing grown with artificial fertilizers. Natural compost only.'

'How long have you been on it?'

'Two years now.' Dempsey breathed deeply and struck his chest a considerable blow. 'Some mornings I run to the lab. Just a dog trot, nothing very strenuous. My best time, so far, is four and a half minutes. You might care to join me one day.

'I don't think so,' said Mark. He made a mental note to change his morning routine. He would leave home earlier or later. He did not intend to break records with David Dempsey.

They reached the top of the rise, and Dempsey flung out one arm like an explorer, or a night club compère about to introduce an act. 'There's the old place,' he said. 'The heart of animal nutrition. The mills of Proto which grind smaller than God.'

'They've not done you much harm.'

'That' said Dempsey, 'is because I am happy in my work. I hope you will be, too.'

'Thank you.' It should not be too difficult, thought Mark. Proto was where he wanted to be, and he was what Proto wanted. He looked down on the complex of buildings, and tried to distinguish his own office. The previous day he had not been afforded this bird's eye view.

Two hundred yards ahead the white concrete gave way to the main road. On the other side, in either direction, Proto property extended for half a mile. There was nothing ostentatious, nothing distinguished in the way of architecture, simply a long, low office block, white like the concrete, which impressed by its insistence, holding the eye, maintaining its level of monotony like one note played on an organ. It was interrupted at several points by doors, the largest of them a confection of gilt and stainless steel in which puppies and small kittens gazed raptly at the brand name Proto, picked out in pure copper. 'That's the main entrance,' said Dempsey. 'We're further down the road.'

Mark looked the way he was pointing. To the south, past the warehouse, the tall chimneys, and the loading bays, was an area enclosed by ash saplings. Behind them stood a high wire fence, more bushes, and then a number of buildings whose roofs shone like oil-skin in the morning sun.

'That's the Contact block,' said Dempsey. 'We're rather exclusive.'

'So I see,' said Mark. He faced Dempsey squarely. 'Are you a Contact man?'

Dempsey scratched his short black hair. 'What an extraordinary question.' He drew himself up, and placed his right hand over his breast pocket. 'Man and boy,' he intoned, 'I have been a follower of Francis Hoover. Will that do you?'

'I didn't mean it like that.'

'I know, I know.' He steered Mark towards the main road, one arm resting lightly on his shoulder. 'What you saw last night was my party piece. I like to make a little mischief, sniff out heretics. You never know when you'll need a good heretic. It's not as pointless as it sounds. You see, as a nutrition man, I have a foot in both camps. I stay friendly. It's in everyone's interests to level with me. I'm there to relay intelligence, to spread the word. Compromise is my middle name.'

'I'll remember that.'

'Good for you.' They crossed the road, and Dempsey glanced at his wristwatch. 'We're still early. The peasants start arriving in about ten minutes time.'

'Which peasants?'

Dempsey sucked his teeth. 'The Proto peasants. The workers. They have their own estate, all fifteen hundred of them, about three miles away. And we have our own little branch line to bring them in, and take the produce out.'

'What about Bell and his lot?'

Dempsey pointed vaguely beyond the factory, and the railway line. 'They have their own ghetto over there, just like ours. You can see how they worked it out. The plant's in the middle, so it's neutral territory. This is where we try to be productive.'

He unlocked a steel gate, and waved Mark into a courtyard, around which single-storey timber buildings formed a long U. The ground was some kind of composition, and dotted at regular intervals with sockets, brimming now with rain water.

'We can put up cages any size we like,' said Dempsey. 'The uprights go in the holes, the frames fit over the top, and we clip nylon mesh where we need it. Reinforced, I might add.'

It was like a tennis court, thought Mark, a place for games. 'I was here yesterday,' he said. 'I know where I am now.'

'You've got an office?'

'Next to Dr Hoover's.'

'Lucky old you.' Dempsey headed across the compound. 'My girls'll be here soon. I'll just get the sheets warm. See you later.'

'See you.' Mark looked around him once more before walking on to his office. His name would be on the door by now; he had seen the painters at work. His appointment with Dr Hoover was fixed for nine forty-five. He had almost an hour in which to convince himself that he really belonged.

'I wanted to be quite sure that everything was all right,' said Louise Hoover. Behind her the grass on the green quivered in a light breeze, and to Biddy, poised in the doorway, the composition looked decidedly heraldic. Buff figure against verdant background. A fertility goddess, she thought.

'Come in,' she said. 'I was just about to bath the baby.'

'I don't want to interrupt you.'

'Come and watch,' said Biddy. 'It's quite a performance.' She was still wearing her housecoat, dappled with Coke, and stained by Sanka. She had bought it two years ago, at a Saks sale, and although its pedigree was still impeccable, the garment itself was in rotten shape. 'You look lovely,' she said, eyeing Louise's leather skirt and jacket. She felt as though she had been dipped in tallow; a slut, caught out in her squalor. She hoped to God that post-breakfast visits were not part of the Proto way of life.

'It's an old outfit,' said Louise. 'I wear it around the place.' She folded her arms, and looked up and down the hall. 'I knew we should have got the decorators in.'

'But then,' said Biddy, 'you wouldn't have known what colours we like.'

Steel chimed faintly on steel. Louise smiled. 'You're absolutely right. Very well. I'll send round some colour charts, and you can choose for yourself. Just let me know what you decide. Francis has to send the authorization to head office, but it's perfectly straightforward.'

'I'll do that.' She led the way into the kitchen, and released James from his high chair. Porridge encrusted his face like war paint, and his top lip was gummy with snot.

'He takes after you,' said Louise.

'Thanks.' She scooped James up and juggled with the door knob. 'In Los Angeles,' she said, 'we had swing doors in the kitchen, like a saloon.'

'What if someone was coming the other way?'

'You just listened hard. I don't remember any collisions.'

The front door bell rang, and both women hesitated. 'Would you mind answering it?' said Biddy. She fled upstairs, and from the bathroom, heard voices below. Resolutely she turned the taps, and submerged an elbow. Nothing, she resolved, was going to break the routine. From the floor, James reached up and caught the flex of Mark's razor. He tugged it and the razor fell on his head. His mouth opened wide, there was a count of three, and then he roared his protest. God in heaven, thought Biddy, what else can go wrong? She picked James up, and cradled him in her arms.

'Can we help?' asked Louise, peering round the door.

Biddy shook her head. 'We had a little accident. It's nothing. Come on in.'

There was another woman behind her, tall and blonde, wearing tartan slacks and a camel-hair sweater. 'This is Peg Dempsey,' said Louise. 'David's wife. She wanted to know how you were settling in.'

Biddy beat a gentle tattoo on the small of James's back. 'Very well,' she said. 'As you can see.' The sobs subsided, and she wiped her son's nose with a tissue.

'Perhaps you'd rather we went away,' said Peg. 'You seem to be having a bit of bother.'

'Situation normal,' said Biddy. She unpopped James's napkin, and waved it in the direction of the lavatory.

Peg lifted the lid, and flushed the basin. 'They're marvellous, the disposable sort,' she said. 'I've never got around to buying them. I can't justify it to David.'

'Get him to wash the others,' said Biddy. She lowered James into the bath, and squeezed the sponge over him. The water darkened his hair, turning it from ginger to ox-blood, and cascaded on to his shoulders like rain from an awning. He grinned broadly, showing the pearly studs of milk teeth. His skin turned pink beneath the suds, and the friction of her hand, and without warning he began to urinate, a small yellow fountain that described a perfect parabola before subsiding like the last trickle from a garden hose.

The women watched it ebb and die, then all three burst out laughing. 'So uninhibited,' said Louise.

'There was a joke I heard once,' said Peg. 'It was a comic alphabet, a whole routine in which every letter stood for something awful. I don't remember much of it, just the odd line. But I do know that P was silent – as in bath.' She looked at their blank faces. 'Silent,' she repeated, 'as in bath.'

'Good grief,' said Louise, 'how corny can you get?' She giggled weakly, and blew her nose.

'It wasn't my joke originally,' said Peg. 'I heard it somewhere.'

Bibby pulled the plug, and bundled James into a bath towel. So ends the first reading from the Proto Bumper Fun Book, she told herself. 'Coffee?' she suggested, and headed downstairs. At the bottom she remembered the filth of the kitchen and handed James to Louise. 'Why not take him into the living room,' she said, 'I'll only be a minute.'

'You mustn't go to any trouble . . .'

'It's no trouble,' said Biddy. 'That is, if you don't mind instant.'

And if you do, it's too bad, she thought, as she measured Nescafé into three hastily rinsed cups. There was no cream, and the silver spoons were still at the bottom of the trunk. If she was to be judged on first impressions the verdict would, undoubtedly, go against her. She watched a blob of white cloud cross the window from east to west, and consciously tried to relax. She stared at her hands, and flexed the fingers. They were nice hands, she thought, with pink, well-trimmed nails: a debutante's hands designed for politely passing unimportant objects. Steam billowed from the kettle, and she mixed the coffee, arranging the cups on a perspex tray, with cold milk in a jug (at least she had unpacked *that*) powdered milk in a can, and lump sugar still in the box. It was like war time, or how her mother had described the war. The muddle spelled emergency, a state, she told herself, for which there was no need to apologize.

'He's a beautiful boy,' said Louise, as she entered the living room.

'Lovely,' said Peg.

Biddy set down the tray. 'Sometimes we don't think so at four in the morning.' She handed Louise her coffee. 'Milk? Sugar?'

'Neither, thank you. He's got your colouring.'

'My skin too. He blisters in the sun.'

James blew bubbles and beamed at the ceiling. The towel slipped from his shoulders, and Louise pressed her cheek to the nape of his neck. 'That's the part I like best,' she said.

'I think I should get him dressed,' said Biddy. The adoration was becoming oppressive. She was reminded of an old people's ward in the hospital at Los Angeles. On the day of her discharge the doctor had suggested paying them a visit. 'They love to see the kids,' he said, 'it's like a transfusion.' And so she had walked between the double line of beds, smiling blindly from left to right, while rheumy eyes watched her progress, and whiskery lips (some of them limned in magenta and blush pink) cooed endearments. Just as she was nearing the exit the doctor had taken James from her arms and presented him, gift-wrapped in a yellow blanket, to the patient in the last bed. 'It's a baby,' he said, and from the nest of sheets a finger had slowly emerged (like a stick insect, recalled Biddy), and crawled towards James's face. She had disgraced herself then, snatching him back, and running from the ward, while behind her the doctor spread his scrubbed hands, and the solitary finger crept back between the sheets. Later she had felt ashamed, but the fear and the anger stayed within like sediment which any threat, or excessive compliment, could stir up.

'I'll take him now,' she said, and, meekly, Louise set the child on her lap.

'Delicious coffee,' said Peg, and Biddy restrained an impulse to snap at her that it was from a tin, and that any fool could make it. She would have to be patient, she thought. They were only trying to be friendly, and it was obvious that she would need friends.

'You have your own school, I believe,' she said, and both women bobbed their heads, like toy birds she had so often seen on West Coast bars poised over glasses of water, nodding tipsily in response to a chemical command.

'We do indeed,' said Louise, 'a very good school. Proto believe in providing the best. We have a kindergarten, too. The children love it.'

'Do you ... ?' Biddy hesitated, 'do you send your children there?'

'I have no children,' said Louise. 'Peg has two boys. I forget their exact ages.'

'Four and six,' said Peg. 'Charles is four, and Robert is six. We named them after their two grandfathers.' She drained her cup of coffee, and winked knowingly. 'Tactics. There's a bit of family money, and we don't want the boys to be left out.'

'Of course not.' Biddy forced herself to smile back. 'I suppose it's something to bear in mind.'

Louise unfastened her handbag and took out a red leather diary. 'I'll make a note to send you those colour charts, then I think we should be off.'

'Yes, we should,' said Peg. 'We just wanted to say welcome, and to let you know that we're on call.' She indicated a small, plastic-bound directory beside the telephone. 'We're all in the Proto book. You're down under the name of Ryman. It's not been corrected yet.'

'Ryman?' Biddy shook her head. 'Was that the family who lived here?'

'That's right,' said Louise. 'They left a few weeks ago.'

'Where did they go?'

'I'm not sure. London, I think.' Louise stood up, and vigorously dusted her skirt. 'I don't know what you do with leather when it wrinkles. Suede goes all greasy, and this stuff just cracks. Do you have any ideas?'

'I'm afraid not.'

'Do you, Peg?'

'I've never worn leather. David says it's kinky.'

'That says a lot about David.'

Let it happen, thought Biddy. Let them talk themselves out of it, or through it and then we can all relax. She hoisted James on to her hip, and glanced hopefully at the door.

'The time!' said Peg. 'I'm having my hair done. They won't *speak* to me if I'm late again.' She squeezed Biddy's waist. 'Don't forget now. Call if you need anything.'

'Call anyway,' said Louise. 'And if you don't, we'll call you.'

The door closed behind them, and Biddy leaned against it, her legs trembling. She kissed the top of James's head, and breathed the scent of his skin as though she was inhaling oxygen. Every day, and in every way, she told herself, it will get better and better. It has to, she thought. And when it does I will ask again about the Rymans.

THREE

'And this,' said Dr Hoover, 'is Boris.' On a screen at the far end of the darkened office a small ape bared his teeth and brushed irritably at his ears – like a man newly released from a barber's chair.

'He's a little disturbed,' said Dr Hoover. 'The grin signifies tension. In extreme cases it is accompanied by head shaking and rocking. You see a lot of it in those appalling television commercials. They're supposed to look as though they're enjoying themselves, but of course they're not. They're scared to death. D'you remember that ape they sent up in the rocket. What did they call him? Something biblical.'

'I think it was Ham,' said Mark.

'That's right. Most inappropriate. Practically blasphemous. The point is, when he came down every idiotic reporter remarked on how happy he looked. Grinning all over his face, they said.' Dr Hoover shifted himself in his chair, and for a moment his shadow cut off the beam from the projector. 'He was absolutely terrified. That's why he was grinning.'

'Public relations,' said Mark. 'You can't be unkind to animals even if it gets you to the moon first.'

Dr Hoover sank lower in his chair. 'I understand about public relations. The louse in the locks of research. I've lived with it for years. We all have. But here we've no need of it. What goes on at Proto is strictly private. We do not seek publicity. We are not in the queue for public money. We have our own funds.'

'We're very lucky,' said Mark.

Dr Hoover shook his head. 'Not lucky. Deserving. We put the money to good use.' He prodded Mark in the ribs, jovially, but hard enough to inflict a minor bruise. 'Don't you think we deserve it?'

'I'm sure we do.' Hand on heart, he thought. For two hours he had watched films demonstrating how the money was spent, and he was distinctly impressed. He was also slightly shaken. There was no doubt that Francis Hoover had a remarkable understanding of primates but it also seemed clear that he was not a man who allowed his affection to interfere with any fruitful line of research.

'This is some of our early work,' he had told Mark as the camera zoomed into a close-up of bloody tissue, tagged like a steak with shiny clamps. 'What we did was remove the prefrontal lobes of the cortex. As brain surgery goes, it's fairly primitive now, but we had an idea that these areas were memory banks, and we wanted to see what would happen when they were taken out. First of all we trained the apes in specific discriminatory habits – the sense of touch, for example, rejecting rough objects, and choosing things that were smooth. Then, when the lesson was learned, we removed the lobes where the information was supposed to be filed away.'

'And what happened?'

'Nothing,' said Dr Hoover. 'There was no loss of memory. They learned just as readily as before.'

'Didn't I read about the same experiments somewhere else?'

Dr Hoover shrugged his shoulders. 'Possibly. There was a man named Carlyle Jacobsen who worked on the same lines at the Yerkes Laboratories. He reduced temper tantrums in chimpanzees by brain lesions, and the idea caught on all over the place.'

'But who came first?'

'I have no idea. Ideas travel in the air. Like radio waves. Anyone can pick them up. It's not important who's first into print.'

Except, thought Mark, that it was Jacobsen. 'Do you still go in for surgery?' he asked.

'Not now.' He gestured towards the screen. 'This is where the real work lies.'

It was still Boris, Mark realized, but he was no longer grinning. In medium close-up he sat placidly on a green-overalled knee, blinking at the lens. The sound track crackled, and then came the ringing of a bell. Boris looked towards the top right-hand corner of the screen, and tapped his ear with his index finger. There was a short silence, and the sound was repeated. Boris tapped his ear again, and stared mildly at the camera.

The focus changed and Mark saw that the knee on which Boris was perched belonged to a girl wearing a laboratory coat, and black levis. Her hair was black, and cut short, and there was a bandage on her left hand. 'That's Dr Bloom,' said Dr Hoover. 'She had an accident with Boris the day before.'

'Nothing serious, I hope.'

Dr Hoover shook his head. 'We thought for a while she might lose a finger. But she was sewn up in time.'

'What's she doing?' asked Mark.

On the screen the girl was tying a bib around the neck of the chimpanzee. She lifted him, like a baby, and sat him in a high chair. A bowl of cereals and chopped fruit was set in front of him, and the chimpanzee began to eat, stirring the discs of banana with skinny yellow fingers, and holding them delicately in his whiskered lips like coins being fed into a slot machine.

The sequence was repeated, but this time the chimpanzee wore no bib. The food was set in front of him, but he did not eat. The girl pushed the bowl towards him, and he shook his head violently, thrashing his arms from side to side.

'Now, see this,' said Dr Hoover.

With his right forefinger the chimpanzee sketched a rough oblong on his chest. He repeated the gesture, tracing, Mark realized, the outline of the missing bib.

'Do you mean . . . ?' he began, but Dr Hoover shook his head impatiently.

'Just watch.'

The girl tied a bib around the chimpanzee's neck, and immediately he began to eat the food. He broke off to scratch an ear, jutting from his head like a pale, freckled leaf, but instantly resumed feeding, ending the meal by lifting the bowl and rotating it on his tongue.

'He wouldn't eat until he was wearing the bib,' said Mark.

Dr Hoover shook his head impatiently. 'You miss the point altogether.'

'But that's what happened.'

'Think again,' said Dr Hoover. 'What did he do with his finger?'

Mark traced the outline of a letter U on his own chest. 'He signalled that his bib was missing.'

Dr Hoover groped for his snuff box. 'That's one way of putting it.' He loaded each nostril and inhaled. 'But think of another construction,' he said. He tucked away the snuff box and sneezed with evident satisfaction. 'Think hard.'

'You mean that he was asking for his bib?'

'Precisely,' said Dr Hoover. 'Boris was asking Dr Bloom for his bib. *Pan troglodytes* was making his desires known to *homo sapiens*. A chimpanzee was communicating with a human being.' He leaned back in his chair, his fingers laced. 'Do you understand the significance of that event?' he demanded.

'I think so.'

'I hope so,' said Dr Hoover. 'If you do not recognize a break-through in communications when you see it there is no place for you in this establishment.'

He hesitated, and Mark realized that a response was called for. 'I recognize it now,' he said. 'I think I was so surprised that I couldn't believe it.' He was aware that the film had run out, and reached over to switch off the projector. The light inscribed deep shadows on Dr Hoover's face, and the gulley marking his mouth suddenly curved upwards at each corner.

'I would prefer you to be sceptical rather than surprised,' he said, and the gulley grew deeper.

'I'll remember,' said Mark, his voice lightening with relief. It was going to be all right, he told himself. Dr Hoover was smiling.

David Dempsey called to collect him for lunch. The canteen stood between the Proto offices and the main factory block, and covered walks led to it from all sides.

'What day is it?' asked Dempsey.

'Tuesday.'

'Cauliflower cheese, fried fish, braised heart, pork chops, or steak if you're feeling rich.'

'What do you recommend?'

'None of it. I put in a standing order for a salad. It's bloody awful, but I can bear it when I think of the cholesterol you're all packing away.'

It was like being back at school, thought Mark. There was no separate executive dining room, but at one end of the hall there was a raised platform on which the tables were covered by cloths, and waitresses hovered, menus in hand.

'Hoover's idea,' said Dempsey. 'Democracy is not the natural order. He likes us to bear it in mind.'

Paintings hung on the walls. Geese flew into a westering sky, elephants trumpeted mutely against an African dawn, springbok bounced, and jaguars sprawled. One picture was set apart. It was a design that might have been made by a child. The colours were muddy, the conception primitive. Roughly speaking, it was a fan. Paint had been spooned on to the hardboard and furrows gouged into it. Mark studied the composition for several seconds. 'Finger painting?' he suggested.

Dempsey nodded. 'Who by?'

'I haven't a clue. One of your kids?'

'I should be so lucky.' Dempsey dug his hands into his trouser pockets, and rocked backwards and forwards on his heels. His voice became sonorous, pedantic. 'An excellent example of primate art, mid-twentieth century. Note the strong radial pattern. Quite uninhibited.' His voice returned to normal. 'Quite pricey, too. It's one of those paintings done by that chimp at London Zoo. What did they call him? Congo. Collector's item. Fifty quid, no questions asked.'

'Did Hoover buy it?'

'Nicked it most likely. He has taking ways.'

They found a vacant table and Mark ordered pork chops. Dempsey was filling a glass with water when he saw someone approaching. 'Oh, Christ. Don't look round.'

'What is it?'

'Nothing. Keep your head down.'

Mark rearranged his knife and fork, and scored the cloth with his fingernail. 'For how long?'

'Too late,' said Dempsey, and aimed a reluctant smile somewhere above Mark's left shoulder.

'Hello there.' A woman's voice, husky and slightly nasal. Mark swivelled in his chair, and as he turned he was conscious of an odour – part human, part animal – a blend of armpit and crotch; both feral, and spicy. His eyes met a zippered fly, clambered over a trim belly and rested briefly on bevelled breasts. He laboured on and realized that he was inspecting the torso of the woman he had seen earlier that day on film. 'Dr Bloom,' he said, scrambling to his feet.

She waved a hand. 'Don't get up. Manners don't belong here.'

'Will you join us?'

'Are you expecting anyone else?'

Dempsey coughed urgently. 'There was just a possibility . . .' he began.

'No one at all,' said Mark.

'OK then.' She sat down and lit a cigarette. Dempsey pulled his chair back six inches, and she grinned. 'I'll put it out when the food comes.'

'My name's Barrow,' said Mark.

'I know. Hoover was supposed to bring you round. How are you fixed tomorrow?' She squinted through the smoke, and Mark notched up a small thrill of recognition. Warner Brothers, vintage 1944; probably Lauren Bacall. He was a connoisseur of styles in cigarette smoking. For months after seeing a season of Bette Davis films he had tried slavishly to imitate Paul Henreid's trick in *Now Voyager*, lighting two cigarettes at once and handing one to his companion. He had abandoned the practice after skinning his lip, time after time. But Dr Bloom was doing rather well.

'Do you like old movies?' he asked, pursuing his discovery.

'Yes I do. Why? What's that got to do with tomorrow?'

'Nothing. I was just checking up.'

She reached across the table for the ashtray, and he was assailed by a fresh gust of sweat, scent, and what else? Images of unmade beds, rumpled by hours of strenuous sex filled his mind's eye. It was like an anthology of hot afternoons and humid nights. Was she aware of her bouquet? he wondered.

'I don't understand about the movies.'

'Personal rating,' said Mark. 'You've just won ten points. What time tomorrow?'

She still looked suspicious. 'Half-past nine. Later if you like.'

'Half-past nine's OK.' He smiled ingratiatingly. 'I saw your chimpanzee film this morning. The new movie.'

'What did you think?'

'Fascinating. Quite remarkable.'

She stubbed out her cigarette. 'You sound like a critic.'

'I mean it.'

'Yes . . . well . . . it's Hoover really. He lays down the programme. All I do is carry out orders.'

The waitress arrived with Dempsey's salad, and Mark's chops, and Dr Bloom peered at each plate in turn. 'I'll take the macaroni cheese,' she said. 'Not that I care about it being kosher,' she told Mark, 'I'm just mad about that farinaceous stuff. It's a race memory, or something.'

'I don't follow.'

'Being Jewish,' she said patiently. 'It's in the blood. All those generations scared of going hungry and filling up on stodge.'

Swiftly, Mark reviewed a selection of his Jewish friends, past and present. Some were thin, some were fat; not one, so far as he could recall, had a great liking for starch. 'What about cannibals?' he demanded. 'Do they have a race memory too?'

Dr Bloom disembowelled a bread roll and wagged the crust in his face. 'It's not the same thing. They never starved. Their psyche wasn't scarred.'

'Really?'

'It was their culture that turned them on to human flesh. They never had a pogrom.'

'I see.'

'I doubt it. Not that it matters.'

'I didn't see you at Hoover's party,' said Dempsey, dusting grit from a lettuce leaf.

'I wasn't asked.'

'I wish I'd known,' said Mark. 'I'd have asked you myself.'

'Would you really?' His response had clearly been unexpected. She touched his hand, and glancing down he saw bitten nails, grimy knuckles, and the unravelled cuff of her cardigan.

'Of course I would.'

'Most likely it was an accident. I've been to Hoover's before.' She made a grimace and her jagged fringe fell and rose again over her forehead. It was deeply lined, Mark observed, and there were dark stains, solid as thumb prints, beneath her eyes.

'You must come round and have coffee,' he said.

'Some time,' she said, 'thanks.' She dug into her macaroni cheese, forking it into her mouth as though she was stoking a fire. 'Those Hoovers' she said finally, wiping her chin with a paper napkin. 'They really stink.'

Walking back to the Contact block with Dempsey, Mark realized that he was breathing deeply, like a boxer at the end of a hard-fought round. He filled his lungs, savouring earth smells, petrol fumes, the fleeting whiff of tar.

'You'll get used to it,' said Dempsey.

'Why doesn't someone tell her?'

'Don't think they haven't. It does no good. It's Bloom's last stand.'

'What do you mean?'

'Independence. Human rights. The bed-rock of personality.' Dempsey took a foil-wrapped package from his pocket and thrust it at Mark. He studied the offering – a dark brown slab, like compressed turds – and shook his head. 'What is it?'

'Dried banana.' Dempsey prised the slab apart, and bit into a length with evident relish. 'Basic energy food. It's what keeps me going.' He chewed vigorously, small polished knobs rotating beneath his cheek bones. 'It's a pity about old Bloom,' he said. 'She had a point to begin with. Before she came here she'd been working with wolves, trying to domesticate them. She used to sit in their cage, reading books, doing the crossword, just keeping still while they wandered around getting used to her. She found they were much happier if she didn't wash. There was no alien smell, you see. Nothing to confuse them. She hadn't much of a social life at the time, so there was no worry there. Anyway, she got results and that's what mattered. Hoover hired her on the strength of a paper she wrote, and she descended on us about a year ago.'

'I saw her film this morning. It's good.'

'Oh, yes, no doubt about it. Bloom knows her stuff.' Dempsey peeled off another baulk of banana and added to his cud. 'The trouble was, she upset Louise. It was one of those drinks evenings. Liberty fabrics, and little things on sticks. And in came Bloom, smelling like a midden. People just melted away, you couldn't help noticing. And Louise took her by the arm and led her off into the kitchen, and Christ knows what she said. What your best friends won't tell you, I suppose. The end of it was that Bloom stormed out, and the next day she told Hoover to stuff his job.'

'How did he talk her out of it?'

'Have you heard Hoover when he really gets going? It's like the Sermon on the Mount, with blood, sweat, and tears thrown in. Bloom says he told her she was irreplaceable, but that she had certain social obligations, and that members of such a closely-knit unit had to consider their colleagues, etcetera, etcetera. And she told him that Mrs Bloody Hoover was no colleague of hers, and she intended to carry on exactly as she had always carried on, otherwise she'd quit there and then.'

'And Hoover gave in.'

'He had to. He's no fool. Bloom was half-way through a programme of research, and doing very nicely, thank you. Mind you, God knows what he'll do when she's delivered the goods. Meanwhile, we all have to suffer.'

Three girls from the factory passed them, their legs twinkling, their nylon dustcoats gaping at the neck. There was a brief, almost sublimal glimpse of brassieres, lace edging and white flesh. Mark watched them until they turned the corner.

'There's a lot of it about,' said Dempsey.

'Obviously.'

'It's an occupational hazard you'll find.'

'It doesn't really bother me.'

'It bothers everyone. There's not much to do round here. You revert to nature.'

'Like Bloom.'

'She's had her share.' Dempsey weighed the bananas in his hand, then slipped them into his pocket. 'She had Ryman.'

'The man I replaced?'

'That's right.' Dempsey hesitated for a moment. 'Did Hoover say that? That you'd replaced him?'

'Not exactly. But we've got his old house.'

'Of course you have. Is everything all right? No leaky taps, no bumps in the night? Just say the word if you need anything. We're only across the way.'

'I'll do that.' It was extraordinary how the picture built up, thought Mark. If you had the nerve and the patience to sit still, the wolves went about their business producing textbook patterns of behaviour, revealing all you wanted to know. He waved goodbye and climbed the stairs to his office. Correction, he told himself; there was no instant revelation. Patterns had to be interpreted, and there were no risks to be considered. He recalled the bandage on Dr Bloom's hand. There was always the chance of a nasty accident. He resolved to be careful.

That evening they finished unpacking. Mark held up a pair of bermuda shorts, mocha brown with a green check overlay. 'Can you see me wearing these, *chez* Hoover?'

'Hardly. What about this?' Biddy leaned back, the top half of a scarlet bikini draped across her chest.

'Better not. You had him going last night.'

'I did not.'

'You should have been where I was. Onlookers see most of the game. He was all hands. Have you checked yourself for bruises?'

'Oh God.' She let the bikini fall. 'I thought he was just being friendly.'

'So he was.' Mark stroked her cheek. His index finger traced the line of her lips. 'You're a bit dim, aren't you.'

'No, I'm not. I accept things at face value.' She leaned against him, making herself heavy, and he put his arms round her, palms cupping her haunches, thighs against thighs, the silence loud in their ears.

'She wanted to know what colour schemes we had in mind.'

'Who did?'

'Louise. Mrs Hoover. She was here this morning. We're going to be redecorated.'

'Fine.' He moved his hands gently and felt the skirt glide over her pants. 'Take them off,' he said.

'Not now. There's too much to do.'

'Nothing that can't wait.' They were speaking in whispers, he realized, a domestic buzz in which confidences were exchanged like delicious morsels from mouth to mouth. It was like entering a small, secret room, a tent made of bed sheets through which the light filtered, rosy as blood. He had been a long time away. 'Biddy,' he said, 'please.'

'Someone might call.'

'They'll go away.'

'Did you lock the door?'

'Locked and bolted.' God knows if it is, he thought. His hand slid under her skirt, and tugged the elastic. She turned her hips and the pants slid over them, peeling off like skin. Stealthily, he bent his knees, lowering himself to the floor. She moaned softly and followed him. 'Darling,' she said, her breath moist on his neck, her teeth stabbing the lobe of his ear. His foot encountered a crate of books, and he pushed it away. They lay side by side, his left arm cradling her neck, his right hand probing between her thighs. She was melting; everything was liquid. 'Now me,' he said, and the zip of his fly purred open. She spread her legs and he rolled on top of her. It was a celebration, thought Mark, a homecoming. He drove inwards and upwards, and saw doors opening, drapes parting. He felt himself harboured by muscles, perfect in detail, mighty in execution. They were joined in flight, held by a rhythm which bound and released them. And then it stopped. 'The phone,' said Biddy.

'Ignore it.'

She did not reply, but he felt her body become rigid.

'Biddy,' he said, 'forget the phone.'

She shook her head. 'I can't.'

He cupped her face in his hands. 'Yes you can.'

She rolled from under him, and he was pitched to one side, his skin crinkling in the sudden chill. He lay back and watched his erection collapse. 'Poor little chap,' he said, and, as though he was covering a corpse, drew up his underpants. He felt extraordinarily clear-headed. The titles of his books advanced from their spines. He was aware of grit in the carpet, of the draught that seeped beneath the door, of Biddy talking brightly to the caller on the hall telephone. 'No patterns,' she said. 'No, really, we both prefer plain colours. Yes, of course. I'll tell you tomorrow. Thank you for calling.' He heard her replace the receiver, and open the door.

'You hadn't locked up,' she said. 'Anyone might have come in.'

'They didn't. Not that it matters now.'

'It matters to me.'

He took a deep breath, and thought of doctors whose advice – formulated in offices six thousand miles away – now seemed irrelevant, even grotesque. 'I'm sorry,' he said. 'I'm sorry about everything. Let's go to bed.'

'I'm going in to see James.'

'Of course.'

'Then I'm going to sleep.'

He picked up the bermuda shorts between his finger and thumb. 'You can burn these.'

'Tomorrow.'

'Naturally, tomorrow.' He followed her to the foot of the stairs, snapping off the lights on the way. 'Was that who I think it was on the phone?'

'It was Louise Hoover.'

'Bidding her flock goodnight.'

'You know why she called.'

'Oh yes, the decorating.' There was no point in going on, thought Mark. No point in anticipating the worst. 'You chose plain colours,' he said. 'That was sensible. You can't go far wrong with those.'

FOUR

Charlotte Bloom awoke at six-thirty, an hour before the alarm was due to go off. She watched the pale light frosting the edge of the curtain and listened, absently at first, then with growing concern, to the drip of a tap in the bathroom basin. She closed her eyes and imagined the water, grey with scum, her face flannel – kept afloat by a pocket of air – hanging in the suds like a suicide. The previous night she had been too tired even to pull the plug. She still ached with fatigue: she felt bruised to the marrow. Her dreams had been about Johannesburg, the ugly apartment in which every surface glittered with cut glass – vases, bowls, ornaments, all of them snaring the light and giving it back in bursts of rapid rainbow fire. She tried to remember who had been there. Her mother, of course, her face foxed with age, her fingers augmenting and orchestrating every statement; her father (dead for three years); her brother and her husband, Gerald, dressed as he had been on the day she left – black mohair suit, white on white shirt, and club tie. There had been an argument, which was nothing new. They had all joined forces, forming a semi-circle, their mouths opening and closing in unison, laying syllables like eggs. She could still hear her mother: 'Ungrateful slut.' Her dreams, she thought, added nothing new to the experience. They were transcripts of the real thing, instant replays of a tape which could not be wiped clean.

She burrowed down in bed, swaddling herself in the blankets, inhaling the smell of her den. The dripping tap persisted and she tried to estimate how long it would be before the overflow was submerged, and water spilled on to the floor. Ten minutes, she decided, in which she could empty her mind and charge her batteries for the day. Miles away a shunting engine echoed against rolling stock. Who else was awake to hear it? At Proto the first shift started work at eight-thirty. She sensed the stirring of a hive; gas rings lit, electric kettles plugged in. But she was not part of it. She was not even a citizen.

When she had arrived in England people had assumed her to be a political refugee, and they had felt betrayed when she denied it. It was so like the English, she thought, to want their liberalism confirmed. At a party in Hampstead she had been introduced to a woman who, she was told, had spent eighteen months in jail for her beliefs.

'But what was she actually doing?' she asked her host.

'She was living with a Cape Coloured.'

'How bloody ridiculous.'

'Courageous, I'd say.'

But mad, she had wanted to argue. The madness was everywhere, and to defy it openly was to compound it. Her own choice had been to opt out, and, even now, she was proud of the systematic way she had gone about it. First, she had sold her jewellery and bought a plane ticket. Next, she had packed her bags and ordered a taxi. Then, half an hour before it arrived, she had told them she was leaving.

'But what about Gerald?' her mother had demanded.

'I don't love him.'

'I love *you*,' her husband had said.

'I can't help that.' She had sat perfectly still, her luggage waiting in the hall cupboard, while they harangued her. Briefly she had been afraid that they might try to detain her by force, but her utter certainty had repelled them. She had felt herself become inviolable, protected by her detachment. When the door bell rang she had picked up her handbag, said goodbye courteously, and driven to the airport.

The next day in London she had paused outside a toyshop in Regent Street. In the window there was a display of miniature spacemen, suited like robots, their heads enclosed in plastic bubbles. It was her own situation exactly, she thought. She went inside the shop and asked to see one of the toys. The dome, she was told, could be unscrewed.

'Leave it as it is.'

'But there's a complete change of uniform.'

'I don't want to see it.'

She had flicked the bubble with her finger nail. It was like flicking the eye of a snake. Protection was guaranteed, the elements did not intrude. She had bought the toy, and for the first year it hung over her bed in a variety of lodgings and apartments. Now she could not remember where she had left it. In any case, she thought, the similarity no longer existed. The situation had altered.

The bed was growing cold, and her feet felt clammy. She swung them out on to the floor, and flexed her toes. The ten minutes were nearly up; she could no longer hear the tap dripping. The light was much stronger, a pallid glare which owed nothing to the sun. That too was English, she thought, a form of concealed lighting peculiar to the climate which neither flattered nor revealed. She threw back the bedclothes and shuffled into the bathroom. She was too late. There was a pool of water beneath the basin. The bath mat had acted as a blotter, and when she trod on it there was a sound like stepping on boggy turf.

She wrenched the plug from the basin, and wrung out the flannel. As she turned, she was arrested by her own reflection. Her nightdress was practically shorn of buttons, and the red flannelette gaped wide from neck to navel. Her skin was sallow, and a faint twist of hair climbed like a fakir's rope from her belly to her sternum. Over her left breast the long furrow of a cigarette burn ended in a charred circle framing a nipple, black as tar. There were food stains at the waist. Random blobs of ink and blood descended towards the hem. Shreds of grimy lace hung from the garment as though it was in moult. Impulsively, she peeled it off, and hurled it into a corner of the room. She was shocked by her own violence. In the mirror she saw a naked, angry woman who stared at her with mad eyes. Jewish eyes, she reminded herself. The pose was an *aide memoire*: arms hugging breasts, knees slightly bent, hair in sweaty points. Candid camera shot, taken on the way to the gas ovens. England could not save her. She was still a fugitive, still in flight.

At that moment Francis Hoover was debating whether or not to show Charlotte Bloom's film to Mrs Deeley. He decided against it. Mrs Deeley, he reasoned, was not a reader of serial stories. What she enjoyed was a complete narrative with a beginning, a middle, and an end. To tell her 'thus far, and no further' would be to antagonize her. He did not wish to do that. He had enough to contend with already.

All the same, he thought, as he rinsed his razor under the tap, everything was under control. His spirits were buoyant. In a voice which made the bathroom vibrate he sang his morning hymn.

All things bright and beautiful,
All creatures great and small,
All things wise and wonderful,
And God made none at all.

Privately he referred to it as 'one of the good old ones', his daily homage to Darwin. He was a fundamentalist, he told interviewers, born into the faith of natural selection and still a believer. Like all his aphorisms it had the texture of tweedy commonsense, but it was skilfully woven, made to measure.

He knotted his tie and strummed the wattles beneath his chin. They were appropriate, he thought, leathery thongs of skin and sinew, the insignia af authority. He was not complacent, far from it. Stamina, as he so often remarked, comprised making long-term plans, while survival lay in carrying them out. For many years he had nursed the notion of Contact, his own unit, free to follow its own line of research, with a generous, non-interfering sponsor. In Proto he had virtually that. There had been and were problems, of course; rivalries to be acknowledged; campaigns to be fought. But he was, by nature, a winner. Success came naturally, if at times its evolution had to be helped. Occasionally, reflected Dr Hoover, he had bloodied a few reputations, and not without relish. There had been Pascoe and his Yeti scalp, a tuft of hair liberated from a Tibetan monastery, and displayed with uncommon reverence, first to the press, then to a company of zoologists, all of them denied the right to laboratory examination.

For a fortnight prior to the unveiling he had grown the nail of his right index finger. When the so-called scalp had been passed to him for inspection he had gouged a small sample of tissue from its underside and, within hours, had conducted a biopsy which proved, beyond doubt, that the hair had come from the skull of a species of Himalayan bear. It was the end of Pascoe, and a victory for the sceptics. 'Hoover makes clean sweep of Snowman' ran a headline at the time, and although he abhorred all puns he did not make himself, he valued the publicity.

He pushed the curtain aside and peered out of the window. The estate was in order. The gnomes beneath the apple tree were all present. The crane studied the lily pads, a dew drop gleaming at the tip of its bill. There was no sun, but it was at least dry and that was a blessing. On the occasion of Mrs Deeley's monthly visit he welcomed fine weather as a natural reinforcer of the optimism he hoped to transmit.

He brushed his hair, counting the strokes: a hundred in the morning, a hundred at night. His barber had once told him that he would never go bald and he intended to make the prophecy come true. Women still found him attractive. The previous month a writer for a woman's magazine had listed him as one of the world's most bedworthy men, a crude and shallow compliment (the writer had not market-tested the goods), but a compliment all the same. When he had married Louise it had been a meeting of not only true and agile minds, but of serviceable bodies too. Over the years, though, there had been a distancing. Louise made him feel that although sex was his right, his energies should be directed elsewhere. She would not actually deny him, but – unmistakeably – she gave him the impression that he was being indulged. She was performing a service, not sharing a pleasure. It was an uncomfortable sensation.

Dr Hoover tiptoed through the bathroom and peeped through the door on the far side. Louise was still asleep. She rarely came down to breakfast before nine, by which time he was out of the house. It was an arrangement which suited them both. He listened to the steady rhythm of her breath, and judged her to be at least an hour from waking. Often he kept watch like this, observing her as raptly as he had once watched animals from bowers of Serengete grass. Her room was now alien territory; not hostile, but unexplored. Its scents and textures were private, and Hoover had learned to keep his distance. He had been trained to respect the environment, to leave it unaltered, and even here the habit persisted. He closed the door quietly and made his way downstairs.

He ate frugally: lemon juice in hot water, honey on wholemeal bread. As he gnawed the crust he found himself counting the number of times he chewed each mouthful of food, and immediately stopped. Compulsive? he wondered, or neurotic? He measured himself against the appropriate behaviour patterns and smiled. It was like being in a self-service store: all psychiatric fittings in stock. Self analysis is the thinking man's vice, he

extemporized, and wrote the phrase in his diary. He would find a
use for it; a good epigram was never wasted.

From his seat at the head of the dining table Hoover could see
across the green. It was a view which had not changed during the
ten years he had lived there. Twice a week in the summer, a gardener
mowed the grass. Daily, a small van edged with a skirt of motorized
brushes swept the road. Half a mile on there was a telephone
exchange and a shopping centre. They were all owned or organized
by Proto. Once, thought Hoover, he would have resented the weight
of welfare, but not now. He had learned to pick and choose. No
man was entirely free of good works, but some were more
independent than others.

He took a filing card from his breast pocket and reviewed the
previous day's itinerary. Items attended to he crossed out. Un-
finished business he transferred to a fresh card. Hoover's little
list was a company joke, but he was past caring. The system
worked and that was what mattered. He read through his jottings
and drew a red star against two of them. 'Introduce Barrow to
Mrs Deeley' said the first. 'Consider Ryman' said the second.
He drank the last of his lemon juice and slipped the card into his
pocket. It promised to be an interesting day.

'When we're with Boris we don't speak,' said Dr Bloom. 'Anything
you want to communicate you have to signal.'

'With my hands, presumably?'

'One hand only. I've based the whole phrase book on the American
Sign Language. ASL for short. The simpler the sign, the easier it is
for him to learn. I'm not trying to make him a brilliant con-
versationalist. I just want to give him enough to get by.'

Through a wall of one-way glass Mark watched Boris at home.
He lived in a single room, built on three levels. The floor was
littered with plastic blocks, a nest of rubber tyres, and a large
red ball. A trapeze hung from the ceiling, and in the corner furthest
away from the door stood a tree buttressed by a cairn of smooth
boulders.

'It's not real,' said Dr Bloom. 'He gets too damn playful. We
made it up from steel tubing with a plastic skin, and he's not put a
dent in it yet.'

So far, thought Mark, the Bloom body odour was quite bearable.

Most likely it ripened as the day wore on. They both wore the regulation green coats, but he noted that while his was freshly laundered, Dr Bloom's bore the rosettes of dried urine left there, he supposed, by an excited chimpanzee. 'Do I go on calling you Dr Bloom?' he asked.

'I was christened Charlotte – after Charlotte Haldane. My father had a revolutionary past.' She brushed her fringe to one side. 'At school they called me Charley. You can call me that if you like.'

'It's better than Dr Bloom.'

'Only just.'

'I prefer it.'

'All right then.' She took a file from the top drawer of her desk, and passed it to Mark. 'The notes are pretty well up to date. You can read them when you have time. All you need to know now is that Boris was taken from the wild when he was about eight months old, and he's been here for the past twenty months. The only people he's been in contact with since then are myself, Hoover, the occasional cleaner, and Ryman.'

'Ryman?'

'He was here before you.'

'But this wasn't his project.'

'No. Boris is all mine. From start to finish.' She folded her arms and pressed her forehead to the glass wall. 'All the time he's been here he's never heard human speech. As I told you, when we're in his presence we communicate only by sign language. The point being, it seems the likeliest way of communicating with Boris. Nobody's certain. Not me. Certainly not Hoover. But, as far as we know, chimps don't speak because they can't. They lack the necessary throat structures and speech centres in the brain. Possibly there are other factors. Maybe they got out of the habit, maybe they've got nothing to say. It's a pretty boring life being an animal. But, person to person – between me and Boris, that is – I've established contact. God knows how long it will last. You know how it goes – a nice, bright juvenile, interested in experiment, sampling flavours and smells, even some trace of an aesthetic sense. And then the glands go to work. He's sexually mature. And all the rest goes to hell. You can't get near him, even, to find out if he wants to think. He's likely to tear your head off.'

'Conspicuous waste,' said Mark.

She nodded vigorously. 'In a way. All that work for such a limited time. It drives me crazy.' She jabbed a thumb to where Boris was examining a banana skin, tracing its surface with his finger tips, sniffing it, exploring each indentation with his lips, licking it, scattering it with sand, and finally jumping on it with shrill rhythmical hoots. 'I want to know how he feels. I want him to be able to tell me.' She traced her initials on the glass, and then rubbed them out. 'I know it's impossible. He doesn't have the capacity. But his vocabulary's building up.'

She opened the file and took out a page of typescript. 'See here. Forty-three phrases up to now. He can tell me when he wants a toothbrush, or when he's hurt himself, or when he wants a crap. He's doing better than that female they had at Nevada. What did they call her? Washoe, or something. I wish I could measure his IQ. I mean, you're supposed to have that for life, if the same rules apply. Just think of him in a couple of years time. All that intelligence fenced in by energy that won't let it function. I won't even know if it still exists.' She unbuttoned her coat, and, instinctively, Mark jerked his head back. It was as though his nose had been jammed into a wet armpit. Clearly, he thought, it was emotion that triggered the Bloom mechanism. She felt strongly about Boris, and her body made known the fact.

'Are we going in with him?' he enquired.

She glanced at the wall clock. 'It's his meal time in ten minutes. I'll get the tray ready.' He made as though to follow her, but she shook her head. 'It's just routine. I won't be long. Skim through the file while you're waiting.'

It was a comprehensive record. Daily observations were rendered down into a weekly summing-up, but the original notes were still attached. Mark's eye was caught by an entry for January the previous year. 'Assisted by Ryman' he read. 'Boris aggrieved by his refusal to surrender apple. Brief tantrum, ending with Boris biting Ryman on left side of neck. Some blood. Boris intensely curious (Query: does he recall own injury?) When Ryman refused to allow close inspection, Boris apologized: clenched right fist drawn to and fro across chest. (Correct ASL form: fist rotated.) Ryman delighted. Permitted Boris to examine bite.'

And all without words, thought Mark. As he looked up his eyes seemed to meet those of the chimpanzee squatting on the other side of the glass. Boris was motionless. His head was cocked to one side, his ears poking through the fur like tubers. He seemed to be listening to or for sounds which, to Mark, were inaudible. Perhaps it was the time of day, he thought, an inbuilt clock advising him that food was shortly due. There was tension in the curve of the body. The eyes were attentive. The mouth, with its white crescent of beard, was puckered as though stitches had been drawn through the lips. Mark tapped on the glass and instantly the chimpanzee sprang across the room, his knuckles propelling him like ski poles, his feet slapping the floor.

'For God's sake. Don't be a tourist.'

Charlotte Bloom stood behind him, a tray held in both hands, her face tight with anger. He felt himself flushing. 'I'm sorry,' he said. 'I didn't think.'

She set the tray on the desk. 'Try to remember next time. I don't want him excited before we go in there. Now we'll have to give him a couple of minutes to calm down.'

Mark peered at the assortment on the tray. It was like an American army issue, the plastic moulded into six sections, each one containing a different food. There was chopped apple, banana, biscuit, raisins, Proto in tablet form, and a small mound of horny shapes whose legs twitched and kicked. 'Why locusts?' he asked.

'Natural protein. I'm not entirely sold on Proto. It's part of the diet, of course. I don't suppose it does any harm, but I don't want him to go short of anything.'

'Of course not.' He was agreeing too readily, he thought, but he felt absurdly eager to please. 'Can we go in now?'

'All right. Remember what I said. No talking. Signals only.'

She unlocked the door, and preceded him into Boris's quarters. She had left the tray behind, he realized, and he almost called after her. He checked himself, and followed on, his hands jammed in his coat pockets. He had no time to take them out before Boris launched himself at his chest, landing feet first, and bouncing away like a wrestler, judging his fall perfectly, and vaulting on to his back, then off again into the cradle of Charlotte Bloom's arms. For a moment he lay there, his eyes as blank as pennies, then in a single movement he was straddling her shoulders, both hands anchored in her hair.

Wincing with pain she kneeled down, and Boris stepped to the floor, his hands clasped about her neck. The shrieks which had accompanied his acrobatics subsided into a soft, querulous hooting, which ceased altogether when he jammed the fingers of his left hand into his mouth and chewed them industriously. Charlotte shook her head, and instantly he backed away, his arms raised, hands dangling at shoulder height, ears flapping as he wagged his head from side to side, his lips drawn back over yellow teeth which parted as the screams resumed their intensity.

She stretched out her arms and Boris scrambled towards her, his fingers back in his mouth. She held him off, and as though checked by a sudden memory he sat down and pressed the palm of his right hand against his chest. He paused, and then rubbed it, clockwise, in a circle. She nodded, and he extended the hand towards her, the pink palm cupped like a begging bowl. She smiled, and catching Mark's eye, fed imaginary objects into her mouth.

'Tray?' he asked silently, and she smiled her thanks, taking hold of Boris's hands while Mark backed out of the door. He returned with the tray, and all three squatted in a semi-circle while the chimpanzee made his meal. He ate rapidly but neatly, crunching the heads off locusts, rotating discs of banana between his lips, spitting out scraps of peel, and picking and choosing from the mixture of Proto tablets. Dempsey would be interested, thought Mark. The green tablets were eaten first, then the brown. Finally a scattering of pink tablets remained, a synthetic rash on the grey plastic.

Boris stirred them with his finger, and watched with mild interest as Mark and Charlotte left the room. She locked the door and leaned against it. 'The finger chewing meant he was hungry,' she said. 'I wouldn't come up with the tray until he asked for it. That's why we got the screams.'

'And he asked for it by rubbing his chest?'

'In a way,' said Charlotte. 'It's that good old American Sign Language again. You can look it up. In the manual the signal means "please".'

The heating was turned full on in Dr Hoover's office. Warm air from two wall radiators edged across the room, only to be driven back by the intense draught from three open windows. It was like being seated in the middle of a weather map.

'You may think,' said Dr Hoover, 'that I have not been completely frank with you. I hope you won't hold it against me.'

Mark shook his head. 'I don't follow you.'

'I have omitted to tell you of certain details. I was not being devious. I merely wished you to form some impression of our work before discussing its application.'

'I think I understand your aims.'

Dr Hoover tipped back his chair and laced his fingers. 'In principle I'm sure you do. But there is one particular aspect which will not have occurred to you.' He waved a reassuring hand. 'I imply no lack of perception. It's what I might describe as a little trade secret.'

'Concerning Proto?'

'Concerning Contact.' Dr Hoover heaved himself out of his chair and closed all three windows. He remained standing, staring abstractedly at the buildings opposite. They were hardly makeshift, thought Mark, but there was something about the unpainted timber frames that spelled emergency. He recalled photographs of the first concentration camps, chalets spawning on empty heathland, a spartan setting for unimagined rigours. He disliked secrets even when he was invited to become one of the conspirators.

'You invited me to join Contact,' he said. 'You weren't specific, but from what you'd written earlier I assumed it was to do with communication. That's why I came.'

'Certainly, certainly.' Dr Hoover patted his shoulder. 'I didn't mislead you. Don't jump to conclusions.' He sat on the edge of his desk and studied his toe caps. 'I want you to meet Mrs Deeley. She'll be here in half an hour. The fact is, I'd welcome your support. She's a generous lady, but – should we say – a little eccentric. We need to maintain her interest.'

'I didn't know it was flagging.'

'It's not. No, I wouldn't say that. But it needs to be nourished occasionally. She likes to feel that there's new activity, new minds.'

'She wants results?'

'We all do.' Dr Hoover sighed deeply. 'I'd better give you the complete picture. I met Mrs Deeley ten years ago, and she agreed then to finance my research. Not personally. It's a book-keeping arrangement; tax deductible, I believe. You could say that Contact is underwritten by Proto. Enlightened capitalism. A way of life for some of us. And it's been worthwhile. We've been economical, whatever Alec Bell may say; we've made progress. Not all of it's apparent, but we've learned *not* to do certain things. We've given the lead. All that surgery I showed you yesterday. It took years to decide, once and for all, that it was getting us nowhere. There are some butchers still cutting and cobbling, but we've demonstrated that it's the wrong approach. You can't wire up an ape like a radio. It's behaviour, not engineering that's taking us where we want to go.'

He helped himself to snuff, and dusted his nose with a handkerchief. 'Last year we began working with three chimpanzees. I introduced you to Rosie; she comes under my wing. By manipulating her lips I've taught her to pronounce one recognizable human word; and there'll be others. You've seen Boris. Dr Bloom's results have been striking, quite remarkable. Then there's Lulu. We had a man here named Ryman who wanted to work on the lines of sleep-teaching.'

'Did he have any success?'

'It's too early to say.' Dr Hoover buried his face in the handkerchief, and blew his nose with evident relish. 'Ryman's not with us now. I thought you might take over his programme.'

'I can't say I think it's very workable.'

'Early days, early days. You must decide for yourself.'

There was something else, Mark thought, something unsaid. It was like attending a play reading, and being given a précis of two and a half acts. He found himself waiting for the final explanation, the swish of the curtain. 'And where's Ryman now?' he prompted.

'In London I believe.'

'Still engaged in research?'

'Not at present. He's been ill.'

'Seriously ill?'

'There was an accident with one of the animals. Ryman disobeyed orders.' Dr Hoover spoke with no particular emphasis. 'His right arm was amputated.'

'Was it Lulu?'

'Good God, no.' Dr Hoover chuckled richly. 'You could put Lulu in your shirt pocket. There's no need to worry about her.'

'Then what happened?' The question came out more sharply than Mark intended. He stared at the desk, and winced as the buzz of the intercom cut across Dr Hoover's answer.

'Mrs Deeley's here.'

'We'll be down in a minute.' He smothered his turbulent hair, and stuffed sugar lumps in his pocket. 'She has favourites,' he said. 'Take some yourself.'

'I don't think I will.'

'Don't be a fool,' said Dr Hoover. 'We can talk later. For as long as you like.'

'Very well.'

'And don't look so grim. You're going to meet your bread and butter.'

'Bread and protein you mean.'

Dr Hoover guffawed loudly, and with some relief. '*Bon appetit*,' he said.

With Mrs Deeley, Mark observed, he was cordial but restrained. There was no arm holding, no obvious playing to the gallery. Dr Hoover was in character, there was no doubt about that. But his well-loved impression of salty eccentric was less robust than usual. In ten years, thought Mark, Mrs Deeley must have learned to distinguish the theme from its variations. It was also possible that Dr Hoover respected her sense of discrimination. He was no fool; and neither, it seemed, was she.

The path was too narrow for more than two people to walk abreast and Mark followed behind, an accidental eavesdropper on their conversation. 'I'll speak to Alec Bell,' said Mrs Deeley. 'He knows how I feel about the budget. I won't have this sniping behind my back.'

'I wouldn't call it sniping,' said Dr Hoover. 'I wasn't implying warfare; nothing so violent. But sometimes there's a whiff of powder in the air.'

'You have a keen sense of smell.'

'Too keen perhaps.'

'The point is,' said Mrs Deeley, 'that I want everyone to prosper. And this feuding doesn't help.'

Even at a distance, Mark felt the chill of her reprimand. She emanated no warmth whatever. She had removed her glove to shake his hand, but her flesh was disconcertingly heavy and cold. When she smiled the corners of her mouth turned upward for a count of three. Then they dropped and her face became impassive, impenetrable.

They were heading, he realized, in a direction that was strange to him. Dr Hoover led the way between two warehouse blocks, behind a car park, and along a cinder track that ended in an iron gate. He unlocked it, and Mrs Deeley stepped ahead of him into what seemed to be a small arena. She glanced up as a bird flew overhead, and following her gaze, Mark saw that they were inside a cage. There was a ceiling of inch-thick bars, sunk into concrete walls. The floor was concrete with a scattering of peat, and in one corner there was a climbing frame, surrounded by a number of hay bales. The area, he estimated, was about sixty square feet, and at its centre there stood a large box – a cell, he thought – made of steel mesh, linked to the far wall by a tunnel of iron ribs. Something moved within it, and Mrs Deeley nodded as though greeting an old acquaintance.

'Is he well?' she asked.

'Well enough,' said Dr Hoover. 'Tranquillized for the moment. He'll be wide awake in fifteen minutes or so.'

She walked steadily towards the box, and Dr Hoover nudged Mark to follow her. 'Behind the wire,' he said conversationally, 'is a male adult chimpanzee. He's the one who tore Ryman's arm off. You should get to know him.'

'Why?'

'He's the reason we're all here,' said Dr Hoover. 'He's the one we're going to talk to when we've found a way of communicating.'

A sudden gust of wind ripped over the top of the wall, and Mark shivered. He turned up his coat collar, but Mrs Deeley did not move. Her face was set firm like lard. Her mouth was bloodless. Her hair, coiled on the nape of her neck, lay still as lead. Only her eyes were alive; large, black, and lustrous. They were beautiful, thought Mark, and they were mad.

FIVE

Above the entrance to the Proto Social Centre, a bronze puppy played pat-a-cake with a bronze kitten. An ascending spiral of wrought iron doves flanked the doors on either side, and in the foyer stood a life-sized figure of St Francis. A small menagerie of vermin gambolled about his feet, and between the fingers of his outstretched hands rested a card which announced in bold red letters 'BINGO, FRIDAY 7.30 p.m.'.

There was a strong smell of cocoa, and Biddy cast around, sniffing from left to right, trying to locate the source. A blonde girl wearing leotards came out of a back room and Biddy smiled hopefully.

'I'm looking for Mrs Hoover.'

'Yes?'

'She asked me to meet her here.'

'What's she on?'

'I beg your pardon.'

'Ballet, dressmaking, music appreciation, current affairs, keep fit.'

'I think she said keep fit.'

'Did she?' The girl looked her up and down professionally. 'You new here?'

'Yes, I am. That is, my husband's just joined the firm.'

'Thought so.' She crossed a leg to inspect the sole of her foot, and peeled something off. 'Bloody chewing gum,' she said. 'Some people live like pigs.'

'I suppose so.'

'You're late,' said the girl. 'Keep fit starts at seven. It's ten past now. Not that it matters. Down the stairs, first on your right, changing rooms to your left as you go in. O.K.?'

'Thank you,' said Biddy. She had resolved to be clubbable, but the prospect seemed less and less inviting. The natives were not unfriendly, but there was not much point in offering them beads. They were not likely to be impressed.

She followed the girl's instructions and found herself in a painted corridor along which piano music jangled distantly. She pushed the door open and was confronted by what, at first glance, looked like a field dressing station. Bodies lay in ranks. They were topped by perspiring faces, and tailed by naked thighs. The faces all swivelled towards her. The thighs quivered to rest. One of the bodies got up and Biddy saw that it was Louise Hoover. She wore an orange aertex shirt, and white shorts, and her hair was tucked back smoothly under an Alice band. 'I'm glad you could come,' she said. 'Did you bring your kit?'

'My kit?'

'Your shorts and plimsolls.'

Biddy shook her head. 'I didn't think I'd be joining the class tonight.'

'No time like the present.' Louise took her elbow and steered her into the changing room. She looked her up and down, just as the girl in leotards had done, and opened a locker. 'You're just a slip of a thing, aren't you. My stuff won't fit you, I'm afraid. But there should be something here. We always keep a few spares handy. Take your pick.'

There was a green shirt, and a yellow shirt, and a purple shirt, and a dozen or so pairs of shorts, black and white, tight and baggy, muddy and clean. 'I'll wait outside,' said Louise. 'Be as quick as you can.' There was no escape; freedom lay several removes back. Biddy held one of the shirts to her nose. It smelled of soap powder, and metal – the essence, she thought, of the fifth form at St Hilda's. She squared her shoulders, and unzipped her skirt. Straight ahead lay the shortest way home. The shorts were loose at the waist, and the shirt (she chose the purple) was tight beneath the arms. As she struggled into it, Louise looked round the door. 'Very nice,' she said. 'How about the plimsolls?'

'There are none my size.'

'That's all right. Bare feet are best.' She beckoned impatiently as Biddy tugged at the waistband of the shorts. 'They won't fall down. It's not important, anyway. We're all girls together.'

Like hell we are, thought Biddy. I am twenty-five years old, and the mother of a son. But her resentment, her identity drained away as she stepped into the gymnasium. She was the new girl, the late starter, the boarder whose arrival had been delayed by illness. She saw faces studying her, heads bobbing in welcome. She did not belong, she told herself; these women had nothing to do with her. But, perversely, she craved the anonymity of the group. To be noticed, to be conspicuous for one second more was unbearable. She joined one of the ranks, standing close to Louise, and to her intense relief the instructor began to speak.

'Ladies, ladies. Let us proceed.' The bidding was so genteel, so incongruous that she expected giggles, if not outright laughter. Instead, there was silence. Rows of sober faces turned north as though about to recite the Creed. Rows of bosoms heaved decorously. In front of her Biddy saw varicose veins, unwanted hair, the ills of the flesh to which the small ads ministered. But they were ignored. They were irrelevant. She recalled the words of her gym mistress, a stringy zealot, whose proudest feat had been to do two hundred push-ups, uninterrupted. 'Fitness,' she had always intoned, 'begins in the mind.'

And it was true, thought Biddy. The evidence was all around her. She sensed dedication, a flexing of wills. They were all thinking fit. She stared straight ahead, and the instructor smiled at her. She was middle aged, perhaps ageless. Her hair was fair and as crisply curled as Biddy's own. Her face and arms were smooth and tanned, and her tunic was like snow. 'Music and movement, ladies,' she said, and the spell was broken. The pianist struck a warning chord. There was a sound like a hundred vacuum tops being pierced as the class drew breath. And then, to the strains of Country Gardens, the company transformed itself into a troupe of suburban bacchantes who twirled, pranced, and gesticulated in jiggling rows of pastel. Dedication was there, thought Biddy, as she joined the revels. But it was not enough.

For the next thirty minutes she touched her toes, swivelled her hips, imitated a bouncing ball, lay on her back, pedalled in the air, racked herself on wall bars, ran an obstacle course, played team games, and climbed a rope while the rest of the class chanted the seconds it took her to reach the top. She clung there for a count of five, dizzily scanning the upturned faces, and then slid down, the sisal scorching her thighs.

'Isn't it marvellous,' panted a fat lady with a fringe. 'It tones you up for days.'

'Do you come every week?'

'Three times.'

The instructor clapped her hands. 'That's all, ladies. The water's nice and hot.'

'Share with me,' said Louise, and, still giddy, sweat clogging her eyes, Biddy stumbled towards the showers. Pink bodies, swathed in towels, bobbed behind plastic curtains. Steam curdled the air. A quartet, veiled in spray, harmonized through three verses of 'Roll Me Over' and then fell silent, leaving the fourth verse and its happy obscenities unsung.

'Women can't do it,' said Louise, tucking her hair inside a shower cap.

'Can't do what?'

'They can't enjoy dirt on their own. They need a man there. It's a kind of display.'

'I suppose you're right. It never occurred to me.'

'It's a zoological fact. According to my husband, that is.' She peeled off her shirt, and was about to step out of her shorts when she saw Biddy's expression. 'Sorry,' she said, 'I wasn't trying to inflame you.' She put on a bath robe, and removed the shorts beneath its cover. 'I'll only be a minute,' she said. 'You can wrap up in my towel.'

Alone in the cubicle, Biddy undressed as quickly as she could. There was a drawstring along one edge of the towel, and she pulled it tightly about her neck. It was an accident, she told herself. There was nothing deliberate about the exposure. Nevertheless, she was shocked. There was a ripeness about the breasts she had seen which made her feel inadequate, undeveloped. It was back to the fifth form, when the haves intimidated the have-nots. But it was she who had the baby, she reminded herself. James was hers. Louise might look like a fertility goddess, or whatever ridiculous compliment it was that Mark, several drinks to the good, had paid her. But she had no family, no children of her own.

Biddy parted the towel and felt her flat stomach. She was in good shape too. She was desirable and desired. The fiasco on the floor the previous night had not been her fault. Next time it would be different. Time was on her side. She was young, years younger than Louise. 'In any case,' she said aloud, 'I hate big tits.'

In the bar of the Proto Social Centre Mark shared a table with Dr Alec Bell and his wife, Kitty. It had been a sticky evening, made worse by the fact that the Bells drank nothing but orange juice. Bell had insisted on buying him whisky, but each time his glass was replenished he had noticed a slight tightening of Mrs Bell's already pursed lips.

'Do you never drink?' he asked recklessly.

'I have no need for it,' she replied. 'No use, whatever. Mind you, I have no objection to other people partaking. So long as they don't expect me to join them.'

'Is it on principle?' A red light flashed on his instrument panel, but he ignored it. For the first time since being introduced to Mrs Bell he saw an individual, however unattractive, taking shape.

'Since you ask,' she said, 'I took the pledge when I was a child.'

'A long time ago?'

'Long enough. I joined the Order of Rechabites when I was eight.'

'The Order of *what*?'

'Rechabites,' said Alec Bell. 'In fact, we both did. It was a temperance organization attached to the chapel. Very practical too. You signed on the dotted line, and right away you had the benefits of a good insurance scheme and sick pay. All before your welfare state, you understand.'

'Perfectly.'

'I doubt whether you do,' said Mrs Bell. 'We were like one happy family.'

'Like Proto?'

'Not at all like Proto,' she said. 'We were joined in spirit. We used to sing hymns.'

'That must have been lovely,' said Mark. 'I can imagine.' But only just, he acknowledged. Mrs Bell was small and dark, like the charred wick of a candle. She had the look of having been consumed from the core. Small spurts of flame still heated the occasional sentence, but her responses were mostly automatic. She was earthed in prejudice and sentimentality. He wondered what she had been doing in the bar in the first place.

'It's not very busy tonight, is it,' he said.

In fact, there were only five other couples. The blue plastic-topped tables were deserted. The turkey-red carpet still bore the furrows of the vacuum cleaner. A selection from 'South Pacific', homogenized by Muzak, lapped the room. Rubber plants stood guard by the door, and a tank of tropical fish embossed the far wall.

'On bingo nights it gets pretty busy,' said Alec Bell. 'Not tonight though. We really come along to show the flag.'

'I don't follow you.'

He spread his hands deprecatingly. 'I think we should make use of the facilities. And show that we're making use of them.'

'Proto provides everything, you know,' said Mrs Bell. 'We believe we should support the enterprise.'

'But where do people go if they don't come here?' Earlier that day he had spent some time poring over an ordnance survey map. As far as he had been able to determine, the nearest village was ten miles away, and London was a ninety minute journey by train.

'They watch television,' said Mrs Bell. 'The older ones, that is. It's hard to say what the younger ones get up to.'

'Some of them join in the activities, of course.' said Alec Bell. 'I believe the keep fit class is very popular. But there's not much for people like us.'

'No chapel?'

'The management have never considered it necessary,' said Mrs Bell. 'We have a weekly meeting. But there's no actual place of worship.' She sipped her orange juice, and looked scornfully about the air-conditioned Gomorrah. In fact, thought Mark, she looked with some care, as if noting who was present and who was not. He followed her gaze and recognized two young men who had been part of Bell's entourage at Hoover's party. Close by sat two of the secretaries from Contact. They looked at each other, but no one spoke. After several minutes the girls got up and left. Mark was reminded of something from his adolescence, a newsreel of British troops entering Germany. The war was won. Trucks brimming with young warriors drove through streets lined with housewives, and plump, adolescent girls. There were no flags. No one waved. There was a tension, an awareness, but no sound beyond the clack of metal treads, and the jerry-baiting prattle of the commentator. And then two words separated themselves from the flow. They were uttered as a sneer, but they were also an explanation. Mark recalled them now: 'No fraternization.' He studied the Bells nursing their glasses of orange juice, and understood their role. They were guardians of a policy, their own brand of apartheid. He understood why the bar was empty, and to his surprise he was suddenly and intensely angry.

'I'll be indenting for some pretty expensive equipment I imagine,' he announced.

Alec Bell smiled warily. 'That's nothing new. No doubt you have Dr Hoover's blessing.'

'No question of it.'

'And Mrs Deeley's?'

'I should think so. I met her this afternoon.'

'And what did you think of her?' It was no idle question. Mark sensed the quickening of Bell's interest.

'We barely spoke. I thought she was very positive.'

Alec Bell folded his arms, and nodded deliberately. 'Oh, yes, she's certainly that.' He was built like a sausage, thought Mark, with no joints between the crown of his head and the base of his spine. His skin, too, was translucent, and the meat that packed it was solid and pink. He hauled his watch from his waistcoat pocket and raised his golden eyebrows. 'My goodness, is that the time? We must be off.'

'Another orange juice.'

'I think not. Moderation in all things.'

'As you say.' Mark pushed back his chair and smiled at them both. 'I'm glad we had a chance to talk.'

'We'll meet again, no doubt.'

'Not here,' said Mark. 'I find it a little inhospitable. I always think a bar should be crowded, a forum for ideas, lots of gossip.' He raised his glass in a mock salute. 'Here's to the social animal.'

'I have met him very infrequently,' said Alec Bell. 'But then, it's not my line.'

They left the room without looking back, without speaking to anyone. The doors swung to and the buzz of conversation instantly doubled. There was time to have another drink, but he decided to make the one he already had last until Biddy came. It was a good resolution, selflessly arrived at, and when he saw her walking towards him he knew this to be one time when virtue might possibly bring its own reward.

They walked home, arm in arm. It was a clear, cold night with a high wind that thrashed the tree tops, and then suddenly dropped to rummage through clumps of daffodils edging the path.

'You wouldn't get those in London,' said Mark.

'Yes you would. On a stall.'

'But these are provided. That's what Mrs Bell said. Proto provides everything.'

'From the cradle to the grave.'

He kissed her on the mouth, marvelling at the contrast between the cold rim of her lips and the warmth inside. 'They didn't provide that.'

The wind pushed them up the hill, moulding their clothes to their bodies. The sky was stripped of cloud, and when they paused and looked back the Proto plant lay beneath them, the concrete white as bone, the roof tops silver-plated by the moon. 'It's like Norway,' said Mark.

Biddy shivered. 'I know what you mean.'

There had been a brilliant moon for one week of their stay on a skiing holiday. But there the resemblance ended. They had stayed in a guest house in the mountains where the altitude had turned a simple cold into something frightening, freezing her sinuses until her face felt ready to burst. Returning to Oslo they had driven into night at four in the afternoon. The entire country was black. There were no towns, no villages, but the churches – far from the main roads – were floodlit. 'God's lanterns,' said their driver, and she had imagined legions of trolls recoiling from the holy radiance.

'Mrs Bell says there's no church here,' said Mark, and she looked at him sharply, imagining for a moment that he had been able to read her thoughts.

'What else did she say?'

'Not much. She's TT, and thinks everyone else should be too. She and her husband sit there keeping an eye on who goes in and out of that bar, marking up their little list.'

'You don't know that.'

'I'm an observer. Trained for it. I saw their beady little eyes.'

'It's horrible.'

Mark took her hand and tucked it into his pocket. 'Not to worry. It doesn't affect us.' He threw back his head and breathed deeply. 'Try it,' he said.

'I've been trying it all evening. I've used muscles I never knew I had. Even my lungs feel twice as big as they did this morning.'

'Anything else?'

'What do you mean?'

'Any other part?'

'I don't think so.'

'Pity.'

She hauled on his arm, and he slowed down, his face puzzled. 'What's wrong? What did I say?'

'Is it really a pity? Do you want me bigger?'

'Do I want *what* bigger?'

'You know. Me. My boobs.'

He stared at her, and then unbuttoned her coat. 'You mean these parts. These rising beauties.' He cupped them gently, and shook his head. 'They pass muster,' he said. 'Just about.'

'I wondered.'

'Then don't.' He re-fastened her coat as though he was wrapping a parcel. 'I like you the way you are.'

'I know it's been difficult the last few months. I'm sorry.'

'It's going to be better.'

'I want it to be.'

The wind swirled down on them as it had when he had stood in the cage with Hoover and Mrs Deeley, and he put his arm around Biddy's shoulders. 'Let's get home.'

They ran the last quarter of a mile, their breath masking their faces. 'I'd better join your class,' panted Mark. 'I'm ruined.'

'Completely?'

'We'll find out.'

There was a special, gentle kind of lechery which they sometimes felt they had invented. It was dreamlike, a montage filmed by a high-speed camera. Images and sensations expanded to infinity. There was no rush. The urgency was cumulative, mounting fractionally until the peak was reached, the impetus irresistible. For six months before their marriage they had lived together. Biddy held a job as a secretary in a publisher's office. Mark had a small grant which subsidized his research at London Zoo. They rented a flat on Primrose Hill, comprising one large bed-sitting room, with a separate kitchen and bathroom. On one side of them was a pub, and on the other lived a married couple. On warm nights they opened the windows to the balcony and heard the lions roaring. Friends they told would not believe them, but the whole summer was like that; nothing was impossible, the extraordinary was commonplace.

One night they heard knocking on the wall of the flat next door. It was hard and rhythmical, as though someone was driving a nail into plaster. Then a woman began to cry, and the cries synchronized with the knocking. Mark telephoned the police and, together, they watched the empty road for twenty minutes until a patrol car pulled up and, without haste, two uniformed men got out. There was no more knocking, but it had been succeeded by a steady, muffled weeping. It stopped when the police went into the house, and the next day they met the woman and her husband in the pub. She had a black eye, but she was smiling. There had been an argument, she told Biddy, in which, to emphasize each point, her husband had banged her head against the wall. She thought it was all a tremendous joke. 'But you're not like that, are you?' she had said, and she had been right. They had been preserved, somehow, like ginger crystallized in sugar. Their juices remained volatile, but their limbs were candied. There was no outside frosting, but their blood was turned to syrup, which flowed languidly towards the same estuary, the same sea.

Marriage had regulated the tides, but not the undertow. They were in love, they were romantically in love, and when Biddy became pregnant it had seemed a simple thing, a budding almost, which had not prepared them for the pain, the shock, and the imminence of death. In more ways than one, America had nearly killed them, and their return home was a return to a way of life.

They breasted the hill, and saw the timbered houses encircling the green like ideal homes, made in toyland. Their symmetry was reassuring. They were orderly, unremarkable. Smoke streamed from their chimneys as storybooks decreed it should do. By choosing to live there, they were entering a tradition. They were protected by it.

At the front door they were met by the babysitter. 'I tried to ring you,' she said. 'They told me you'd just left.'

Biddy pushed her aside. 'What's wrong?'

'The baby fell out of his cot. I was going to put the rail up, but I just turned my back and he was out.'

'And what happened?'

'He's hurt his arm. I called the doctor. He says he thinks it's broken.'

'Oh, my God.' Biddy pounded up the stairs. Half-way, she turned. 'You stupid bitch,' she screamed. 'Get out of my house.'

Mark held out the babysitter's coat and a pound note. 'Don't worry. I'm sure you're not to blame. My wife's upset. You can understand that.'

'I'm sorry,' she said. 'I really am. But it wasn't my fault.' She gave him a scrap of paper. 'There was a message for you. He said it wasn't important, but I took down the name.'

'Thank you,' said Mark, 'and good night.' He shut the door and turned to go upstairs. His head throbbed, and he could taste bile at the back of his throat. Above him he heard the flutter of bedclothes, like a large bird re-making its nest. Biddy would be spending the night with James, unless he could persuade her to bring him in with them. He looked at the piece of paper and read the pencilled words: 'Mr Ryman called. Will call again.'

SIX

'But can't you see,' said Louise Hoover, 'adoption would be for the best. I mean for everyone . . . nobody would blame you. How can a sixteen-year-old girl be expected to bring up a baby?'

'My mum were sixteen when she had me.'

'But she was married.'

'Only just.'

'The point is,' said Louise, 'she actually had a husband. It doesn't matter that she caught him in the nick of time. He was there. In the flesh. Your case is different. You can't even say who the father is.'

'I *have* said.'

'You've named a committee. You've told me about five boys who had intercourse with you, and any one of them could be the father. They were all in the same week.'

'We were all at the dance,' said Linda Gillis. 'We got a lift in the same van.'

Sitting on the sun verandah of the Proto hospital, her hair tied back with a pink ribbon, a woolly bedjacket round her shoulders, and Mickey Mouse slippers on her feet, she looked no more than a child. But the facts were different. Linda came from local stock. She was a country girl, and she had matured almost exactly on schedule. Sixteen was the age at which seventy-five per cent of her contemporaries had their first baby. Most of them married at eighteen. After twenty, if they were still on the shelf (the expression still persisted) they were likely to remain spinsters for life, unless, of course, they moved to London where their instincts could be turned to profit. Their rhythms were those of the seasons. They were feckless and fecund. After two years at Proto Louise had come to an arrangement with a metropolitan adoption agency which had an inexhaustible supply of clients eager to take on the progeny of Proto's unmarried mothers. So far, the supply had not exceeded the demand. But there had been times when both lists had run neck and neck.

Louise offered the girl a cigarette. 'Look at it this way,' she urged. 'You live at home, and there are six people in the house already. Your grandfather has asthma. Your father works the night shift. Your brother and two sisters have to share a bedroom. And your mother has trouble with her legs.'

She repressed a shudder. Mrs Gillis's legs, festooned with ulcers the size of army cap badges, filled her with a peculiar horror. They were a family affliction, and in a way Mrs Gillis was proud of them. She claimed that they warned her of any imminent change in the weather. Rain made them ache. Frost made them throb. Without encouragement, she would unreel her bandages to display them to any visitor. The company doctor had been sufficiently interested to conduct an investigation, and his report had become part of Proto folklore. The ulcers first made their appearance when Mrs Gillis was twenty-two. Her mother had borne the same stigmata at an early age, and her mother before her. The complaint seemed to stretch back to the Conquest, an unbroken line of infestation, proof against disinfectant, immune to antibiotics, an emblem of peasant origins, as venerable as a coat of arms.

'I don't mind about the legs,' said Linda.

'But think of the baby.'

'She's lovely. She's got my eyes.'

It was useless, at least for the time being, decided Louise. There came a point in all her welfare negotiations when she had to restrain herself. It was like feeding yeast into a bowl of dough. She had to allow time for the facts to do their work. Linda would weigh the pros and cons. If she could see any advantage to herself she would keep the baby. If not, she would consign it to Louise and the agency, and that would be an end to it. When there was another baby – and there was little doubt that Linda would repeat the performance – the same questions would be considered with the same lack of anxiety.

It was awful, but it was enviable. As the wife of the Scientific Director of Proto, and the Director of Contact (the titles still consoled her) Louise wanted an ideal society. Not for its own sake, but as a setting in which she could display herself, as part-architect and prime adornment. She wanted it to reflect her competence, her perspicacity, her humanity. Girls like Linda were an irritant because they were unaware of any Plan. They were not so much obstinate, as obtuse. They lacked imagination. They allowed life to happen without attempting to shape it. They did not co-operate.

'I'll come and see you tomorrow,' she said.

'My mum's coming in the afternoon.'

'Then I'll come in the morning.'

'It's not visiting hours then.'

'I don't think that applies to me,' said Louise. 'It's not exactly a social call.'

Linda stretched herself luxuriously. 'I like it here. I could put up with a lot of this. Any amount.'

'Did you report sick at work?'

'I wasn't sick, was I.'

'You know what I mean.' Louise felt her exasperation mounting. It was a moment to beware. There was a watershed of stupidity, and on its far side was insolence. It was the Proto secret weapon, difficult to pinpoint, impossible to counter. She sweetened her tone. 'Did you tell them at work you would be away?'

'Yes, I told them.'

Linda worked in the bottling department. The process was largely automated, but at intervals along the production line sat girls monitoring the jars, drums, and capsules, as they filed past. What did they think of? wondered Louise. 'Rabbits,' one girl had told her, but it was hard to say whether she was telling the truth. Nor did the industrial psychologists help. 'As far as I can determine,' read one report, 'the monotony of the work constitutes no safety hazard.' Privately he had explained: 'They have no imagination. They're not bored because there's nothing else they'd rather be doing. They can't see themselves in any other situation.'

That part of Proto, Louise recognized, was beyond her control. It was, in any case, the least interesting part. But it was closest to hand, while Contact, her husband's own unit, was out of reach. Blandly, but stoutly, he denied her access. Years ago she had introduced him to Mrs Deeley; as Proto's first public relations officer it had amused her to set up force fields, to act as an honest broker. And he had recognized her usefulness by marrying her. She was a born executive, she had been told; but the decisions she was allowed to make now were merely domestic. She was curious about her own potential, and unless she tested the ground she did not know how far she could go. At times, she felt that the welfare work was merely a rehearsal for something vast, something global. She was an impresario, able to divine talent, to change lives, even, she thought, if the lives were only those of girls like Linda.

'If you keep the baby you'll need another sort of job,' she said.

'Lots of the girls have babies.'

'They don't find it easy.'

'What would I do then?'

'Let me have a think about it,' said Louise. 'You might do something in the house.'

It was strange how ideas were sometimes given to her, she thought, like a bar of cooking chocolate, weight and date stamped, ready to use. Through the swing doors at the end of the verandah she had seen Biddy and Mark, each of them clutching the straps of a carry-cot. She got up smiling. She had work to do.

They got through breakfast without an argument. The trouble began when Mark lifted James out of his high chair, and jogged his arm. His screams brought Biddy running into the kitchen, a blob of mascara hanging from one eyelid.

'What are you doing to him?'

'I'm not doing anything. I just jogged him.'

'Why can't you be more careful?'

'It was an accident. I was lifting him and he slipped.'

She took her son, and buried his crimson face in her cashmere. When he heaved back to draw breath the sweater was streaked with mucus and tears. It looked as though snails had been mating on her shoulder.

'What time's the car coming?'

'Half-nine.' David Dempsey had offered to drive them to the hospital where James was to be x-rayed. It was not going to be a creative morning, thought Mark.

'We should have checked up on that babysitter.'

'Look,' he said. 'I don't believe it was her fault. You know how restless James can be. Most likely, he threw himself out of the cot, just like she said.

Biddy stroked the baby's head. 'I don't believe it.'

'What is it you find so unbelievable?'

'I don't know.' She drew James closer, and rocked him from side to side. 'But we just went out and left him. She was a stranger. He could have been killed.'

'Jesus Christ!' He sat down heavily, and let his hands fall into his
lap. He was oppressed by the sheer physical weight of Biddy's
neurosis. He felt shackles on each wrist, a ball and chain tethering
each ankle. 'She was a perfectly responsible woman. She was
recommended to us by the Dempseys. The other night we even
said it was O.K. for her to leave before we got home. Accidents
happen. He'll be in plenty more before he grows up.'

'*If* he grows up.'

'Don't be melodramatic,' he snapped.

'Don't be unfeeling.'

Checkmate had been reached. Mark twitched the curtains to one
side, but the road was empty. They would have to get a car, he
thought, otherwise his time at Proto would be a prison sentence.
The trouble was they had very little ready cash. 'How much do we
have in the bank?' he asked.

She affected not to hear, and he repeated the question, enunciating
each word with immense care. 'Three hundred pounds, sixteen
pence,' replied Biddy. 'And most of it we owe to Mummy.'

'She doesn't expect it back.'

'That's just the point. It's up to us.'

Mark strode over to his jacket, and pulled the cheque book from
his inside pocket. 'How much exactly?'

'Don't be ridiculous.'

'I want you to tell me. I want to pay the old bag off and have done
with it.'

'We can't afford to. Not at present.'

'Then for God's sake,' said Mark. 'Don't be so bloody silly.'

It was all wrong, he realized. This was one of the times when
they should be united, supporting each other, standing shoulder to
shoulder, although, he reasoned that too was tactical folly. Side by
side they presented a bigger target for whatever slings and arrows
were flying. In Los Angeles they had once turned the corner and
walked into a riot, and the lesson had been well learned: head down
and get the hell out. Biddy had hauled him away from danger, his
eyes streaming with MACE, and that night they had made love as
though they had been granted a reprieve in which to decide what
was most precious in their lives.

It was ironical, thought Mark, that they now had less and less of
what they had come to enjoy more and more. A car hooter sounded

outside, and he waved through the window. 'All set then?' he asked.

It was important to speak, to actually utter words. It signified a truce. 'All set,' she said.

And so, for the time being, it was over. They drove to the hospital, Biddy and James in the front, Mark in the back with an assortment of boots and bats, and screwed-up toffee papers. 'It's a bit squalid,' Dempsey apologized. 'But they're not really house-trained yet, let alone fit for the car.'

'It doesn't matter,' said Mark.

'You learn to live with it, I suppose,' said Biddy.

Dempsey nodded cheerfully. 'Under protest. You keep on hoping they'll become human beings.'

'They do, of course.'

'In the end.' He thumped his fist on the hooter as a large brown dog ambled across the road. 'You can trust the hospital,' he said. 'It's small, but it's efficient. We had both boys in last year to have their tonsils out. They never wanted to leave.'

'I hate hospitals,' said Biddy. 'Even the good ones.'

Dempsey grunted. 'The only thing really wrong with this one is the food. I'd like to get my hands on that diet sheet.'

'Proto on prescription,' said Mark. 'All those guinea pigs.' He watched the concrete flow behind the car. It was white, like the wall surrounding the factory. The houses they were passing were white also, small terraces alternating with semis, their doors and window-frames a uniform green, their wet roofs black as sealskin. In the summer, he thought, they would be purple. His childhood house had been roofed in slate, and its colour had been more reliable as a weather prophet than the tassel of seaweed that hung outside the study window.

'Not a bad bit of town planning,' said Dempsey. 'Nineteen thirty-six, thirty-seven; thereabouts. It was old Deeley's idea. He went up to Jarrow and took half his labour force from the dole queue. Social engineering he called it. He liked to experiment.'

'What happened to him?'

Dempsey looked across at Biddy and hesitated before speaking. 'He died,' he said finally.

'And now Mrs Deeley's the boss.'

'She is indeed.'

'I met her yesterday,' said Mark. 'Strange lady.'

Dempsey leaned on the hooter as four more dogs trotted across the road, their noses rooted in each other's hindquarters. 'Bloody animals,' he said, 'the place is crawling with them. Yes, she's strange. There were no kids, you know. She's all on her own. All that money and no one to give it to.'

'Look no further.'

'Not a chance,' said Dempsey. 'Proto's her baby, especially your part of it. They say old Hoover's got her in the palm of his hand.'

'I doubt it.' He thought of the squat, black figure walking towards the cage. 'I don't think anyone has.'

'Well I haven't. That's for certain.' Dempsey drew up outside the hospital, and opened the car door. 'Best of luck. I'm sure it's not as bad as you think. They'll run you back in the ambulance.' During the drive he had avoided all mention of the accident, Mark realized. Dempsey's tact took on a new dimension.

He was an accurate forecaster too, they agreed later. The x-ray pictures showed a greenstick fracture. 'It'll mend in no time,' said the doctor. 'Keep him as still as you can. And don't worry.'

'Except about finding better babysitters,' said Biddy.

They saw Louise waving at them through the swing doors, and Mark steered the carry-cot in her direction. 'Ask madame,' he said. 'She's bound to have ideas.'

He met Dr Hoover for lunch. They sat beneath a large painting of stags duelling on a blasted heath, watched by a herd of nubile hinds.

'Ever done any?' asked Hoover.

'Any what?'

'Deer-stalking. I had a fellow here who did it every summer. Dreadful business. He used to come back covered in lumps like billiard balls. Horse-flies, he said. Covered in bites from head to toe.'

'Very nasty.'

Dr Hoover waved a stick of celery judiciously. 'It's all in the game. I've had worse.'

'I'm sure you have.'

'Snakes, scorpions, centipedes a foot long. Worst of all were the chiggers.'

'Chiggers?'

'Used to lay their eggs under your toe nails. Had to dig them out with a knife.' He thrust the cheeseboard across the table. 'Have some gorgonzola. It's nice and ripe.'

Mark studied the marbled slab that seemed to pulsate gently beneath his nose. 'I don't think I will.'

'Really?' Dr Hoover cut off a slice. 'The trouble is, persuading them to let it mature. This is just about right. Some people like it actually crawling.'

'I think that's what this is.' Mark indicated a number of pallid worms waving from holes in the section newly-excavated by Dr Hoover.

'You're right. I doubt whether anyone else will want it then.' He beckoned the waitress over. 'I'll take this away with me. Be a good girl and wrap it up.' He leaned across the table. 'Doesn't do to waste good food.'

'Of course not.' Mark sipped his coffee, and debated whether or not to mention the message from Ryman. He decided against it, some unidentifiable caution censoring his conversation. 'I wonder' he said finally, 'if I could see Ryman's notes.'

'By all means. I've already looked them out for you.'

'How long do they cover?'

'One year, perhaps eighteen months. They're not complete, of course. He had the accident.'

'I was going to ask you about that.' Mark dabbed his lips with the table napkin. 'How did it happen?'

For a while he thought Dr Hoover had not heard him. He sat massively in his chair, staring at the tablecloth. Behind his head the stags fought on, their eyes bloodshot, their antlers locked. Hoover sighed, and an avalanche of crumbs rolled towards the water jug. 'Carelessness,' he said. 'Pure carelessness. He was an experienced man, and he failed to take the proper precautions. He entered the large cage alone, and Otto was waiting for him.'

'Otto?'

'Didn't I tell you? That's the name of the ape. They all have names. It's simpler than calling them A, B, and C. Anyway, Ryman was lucky. One of the keepers was near by and heard him call, and they got him out before any more damage was done.'

'Does *he* think he's lucky, with an arm gone?'

Dr Hoover raised his eyebrows. 'Ryman is a realist. He's well aware what might have happened. He could easily have been killed. Otto's thirteen or fifteen years old, we're not sure. He's lived alone for the last few years. He's morose, and quite unpredictable.' He felt in his waistcoat pocket. 'Did you notice his teeth?'

'I'm afraid not.'

'They're weapons. Have a look at this.' Dr Hoover handed Mark what appeared to be the head of a small pick carved from bone. One end was shaped like a chisel, the other like a claw. 'We took that from a beast we had to shoot. I've carried it round with me for ages. Just as a reminder.'

Mark weighed the tooth in his hand. It was an odd sensation, as though shutters, silent and spring-loaded, had been released in his mind, opening on to vistas of pre-history. He felt as though he was being introduced to his own past. 'I imagine they could do a fair amount of damage,' he said.

'Teeth are only part of it. The real weapons are the hands and arms. I saw Otto with an Alsatian once. Tore it to pieces, limb from limb.'

'Then why keep him?' Mark handed the tooth back, glad to be rid of it.

'Because he's a valuable animal, part of the programme. We've improved security since Ryman's accident. There's no danger, so long as the rules are obeyed.'

'I'll take your word for it.'

Dr Hoover smiled benevolently. 'You may have to look at the arrangements a little more closely than that.'

'What do you mean?'

'Otto's not there as a pet. The idea is to try and establish contact.'

'But how?'

'By whatever means seems to be the most rewarding.' The smile was a fixture, thought Mark, but it was devoid of humour. It was the cast of a public face in a public place. What went on behind it was unguessable.

'And the other animals? Dr Bloom's work? Your own?'

'Promising, promising.' Dr Hoover leaned across the table, bringing their faces closer together. 'Research means investigation. That's elementary. If we establish facts and methods, the next stage is to apply them.' The smile dimmed and then re-kindled. 'Don't you agree?'

'Yes, of course. But *where* do we apply them?'

The waitress brought the parcel of cheese, and Dr Hoover beamed his thanks. 'My dear boy,' he said. 'You have the salient facts. Use your imagination.'

Sitting alone at the kitchen table, Biddy Barrow reviewed the events of the morning. The doctor's verdict had been a relief, and James was now asleep. She gave silent thanks, and munched an apple. She disliked lunching alone, but she had refused Louise's invitation to join her. A little of Louise Hoover went a long way. She had insisted on driving Mark to his office, and then, as soon as the car had its nose in the road she had launched into her sales pitch. There had been no need for Biddy to raise the subject.

'What you need is someone to give you a hand,' she began. 'Someone in the house, I mean.'

'I don't think we could afford it.'

'Nonsense.' Louise drove as she spoke, assertively, and with the utter conviction that she was in the right. A brace of cyclists took evasive action, and in the wing mirror Biddy saw them glaring after the car.

'Mark hates to share the house with anyone. He was impossible when my mother stayed with us.'

'He's just selfish. He doesn't have the baby to look after.'

'I love looking after James.'

'But it's too much for you.' The car drove through a large puddle, and water pummelled the underside of the floor boards. Louise gave no sign that she had noticed. Her hands on the wheel were gloved in black kid. They looked trim, competent, unhesitating.

'I do get tired sometimes,' Biddy confessed. 'And I worry. The accident last night upset me. I can't help blaming the babysitter. Mark says I mustn't. But it was such an unnecessary thing to happen. So careless.' She felt tears flooding her eyes, and crossly blinked them back. The needlessness of the mishap was something that Mark did not, or would not understand. In his view there was no guilt to be apportioned. He did not feel responsible.

'We've had this problem before,' said Louise.

'Accidents?'

'No, no. I didn't mean that. Lack of understanding.' She changed gear smoothly, her eyes on the road ahead. 'The men here get so preoccupied with their own business. What happens at home doesn't concern them.'

Biddy glimpsed herself as one of a long line of case histories, and her resentment changed direction. 'It's not like that. Mark's not neglectful.' Her voice faltered. She was no longer sure whose case she was pleading.

'I have a suggestion,' said Louise. 'Nothing more. I wouldn't dream of interfering, but I was talking to a girl this morning – she's just had a baby, in fact – who might be just the person you're looking for. She's perfectly capable of looking after James, and helping you in the house, and it would be doing her a good turn at the same time.'

It was all going too fast, thought Biddy. She wished, desperately, that Mark was with her. 'What about her husband?' she asked.

'There isn't one,' said Louise. 'Of course, if you have some sort of moral objection . . . '

'Oh, no,' said Biddy. 'Not at all.'

Louise tucked her chin briefly against her chest, a small bob of satisfaction, neat as the curtsy of a water bird. 'I'm glad about that. I don't condone promiscuity, of course, but it's important to put first things first. She's living at home at present, but it seems that she wants to keep the baby, and it's quite unsuitable where she is.'

Biddy sensed a change of emphasis in the discussion. The helper and the helped seemed to have exchanged roles. 'Have you mentioned this to . . . whatever her name is?' she asked.

'Linda,' said Louise. 'No. Not yet. But the idea came to me when I saw you both in the hospital.'

'Perhaps she won't want to come.'

'I think that she will.'

'I shall have to discuss it with Mark.'

'I'm sure he'll see reason.'

'I'll let you know then.'

'I'll telephone you this evening,' said Louise firmly.

And, without doubt, she would, thought Biddy. She gnawed the apple core, top and tail, and aimed it at the rubbish bin beneath the sink. It was too light to tilt the swing lid and bounced off on to the floor. Something else for her to pick up, she thought. Perhaps she did need help after all.

SEVEN

Ryman had not been an animal lover; that much was clear from a first reading of his notes. They were kept less methodically than Charlotte Bloom's. Scrolls of red ink rambled across the page, ignoring the ruled lines. There were crossings-out, and afterthoughts added in the margins. Also, Mark discovered, there were personal paragraphs. Ryman had made no distinction between the scientific record and his own random journal. Doubtless he would have edited the manuscript if he had not been disabled, but as Mark pored over the erratic script he felt a growing awareness of the writer's identity. Ryman, he decided, was a bit of a bastard; but he was wholly flesh and blood.

The entries began in September, a year and a half previously. 'Inspected quarters' Ryman had written. 'Inadequate as expected, but will exert pressure. Hoover introduced me to chimpanzee subject. He calls her Lulu. Is the name a consequence of pop zoology? Or in anticipation of same? Hoover suggests desirability of my establishing relationship with chimp. What does he want? Shared digs? My Life in the Wild as told to . . . ? See no necessity for this. Lulu (I accept the name for the sake of convenience) needs to be intimate only with the apparatus. Old maxims apply: the devil finds work for idle hands to do. For devil substitute Proto. Create vacuum, i.e. boredom, to be filled with desired activity. Create *need* for education. Lulu said to be intelligent. Devise tests.'

Most of them, Mark decided as he read on, were routine. There was the grape shy: a board on which grapes were poised on small wooden tees to be knocked off by a ball at the end of a string. After the first day Lulu had done well, scoring an average of four out of six. 'Twenty minutes maximum' Ryman had noted. 'Lulu becomes irritable after time limit expires. Co-ordination excellent. Quick to capitalize on my inattention. Grabs grapes when my back is turned.' She had been less successful with the slot machine, but Ryman made allowances. 'Small thumb makes it difficult for her to insert penny in slot' he had written. 'Succeeds at fifth attempt. Imitates me and pulls out drawer. Reward: two grapes.'

It was all good television material, thought Mark, men and animals at creative play. But other tests were definitely not for family viewing. In December Ryman devised his pushbutton test: 'Four buttons. One, two, and four, deliver grapes. Button three administers slight electric shock. Maintain sequence for one week, then vary. Increase shock.' There was an obstacle course designed on similar lines, and a maze in which one wall was laced with live wires. The entry for January 30 noted: 'Limited use of pain stimulates ability to learn. Reinforces lesson. Secondary effect, however, is to reduce desire to experiment. Lulu now takes few chances. Time, perhaps, to try Hoover's all-friends-together technique.'

Mark lit a cigarette and walked to the window. Behind the raw timber building opposite stood a row of birches, the new leaves on their branches glinting like green sparks. There was no one in he yard, but in his mind's eye, Mark saw it ringed by a procession of tmen wearing suits of striped canvas. He blinked and they were gone, but the memory remained like a line on paper scored by a fingernail. It was ridiculous, he told himself. There was nothing sinister in Ryman's notes. A flock of rooks laboured overhead, battling against a head wind. A door in the end building burst open and two girls raced towards the canteen, one chasing the other. He stubbed out the cigarette and sat down. It was the tone that he disliked, he decided. He was being influenced by the form and overlooking the content.

He read on. 'February 19. Discussed possibility of using a sonograph, i.e. sound spectrograph, to record chimpanzee sounds in visual form for analysis. Hoover objects. Queries value – and expenditure involved – of amassing ape vocabulary. Why reverse the process? he asks. Are we to converse in grunts and groans? Incredibly obtuse. Is there something in his own character which denies the possibility of purely animal communication? Refer him to examples of similar techniques being used to study songs and call notes in birds. Accounts describe different calls to indicate fear or alarm, flocking and flight, leading to analysis of behaviour. Why not similar study with chimpanzees? Try to enlist support from Bloom.'

It was the first mention of Charlotte, Mark noticed, but turning the pages he saw her name repeated again and again. Most of the entries referred to work: 'Bloom encouraged by chimpanzee response . . . Bloom suggests supplementing diet with natural protein . . . Bloom advocates extension of play facilities. Quarrels with boredom theory. Counters with saying of her own choice – all work and no play, etc.' There was no continuity to Ryman's notes, but as the dates multiplied, Mark sensed a dialogue developing. He was merely the eavesdropper. The journal was becoming increasingly intimate.

He ran his finger down the page, and paused against the entry for June 3. 'Situation worsens. Moral: professional and personal relationships don't mix. No surprise. Hoover critical but uncommunicative. Mounting tension at home. What's to be done? No easy answer. Isolation creates the trouble and sustains it. Bloom not pregnant: for this relief much thanks. Query resignation. Hers or mine.' The entry ran to the bottom of the page, but it did not continue overleaf.

In July Ryman made his first reference to sleep teaching. 'Why not? Lulu's intelligence proven to my satisfaction. Resist comparisons, but not unlike simple computer with unvoiced wish to be programmed. Possible procedure. (1) associate object with spoken name, e.g. cup. Word reiterated until connection beyond doubt: query lip manipulation. (2) display object in chimpanzee quarters. Arrange lighting so that object is centre of visual spectrum. Repeat word on tape, dimming light and reducing volume as chimpanzee goes to sleep. (3) at intervals – perhaps hourly – increase light and volume, waking chimpanzee and reinforcing lesson.'

It was pure Heath-Robinson, thought Mark, a précis prepared by a crank inventor, fitting within the framework of a superficial logic, but surely unworkable. He thumbed through the rest of the notes. In August Ryman began the new programme. Three weeks later he wrote: 'Lulu picked up cup this morning and enunciated word clearly and correctly. No reward.' And then, without interruption: 'Talk of divorce, but difficulties considerable. Consider S. African end. Also position of self and family with Proto.' The next page was empty, except for one sentence in capital letters: 'WOULD METHOD SUIT OTTO?' There were no more entries. Mark put the notes into his desk and locked the drawer.

Charlotte Bloom was in the kitchen behind her office. She turned the handle of a hydroponics machine, and trays of wheat shoots rotated like a choice of hors d'œuvres on a restaurant trolley. It was a simple but ingenious way of growing fresh greenstuffs throughout the winter. In his first laboratory Mark had reserved a tray for his own supply of mustard and cress.

'I had no idea you were married,' he said.

'Christ, yes. It's no secret.' She shook the shoots out into a plastic sieve. 'How did the question arise anyway?'

'I was reading Ryman's notes.'

'And he mentions me?'

'Here and there.' Mark perched on the edge of the table. 'He mentions divorce. Yours, I presume.'

'His too. He was married as well.' She corrected herself. 'He still is married. Her name's Dorothy, a very nice lady I'm told. Very keen on protocol. She asked Hoover what she should do about me. He told her to weather the storm. It was bound to blow over.' She rinsed the shoots under the tap, and tipped them into a tea cloth. 'I don't know how to put it, quite. But are the notes . . . very personal?'

'Descriptive, you mean. No, they're not.'

'And Hoover's seen them?'

'I assume so. He gave them to me.'

'Bloody hell.' She swung the tea towel and water sprayed the kitchen. 'Well, I'm not resigning. I'm staying where I am, and they can fire me if they want to.'

'I can't imagine them wanting to do that. No one's sitting in judgment.'

'Oh, no? And how well do you know Mrs Hoover?'

'Hardly at all.'

'You will. I promise you that. It's one of the penalties of working for Proto. She's the Great White Mother of us all.' She stowed the cloth containing the wheat shoots into the bottom of the refrigerator, and took a bottle from the shelf above. 'Care for a drink?'

'What is it, vodka?'

'Straight from Moscow. Last year's visiting fireman was Comrade Poliakoff, and this was his little gift. She raised her glass. 'Here's to progress.'

'Cheers.' The vodka lifted the top of his skull quite gently, and he waited until it dropped back into place. 'Do you get many visitors?'

'We used to get more than we do now. Most of them come to pay their respects to the old man, but we've had a few researchers too.'

'Any useful give and take?'

She shook her head. 'We've taken an idea now and then, but I don't think we've given much back. Hoover's warned us not to discuss what we're doing. In detail, I mean. He likes to make the announcements himself.'

'How did he get on with Ryman?'

'They weren't exactly close. Ryman was too independent. More than that, he made damn sure that Hoover knew he was independent. He made a production of it.'

Mark swilled the vodka in his glass and held it up to the light. The drink was the colour of mulberry, a fruity, sullen red. 'What do they put in it?' he asked.

'Mare's piss,' said Charlotte. 'That's what they tell me. The czar used to wax his moustache in it.' She took a sip and clicked her tongue like a taster. 'Imperial stables, vintage '69.'

'A good year?'

'The best.' She smiled at him as she drank, and he thought how much more attractive she looked when the lines of strain – or was it simply belligerence? – were eased from her face.

'Can I ask you about Ryman?'

'It depends on what you want to know.'

'Was he any good?'

'At his job, yes. In every other respect he was a disaster. He married too young. He hated his wife by the time they came here, and he made sure she knew it. I used to feel sorry for her.' Involuntarily, Mark raised his eyebrows, and she laughed. 'I did, really. It's not hard to sympathize with the wife of someone you're screwing. You have a lot in common. There's the man himself for a start. If you both go for him your tastes must coincide somewhere along the line. Maybe that's all there is. Except that you're both female. You've got the same plagues and ailments, and men haven't a clue what its like to have a belly-ache that lasts for days. I knew how she was feeling when he complained how bloody-minded she was. Of course, I'd think that if I was her I'd do it all differently, and what a silly bitch she was. But it's not true. Not then, and not now. Most likely I'd act in exactly the same way because he'd be the same. He's set in his particular behaviour pattern, and whoever he's with keeps on manufacturing the same situations, and you know in advance how they'll work out.'

'Then why get into it? What's the attraction?'

She looked at him over the rim of her glass. 'You're not asking me about Ryman any more.'

'I'm sorry.'

'Ryman was treated badly here,' said Charlotte. 'He lost his right arm when he went into that cage. It was his own fault. Everyone keeps repeating that, and they're right. He was careless and he should have known better. Proto settled his hospital bills, and gave him an ex gratia payment, but Hoover made it very clear that he hadn't a hope if he sued for compensation. He doesn't even have a claim on the research he was doing. That belongs to Proto too.'

'He telephoned the other evening,' said Mark. 'I was out, but he left a message.'

Charlotte refilled their glasses. 'He's a great one for telephoning. Wait till they start at two in the morning.'

'Why would he do that?'

'He likes to create unease. He even has this line in heavy breathing. No words. No station identification. Just this person, this presence at the other end. He did it to me when we broke up.'

'I still don't understand.'

'I don't suppose he does either.' She put down her glass and spread her hands. 'Look at it this way. You're feeling alone, and miserable, and betrayed, and it's suddenly more than you can bear. So what can you do about it? The simplest thing is to shed some of the load. Spread it around. Let other people worry a bit. I shouldn't imagine for one second that he's worked it out. But I'm sure about the reasons.'

'I hope to God he doesn't get Biddy.'

'That's your wife? She'll be all right. He only goes after the people he feels have let him down. It's a very limited kind of persecution.'

'Why me then?'

'You don't know what he wanted to say. Maybe it was just hello.'

'Is that what you think?'

'Hardly.' She put the bottle back into the refrigerator. 'Maybe he resents you for taking over his research. He might even want to warn you about Otto.'

'I know about Otto.'

'Not like Ryman does. He never stopped talking about that damned ape. He thought he had him taped.'

'That's a terrible joke,' said Mark.

'Joke?'

'He thought Otto was ready for his tapes. It's in the notes.'

'Along with the true confessions.' Charlotte took off her coat and hung it behind the door. 'I've had enough for today. I'm going home.'

'Me too.'

'I'll see you tomorrow then.' She pressed his arm. 'Don't worry about the phone calls.'

They walked side by side to the yard, and at the steps leading up to his office Mark turned to watch her stride away into the chilly dusk. She was not a big woman, but she was solid. With each step her thighs and buttocks trembled briefly as if they had been slapped. There was a run in one leg of her tights, and the lining of her reefer jacket hung below the hem. He could understand why she irritated Louise Hoover, but perhaps he was becoming conditioned, he thought. For the first time he had hardly been aware of her body odour.

During dinner Biddy brought up the subject of Linda Gillis. 'I've not committed us to anything,' she said. 'It's just an idea.'

'It's a rotten idea,' said Mark.

Between them a dish of stroganoff slowly congealed. Biddy had lit candles and melted wax spilled down their sides like tears. She had unpacked their collection of records and on the turntable Cream gave way to the Beatles. It was an old album. He had last heard it, Mark recalled, in a restaurant on Catalina Island. By accident they had chosen to go there on the night of a film première and the waiter had brought them a bottle of champagne – domestic and unasked for. When he had tried to refuse it the waiter had walked away and he had been left standing, bottle in hand, while the freeloaders pelted him with olives.

The boat back to the mainland had been full of drunks. An actor wearing a trilby hat with a tiny brim had joined them at the ship's rail, and together they had stood watching the mushrooms of burst water marking their passage. Then Biddy had screamed, not loudly but in genuine surprise, and he had seen the actor's hand rucking her skirt. When he stepped between them the actor had been sarcastic, then abusive, and there had been a brawl in which Mark had made the actor's nose bleed. Other drunks had separated them, but at the dock they had been foolish enough to accept the offer of a lift home from a film publicist. Once inside the car they realized that the publicist was drunk also, but Biddy had managed to head him off the freeway into a complex of side streets where traffic lights checked them at two hundred yard intervals. They had got home safely, and for a while they stood on the sidewalk, their arms about each other's waists, the night air cool on their damp bodies. What they had shared was a feeling of deliverance, of danger past.

'She loves you' sang the Beatles, and he glimpsed the depth of the chasm that now lay between them.

'All right,' he said. 'Let's talk about it. Have you signed up with the do-gooders, or do you really need someone in the house?'

Biddy sipped her wine. 'It would make life easier.'

'Is it so hard then? You've hardly had time to find out.'

'It would give me a chance to do something on my own.'

'For instance?'

'I don't know. I could get a part-time job.'

'With Louise Hoover?'

'Not with Louise Hoover.'

Mark picked at the candles, pinching the soft wax between his fingers. 'Where would she live?' he asked. 'There's only one spare room for her and the baby. We'd be on top of each other all the time.'

'It's more than she has at home.'

'I wasn't thinking about her. I was thinking about us. About me.' Bitterly he recalled the last time that Biddy's mother had stayed with them, commandeering the lavatory at eight a.m. every day, remaining there for twenty minutes. Strangers in the house always made him constipated, and the visit had lasted for six months.

'Keep her out of the bog in the mornings,' he said.

'I can try.'

'Better than try.'

'I'll keep her out,' said Biddy.

'Would she do the cooking?'

'Breakfasts maybe, nothing else.'

'Can she make coffee?'

'I haven't asked her. She can learn.'

'What about money?'

'We'd arrange something.'

The record clicked to a full stop and Mark got up to turn it over. He sat down again heavily and waited.

'We can afford her,' said Biddy, 'after all, we're not paying rent.'

'That's not the point.'

'I know it's not. The point is that there'll be more time for other things. I won't be so tired.' She stood behind him and stroked his forehead, thinking as she did so 'What a knavish trick'. It had been one of their jokes when they had first lived together, a phrase coined in private to be used in public. The code was rusty, but it was still intelligible.

He pressed his head backwards and felt her breasts divide. 'You're acting like a tart,' he said hopefully.

'Your tart.'

They both paused, half expecting a cry from the nursery. There was no sound, and he reached behind him and ran his hand up her leg. She did not pull away and he encountered a dear, familiar warmth. Sitting down became uncomfortable and he stood up, his shirt slithering against her dress. 'Come on,' he said, and they stumbled upstairs, their mouths glued together, their bodies joined at the hip. On the landing he unzipped her dress and she stepped out of it, letting it fall in a soft puddle, kicking it to one side as he pulled her into the bedroom. A feather from the eiderdown stabbed her back. His tongue lapped her eyelids, and his hands stripped off tights and underclothes. She arched her body to meet him. She saw lights, colours, the tail of a comet, and then it was over, his breath soughing in her ear, his beard grazing her cheek.

Later she heard the record player switch itself off, and while Mark slept she went downstairs to snuff what was left of the candles.

The yellow light moulded the globe of her belly, and as she doused the flame she touched herself reminiscently, tucking a table napkin between her legs to stem the leak.

It had been a knavish trick, she told herself, there was no doubt about that. But the matter was resolved. Now she could talk to Linda Gillis.

EIGHT

'We've had this enquiry,' said Rupert Lacey-Jones. 'Right out of the blue. Chap from the *Sunday Times* rang up, wanting to come down and take a look at your research. Caught me on the hop, I'm afraid. Had to tell him I'd let him know.' He looked expectantly at Mark, then at Dr Hoover. 'I presume it's all in order. Good for the old image, you know.'

Dr Hoover cleared his throat. 'Whose image?'

'Proto's, naturally. Profits subsidizing pure research. Very trendy subject. Couldn't be better.'

'Trendy?' said Dr Hoover with deep distaste. 'What on earth makes a subject trendy?' He rid himself of the word as though it was rancid, a scrap of food from a rotten tooth.

'Topical then. Of current interest.' Lacey-Jones smiled brilliantly. 'Everyone's on about communication these days. It's close to my own heart. Professionally, I mean.'

Briefly, Mark felt some compassion for the visitor. He had arrived on a wave of euphoria, sure of his welcome, confident that all would be plain sailing. Nothing had prepared him for Dr Hoover. Lacey-Jones was about thirty: fresh-faced and blue-suited. He wore a striped tie with a tiny knot which jutted from his stiff white collar in an arc like the tail of a horse about to defecate. His hair was black and wavy with a precise parting. His company, he explained, handled public relations for Proto. It was one of his favourite accounts.

Dr Hoover charged each of his nostrils with snuff, and dusted his upper lip with his handkerchief. 'There's nothing for you here,' he said.

'But I've told you, we represent Proto.'

'That is no concern of mine.'

Lacey-Jones adjusted his smile. 'I don't think you understand. We're *paid* to represent you.'

'I have no wish to be represented.'

Lacey-Jones appealed to Mark. 'We have a contract. We've looked after you for years. It's normal business practice.' He leafed through his diary. 'I was here two months ago. I saw Dr Bell.'

Dr Hoover leaned across his desk. 'Did he tell you to pester me?'

'Of course not. I told you, we had a newspaper enquiry.'

'And what prompted that, I wonder.'

Lacey-Jones shrugged his shoulders. 'I've no idea. It's usually something they've read in one of the scientific journals, or a tip from someone in the know.'

'Could you find out?'

'I very much doubt it.' Lacey-Jones tugged his lapels, and spread his buttocks more firmly in the chair. He was like a hen, thought Mark, unexpectedly ruffled but bearing down on the nest egg that was his future. 'It's a question of ethics,' he said. 'I could ask, of course, but journalists don't like to reveal their sources of information.' He was assailed by a sudden doubt. 'There's nothing peculiar going on is there? Nothing they might call cruelty?'

'Don't be impudent.'

'The point is,' said Mark, 'Dr Hoover doesn't wish to discuss his research. The time isn't right.' He cast around for some crumb of comfort. 'Perhaps in six months we'll have something for you. Couldn't you put them off till then?'

Lacey-Jones ran a finger along the knife edge of his collar. 'It isn't easy. Journalists have suspicious minds.'

And rightly, thought Mark. Suspicion was a form of insurance that everyone should carry. He tried to catch Dr Hoover's eye. 'What if I showed Mr Lacey-Jones round,' he said tentatively, 'just to put him in the picture.' He raised a hand, stilling the imminent protest. 'I could give him a general idea of the work in progress. Just a rough outline. I'm sure he'll understand why we don't want to make any announcement at present.' There was a system employed by mind-readers, he recalled, a use of key words which transmitted a message within a message. It was the language of diplomacy. He stared across the desk, willing Dr Hoover to understand.

The seconds ticked by. The shaggy eyebrows rose and fell. 'I take your point,' said Dr Hoover. 'We don't want to appear inhospitable.' He pushed back his chair with a squeal of castors, and spread his arms. 'There's nothing we wish to conceal, but the point about research is that it's a continuing enquiry, a business of trial and error. Possibly I'm over-sensitive, but when I'm asked questions – quite innocent questions – I feel that I'm back at school. The interrogation is on. It makes me uneasy. The hairs on the back of my neck stand up. Quite literally. I'm sure you can understand that.'

'Of course,' said Lacey-Jones. 'It must be very off-putting.'

'Precisely.' Dr Hoover snapped his fingers implying, thought Mark, how lucky he was to know a man so astute, so comprehending as Lacey-Jones, ready to furnish him with the exact expression that he sought.

Lacey-Jones writhed with pleasure. His cheeks flamed, and he lunged forward as though a pin had been jabbed in his rump. 'Dr Hoover,' he said. 'I can assure you that I am not here to intrude. 'My wish, *our* wish is merely to serve. I only ask, that is to say *we* only ask to be taken into your confidence. Not entirely. But in part. We need to know what *not* to say. Eight-tenths of an iceberg is under water. I need to know, that is to say *we* need to know what areas to avoid. Do I make myself clear?' He perched on the edge of his chair, his face burnished with hope. What he was witnessing, Mark realized, was something on the lines of a courtship display. Mentally, he classified it as rampant grovelling. It was practically the stuff of a thesis.

Dr Hoover stood up noisily, and rested a hand on Lacey-Jones's shoulder. 'Say no more. Dr Barrow will show you what there is to be seen. Then perhaps you will join us for lunch.'

'Delighted,' Lacey-Jones stammered. 'Really delighted.'

'We'll see you later,' said Mark. He awarded Hoover full marks. The atmosphere in the room was changed as though by instant dialysis. Each particle of ill feeling and suspicion had been scrubbed and rinsed clean. All he had needed to do was give the line, and – like the old pro he was – Hoover had taken his cue. He herded them into the corridor, children off on an outing. His farewell smile was a blessing.

'An amazing old boy,' said Lacey-Jones.

'Quite.'

'A real character.'

'Yes, indeed.'

'Not many like him left, I should imagine.'

'Practically unique.'

'I'm so glad we came to terms.'

End of sequence, thought Mark. He was fairly adept at small talk, batting puff-balls of conversation across a courtesy net, but there was a limit to his enthusiasm for the game. Lacey-Jones, he decided, was a twit, and he was not in the mood for a guided tour. He felt decidedly languid after the night's activities. He had woken up shortly before dawn, and found Biddy naked beside him. They had made love a second and third time, and after she had gone back to sleep, curled against his chest, he had remained awake, reviewing the concession he had made. It rankled now. She would hold him to the bargain, and he could not risk defaulting.

'Where do we start?' asked Lacey-Jones.

Mark stifled a sigh. 'I think, perhaps, you should meet Rosie,' he said.

Two hours, and a full programme of intelligence tests later, his feet were aching and his patience was starting to fray. He had avoided all mention of Otto. He had glossed over Ryman's accident. He had steered clear of Charlotte. His patter, he thought, had been glib, colourful, and entertaining. He had given value for money, but Lacey-Jones was indefatigable.

'I envy you,' he said. 'I can see how satisfying the work must be.'

On a stool between them Rosie sat peeling a banana. Her fingers were deft, her eyes were bright, and she ate with finicky precision. Any moment now, thought Mark, he would say that she looked almost human.

'You know,' said Lacey-Jones, 'she looks almost human.'

'But she's not.'

'I realize that. But you know what I mean.'

'Proto makes bonny babies.'

'I beg your pardon.'

'I was just thinking of a slogan. Next year's campaign.' Mark remembered to smile; an exercise, he reminded himself, which he had performed a good deal that day.

'That's not my line,' said Lacey-Jones. 'I've nothing to do with the actual advertising.' He watched the banana disappear. 'All the same,' he said, 'it's worth passing on.'

'By all means.'

Rosie wiped her lips with the back of her hand, and rocked backwards and forwards on the stool. 'Do you think I might pick her up?' asked Lacey-Jones. 'I'd be very careful.'

Mark hesitated. 'I wouldn't advise it.'

'She *wants* me to pick her up.'

'All right, go ahead. But don't excite her.' He had done his duty, thought Mark. He had delivered the statutory warning but Lacey-Jones would not be warned. There had been no overall to fit him, and already his blue suit was flecked with chimpanzee hair. 'Not to worry,' he said, 'it'll brush off.' He bent down and Rosie embraced his neck and ran up his body, her flat feet drumming against his chest. 'Steady on,' said Lacey-Jones, 'take a little nap.' He tipped Rosie backwards, and cradled her in one arm, tickling her with his free hand. Rosie bared her teeth in ecstasy. She rolled her head from side to side, and her arms flailed like apron strings.

'If I were you . . .' began Mark, but Lacey-Jones ignored him.

'She likes me,' he said triumphantly. His fingers raked through the short fur on Rosie's ribs, and the chimpanzee squirmed in his grasp. Her toes curled, and Mark reached out to pluck her away. But he was too late. A jet of urine hosed the front of Lacey-Jones's waistcoat, darkening the blue of the material, and saturating his shirt.

For several seconds he stood motionless while Rosie lay perfectly still in his arms, her grin relaxed, her eyes dreamily contented. Water plopped on to the floor, widening the pool between Lacey-Jones's glittering shoes. 'Christ!' he said in a small, shocked voice. 'I'm wet through.'

'I tried to tell you,' said Mark.

'But I'm drenched.'

'It always happens when she gets too excited.'

Lacey-Jones straightened his arms in a spasm of disgust, and Rosie slid to the floor, whimpering softly. She dipped a finger into the puddle, and stopped to study the trail it made as she backed away. Really, thought Mark, she was conducting an experiment. Dr Hoover would be interested. It was he who had called Rosie a genius.

Louise Hoover and Biddy sat side by side on the settee in Mrs

Gillis's front room. It was part of a three-piece suite upholstered in brown rexine and grained to resemble leather. Biddy inched her way forward but the rexine clung to the backs of her thighs, sucking moisture from the skin and dispensing it in an unpleasant dew. It was very cold. There was a red paper fan in the grate, and an electric fire glowed dispiritedly beside it, releasing a strong smell of roasted dust.

'Will she be long?' hissed Biddy.

Louise shook her head. 'I can hear her coming.'

There was a succession of heavy bumps overhead, followed by the sound of something inert being dragged along the passage. The door opened and Mrs Gillis limped towards them. She wore a yellow hair net, a long grey cardigan, and slippers which oozed a dingy fleece from assorted pressure points. Her legs, Biddy saw thankfully, were bandaged. As she lowered herself into a chair beside the electric fire, she patted them like a plumber making sure that his pipes were properly lagged.

'Terrible today,' she said.

Biddy smiled blankly. 'What is?'

'My legs,' explained Mrs Gillis. 'Pain morning, noon, and night. Nobody knows how I suffer.' She stroked the bandages with evident pride. 'The doctor can't do anything for me. I've seen specialists. Useless.'

'We came to ask you about Linda,' said Louise. 'Mrs Barrow wants to offer her a job.'

'All useless,' said Mrs Gillis, deaf to interruptions. 'One of them told me I represented a defeat for science. His very words. I've seen the top men. Mrs Hoover knows.'

'I certainly do,' said Louise.

'Mrs Hoover took me herself to see one of them.'

'Yes I did,' said Louise.

'Up to London by car. One of them big hospitals. Test after test. Useless.' She nodded with grim satisfaction.

A silence fell during which Biddy realized a contribution was now required from her. She reached into her bin of platitudes. 'Science doesn't know everything,' she said.

Mrs Gillis accepted the tribute. 'Very true.'

'We must keep trying though,' said Louise. 'That's what we're here for.'

The smell of burning dust became stronger, but only their breath smoked in the chilly room. Louise should have warned her, thought Biddy. The sense of ritual was overwhelming. Next, she guessed, there would be a token offering, a gift to the shaman. And then, perhaps, a cup of tea – Proto's equivalent of a peace pipe. Then they could proceed with the business in hand.

Her instinct was sound. Louise opened her handbag, and took out a paper bag. 'I brought some of your peppermints. The extra strong.'

'Very kind of you. The kettle's boiling.'

They were left alone while Mrs Gillis clashed cups and saucers in the kitchen. The door was ajar and they spoke in whispers. 'She won't be hurried,' mouthed Louise. 'We have to proceed in stages.'

Biddy nodded. 'How long will it take?' Peg Dempsey was looking after James. She had promised to be back within the hour.

'Can't tell.'

'But can't Linda decide for herself?'

'Linda does as she's told.' Mrs Gillis appeared in the doorway, the tea tray in front of her. She waited while Louise unhitched a nest of tables, and then put the tray down. 'Milk and sugar?'

'Both please,' said Biddy. She cradled the cup in her hands and peered through the steam. 'We know Linda takes your advice,' she said, 'but Mrs Hoover thought she might like to work for me.'

'Linda's got a job.'

'The point is that Linda wants to keep her baby,' said Louise, 'and Mrs Barrow could give her a nice home.'

'She got a nice home already.'

'But rather crowded.'

'There's room enough.' Mrs Gillis saw the weakness of her argument and tried to reinforce it. 'We'd make room.'

'Of course you would, but there's no need.' Biddy shot a warning glance at Louise: leave her to me. 'She'd be quite close. She could come and see you whenever she wanted to.'

'Umm.' Mrs Gillis sucked at her cup. 'What about wages?'

'Whatever's reasonable. I thought five pounds a week, with full board.'

'Maybe. What about your husband?'

Biddy frowned. 'I don't know what you mean.'

'Will he keep himself to himself?'

'I don't follow.'

'We don't want any hanky-panky. My Linda's a good girl.'

With one bastard already to prove it, thought Biddy. 'But unlucky,' she suggested. 'Unlucky in her friends.'

It was a palpable hit. Mrs Gillis sighed, and conceded the point. 'She always was too trusting. She needs looking after.'

'I could keep my eye on her,' said Biddy. She felt a surge of elation, the quickening of a bargain about to be struck. Louise Hoover, she realized, was looking at her with a new respect. But even as she gathered herself to clinch the deal, she was struck by another thought. She had not particularly wanted to employ Linda Gillis, and Mark, she knew, was actively hostile to the idea.

Somehow, she had allowed herself to become involved in a course of action. The reins had been passed to her, and instinctively she had run the race. 'A drop of something to keep out the cold?' said Mrs Gillis, and, almost absent-mindedly, Biddy looked up to see her with a miniature bottle of whisky poised over her cup.

She nodded, and Mrs. Gillis smiled broadly. 'Good health, then,' she said. 'I reckon you and our Linda'll suit each other fine.'

After lunch (eaten in borrowed slacks and sweater) Lacey-Jones left for London. Mark walked with him to the car park and waited, hands in overall pockets, while he polished his windscreen. The car was a Morgan – canary-yellow, low-slung, and sporty. It was, almost too blatantly, a piece of image-making equipment. A work of fiction, thought Mark, and not to be taken seriously; but he felt jealous all the same.

'Sorry about Rosie,' he said.

'Not your fault,' said Lacey-Jones. 'And thanks for the loan of the clobber. I'll return it.'

'There's no hurry.'

Lacey-Jones breathed on the glass, and rubbed it vigorously. 'I enjoyed the tour.'

'I'm glad.'

'What there was of it.'

'I'm not with you.'

Lacey-Jones shook the duster, and folded it into a neat square. 'Balls,' he said. 'The last time I got this kind of treatment was at some government place where they made nerve gas. Something's going on here that I'm not supposed to know about. It sticks out a mile. You don't have to tell me, of course, but someone's got the smell of it. Reporters don't ring up to pass the time of day. I'll do what I can, naturally. But there'll be more enquiries. It won't stop here.'

Lacey-Jones was brighter than he had realized, thought Mark. 'I haven't told you any lies,' he said.

'I'm not saying that you have. But you've been . . . selective.'

'I suppose so.'

'You ought to work on the old boy. Get him to open up a bit.' Lacey-Jones gave his windscreen a last caress, and climbed into the car. The engine roared and cinders spurted from beneath the wheels. 'I'll be in touch.'

'Right you are.'

The Morgan slewed on to the road, and disappeared in a blue haze of exhaust fumes. Mark stood with his hand raised in farewell. It was unsettling to be caught out so easily; even more unsettling not to have known that the deception was plain to see. All his life Mark had despised the Lacey-Jones's of his acquaintance, but he acknowledged their uses. In a war they would make superb interrogators. Their blandness was a box, an ornamental casket containing machinery which worked efficiently, without conscience and without scruple. He was mercenary, attuned to the main chance. It was instinct, rather than intelligence which sharpened his wits. But it was also instinct, thought Mark, which had prompted him to censor his own account of Contact's work programme.

Clearly, Hoover had approved. At lunch he had been the ribald host, bawdly informative about mating habits, marriage rites, and native customs in East Africa; a National Geographic lecture with extra spice. He had talked almost exclusively about the past. 'At my age,' he told Lacey-Jones, 'I step lightly towards the future. I have no wish to surprise the echoes.'

A resonant observation, thought Mark, but meaningless. He recalled the Thurber drawing of a harassed male quizzing his broody mate: 'What do you want to be inscrutable for, Marcia?' The same question could be put to Proto, but it was doubtful whether it would be understood, let alone answered. Zoologists, researchers, manufacturing chemists were all bound to keep trade secrets, but discretion had somehow become a passion for plotting, to which he himself had succumbed. For no good reason that he could think of he had played games with Lacey-Jones, when it would surely have been in everyone's interest to tell all, and then indicate where embargoes were necessary. It was in the air, he decided. Duplicity was like the common cold, and he had caught the virus.

At the edge of the car park, he saw Mrs Deeley's Bentley, a sitting room on wheels. She was not inside it, and looking round, Mark realized that he was near Otto's enclosure. He took the cinder track, and found the gate at the end of it unlocked. The arena was just as he had last seen it, but in front of the cage sat Mrs Deeley on a green canvas stool, a thermos flask in her lap.

She turned slowly, and studied him without any change of expression. 'Good afternoon,' said Mark.

'Good afternoon.'

As she spoke the straw in the cage erupted, and Otto hurled himself against the bars. 'He dislikes me,' said Mrs Deeley.

'Why is that?'

'He thinks I intrude.'

'But it's your place,' said Mark. 'You should tell him that.'

Mrs Deeley compressed her pale lips. 'Don't humour me.'

'I wouldn't dream of it.'

'And do not be facetious. I find it irritating.'

'I'm sorry.' He swallowed hard and waited to be dismissed. He was angry, but he was also intrigued. She must have been there for hours, he thought. Beneath her stool there was a knife, fork and plate on which there remained some scraps of smoked salmon. There was a small wicker basket containing fruit, and beside it there was a box of chocolate mints. 'Isn't it chilly for a picnic?' he asked.

'I don't feel the cold.'

He believed her. She was a Snow Queen already. He was reminded of photographs he had once seen of Victoria in mourning; grief holding her firm like aspic. Mrs Deeley had the same air of ceaseless vigil, of waiting because it was both her inclination and her duty. 'Have you tried Otto with the fruit?' he asked.

'He takes nothing from me now.'

'Did he ever?'

'Oh, yes,' said Mrs Deeley. 'At one time he did. At one time we were friends.'

'What happened?'

'He betrayed me,' said Mrs Deeley. She stood up, and stepped to one side, so that Mark instinctively reached for her stool. 'The driver will collect the rest,' she said.

As she turned away the chimpanzee threw himself against the bars, ricochetting from one wall to another, hurling dung and straw after them, his screams collecting and colliding within the arena so that Mark saw the echo as a hoop of sound spinning endlessly about them. Mrs Deeley did not look back. She walked briskly towards the gate where the driver met them. 'Thank you, Dr Barrow,' she said.

'You know that I'll be working with Otto from now on?'

'Dr Hoover told me.'

'I think you could be of help.'

'I doubt it.'

'Mrs Deeley,' said Mark. 'You pay me for whatever I do here. Aren't you in the least economy-minded?'

She shook her head once. 'Single-minded.'

Fat, isolated drops of rain began to fall, and the driver put up an umbrella. 'You'll get wet,' said Mrs Deeley. 'Can I drive you to your office?'

'I don't think so, thank you. I need the air.'

'Just as you wish.'

The rain was heavy when the Bentley overtook him, but he did not regret his decision to walk. The dialogue had run into a dead end. What do you want to be inscrutable *for*, Marcia?, he asked silently as the rear-lights bobbed out of sight. Mrs Deeley was not going to tell him. But it was time, thought Mark, to put the question to Dr Hoover.

NINE

That evening, while watching the nine o'clock news, Dr Hoover had an accident. He was enjoying the programme: street riots and a murder hunt at home, guerilla training in the Middle East, a hurricane in Florida. Colour, he always argued, helped catastrophe to realise its true potential as entertainment. He was not concerned with the subtleties. On Hoover's screen, faces glowed as succulently as prime steak; skies were cobalt; forests, inky green. He preferred quantity to quality.

The day, he thought, had gone well. Barrow had disposed of Lacey-Jones with uncommon tact. Mrs Deeley's visit had been no more than a social call. The research projects were ticking over nicely. He reached for the pot of coffee on the table beside him, and as he tilted it over his cup, felt the handle jerk free like a plug from its socket. The coffee pot dropped into his lap. In the fraction of time that elapsed before pain laved his thighs he saw a rooftop, scalped by gale force winds, sail like a discus across the screen and disappear down an alley of telegraph poles. 'More than three hundred people are feared dead,' said the newscaster.

Dr Hoover reared up from his chair, plucking at the trousers which clung to him like a compress. He heard himself roaring wordlessly. The heat was impossible, unbearable. He danced on one leg, and then the other, wrenching off his jacket and waistcoat. Buttons sang across the room. He stripped off his braces, unzipped his fly, and as his trousers fell, sighed as the cool air struck his steaming flanks.

'What on earth . . . ?' In the open doorway Louise gaped at her husband. Behind him armoured cars, their guns blazing, traversed the television screen. She switched it off, and peeled away his undershorts. 'Does it hurt?'

'Of course it hurts!'

'Cold water,' she said. 'I'll fill the bath.' She sprinted to the foot of the stairs, and then ran back. 'Hurry! Before it blisters.'

Dr Hoover limped after her, wincing with every step. 'It was that coffee pot,' he bellowed. 'It came away in my hand.'

'What?' Louise peered over the banisters.

'The handle. It came clean away.'

'Alec Bell gave it to us.'

'I'm not surprised.' Years earlier the Bells had tried to institute a ritual exchange of Christmas presents, but the traffic had been one way. As overlord of Proto, Dr Hoover had considered the gifts as a tithe that was no more than his proper due. He was not put out when they ceased. Alec Bell had grown up. Evolution took its toll.

In the bathroom he stood awkwardly while Louise unbuttoned his shirt. At any other time he would have enjoyed the attention, but now the pain was too intense. 'My legs,' he said.

'Get in the bath.'

'What about my shoes?'

'Forget about your shoes. Sit on the edge.'

He did as he was told, and Louise tipped him gently into the water. He slid down the porcelain, gasping as the cold punched out his breath. It was like being back at school, a non-swimmer then, clinging to the rail at the shallow end and staring pitifully up at the games master who supervised the morning plunge. The chill was the same. So was the feeling of desolation. But now he sat in his own bathroom watching his brogues drown beneath the rising tide.

'I'll ring the hospital,' said Louise.

'I don't want to go to hospital.'

'I think you should.'

The water rose higher, and Dr Hoover shivered violently. 'All right.'

In the ambulance he wore his bathrobe, striped like a marquee. 'I suppose you'd better let Bell know,' he said.

'What should I tell him?'

'Tell him it's not serious. Say I'll be back in a couple of days.'

'I think I should ask the doctor.'

'Damn the doctor! Tell him a couple of days.'

He was unloaded on a stretcher, an aluminium cradle keeping the blankets from his legs. His teeth chattered while his thighs were on fire. 'I didn't sponge the carpet,' said Louise.

'The carpet?'

'There'll be a terrible stain.'

Dr Hoover closed his eyes, and turned his head away. He longed for oblivion. On safari once he had caught malaria. For three days and nights the bearers had carried him through forest and savannah, and for most of the journey – they told him later – he had sung 'Pack Up Your Troubles'. But he was younger then. Joggling over the wet tarmac he felt a thousand years old and maimed more brutally than he dared imagine.

Doors swung open, and he was carried inside. The ceiling flowed above him, and he was ringed by faces. 'Something to take the pain away,' said a voice, and he felt a sting on his left arm. Then darkness blotted the faces, the ceiling shrank like the pupil of an eye, and suddenly, it too was shuttered, and he was away.

'It's been a busy night,' the matron told Louise after she had seen Francis wheeled into a private ward – his lower belly, genitals, and thighs painted a deep orange. 'That Linda Gillis discharged herself.'

'Why did she do that?'

The matron pursed her lips. 'She's a little madame, that one. The ward sister told her it was after hours for smoking, and she gave her a proper mouthful.'

'How dreadful!'

'No more than you'd expect. Sister came to fetch me, and when I got there our Miss Gillis was up and dressed and shouting for the baby.'

'And you let her take it?'

'What else could I do? She's got a home to go to. We couldn't keep her by force.'

'I wish you'd let me know.'

'You had enough on your plate, Mrs Hoover.'

'But she was my concern.'

The matron drew herself up so that her starched collar and cuffs clanked a warning. 'First things first,' she said. 'We can't do everything. The girl was perfectly fit. In the ordinary course of events she'd have gone home the day after tomorrow. And I don't like my staff being insulted.'

That was the heart of the matter, thought Louise. And the boundary had been drawn for her too. Trespassers would be denied help, sympathy, co-operation. She was too tired to argue. 'I suppose she'll be all right. I'll call in and see.'

'Just as you like. But take my word, Mrs Hoover. There's no need to worry about *that* one.'

They had reached the entrance, and she saw Alec Bell waiting, hat in hand. 'They telephoned me,' he said. 'Is he going to be all right?'

'Of course,' said Louise. 'I was going to ring you myself.'

He smiled, so briefly that he appeared to be wincing. 'I'm sure you were. But there was no need. They keep me informed.' He pushed the door open and waved her on. 'I'll drive you home.'

'That's kind of you.'

'No trouble at all.'

'It was the coffee-pot that did it,' said Louise. 'The one you gave us. The handle came off.' She pulled on her gloves, and straightened the seams. The apology, she thought, was a long time coming.

'That's terrible,' said Alec Bell, at last. 'But we might be able to fix it. Some of the glues you can buy these days mend anything.'

It was ten minutes to seven when Mark left the Contact block. After the meeting with Mrs Deeley he had returned to his office and read through Ryman's notes for a second and third time and it was not until he heard the Proto clock, half a mile away, chime the third quarter that he realized how late it was.

He telephoned Biddy. 'I'm on my way.'

'David Dempsey got home an hour ago.'

'He's not Hoover's right hand,' said Mark. He told her about Lacey-Jones.

'Is that part of the job?'

'Absolutely.'

'Well, make haste now. You've missed seeing James.'

'How was he?'

'Absolute hell. I've put him to bed.'

'Lucky old James.'

'Just hurry back.' She broke the connection, and Mark stood thoughtfully for a moment before replacing his own receiver. Biddy's telephone manner intrigued him. It was brisk but intimate, like a commercial for toothpaste which hinted at all things nice, but distantly. Promise and fulfilment were kept apart like separate entities, cousins maybe, but coming from branches of the family which seldom spoke.

On an impulse he put Ryman's notes into his briefcase, and locking the door behind him, walked down the corridor. The rain had dwindled to a fine drizzle, and crossing the courtyard he saw Charlotte Bloom, her collar turned up, her hands thrust into her coat pockets. He caught up with her, and got into step. 'Terrible night.'

'Terrible.'

'I've got to do something about getting a car. No one told me about the daily hike.'

'Hoover calls it his constitutional.'

Mark trod in a puddle and felt a cold patch blossom on his ankle. 'Dempsey says he can make it to the lab in four and a half minutes. He wants to get me in training.'

'You look fit enough.'

'How wrong can you be.' He coughed theatrically. 'Hoover wants me to stop smoking too.'

'You should expect that,' said Charlotte. 'They'll all try to reform you.' Rain pebbled her short black hair, and when she wiped it off, her fringe was plastered to her forehead. She pointed to the left. 'I go that way.'

'Do you pass the club?'

'Invariably. I mean, I never go in.'

'Break your rule. Have a drink with me.'

'Are you sure?'

'Of course I'm sure.' He cupped her elbow in one hand, and steered her down the road. 'I want to ask you about Ryman.'

'What about him?'

'Did he ever tell you about Mrs Deeley?'

'Now and then. Nothing special. He didn't have much to do with her.'

'Did he tell you about her visiting Otto?'

'Yes. He warned her not to get too close. Funny, the way things turned out.'

'Did he say anything about how Otto betrayed her?'

Charlotte stopped short, and peered at him through the dusk. 'Did you say betrayed?'

'That's right.' He nudged her towards the lights of the club. 'That's what Mrs Deeley said to me this afternoon. She said they used to be friends, but Otto betrayed her.'

'She said nothing like that to Ryman. At least, he didn't tell me if she did.'

They passed St Francis in the foyer, and went into the bar. 'What's it to be?' said Mark.

'Vodka and tonic.'

'It won't be vodka like yours.'

'It'll be fine.'

The Bells were not there he observed thankfully, the chances were that it was too early. He made a mental note of the time: seven twenty-five. Ten minutes and then home, he told himself. Biddy was waiting, and there were matters to discuss. He intended to return to the subject of home helps. There was more to be said on both sides.

'Thank you for keeping that PR away,' said Charlotte.

He raised his glass. 'Cheers. It was easy enough. I didn't think you'd want to be bothered.'

'Quite right. I heard he had an accident.'

'A small soaking. He wasn't so bad, all things considered. He thinks the old man has secrets.'

'And what do you think?'

'I think he's right.' Mark opened his briefcase, and took out Ryman's notes. 'I was going through these again tonight. Ryman says that you disagreed about methods.'

She nodded, and poured more tonic water into her glass. 'Sometimes I thought he was round the bend.'

'Were you involved in the sleep-teaching?'

'Early on. We weren't seeing much of each other towards the end.'

'Why was that?'

'I don't know, quite. I think I decided that he was too much like my husband. He'd go so far in argument, and then he'd dig his heels in. Papal infallibility. The point in question became an article of faith.' She shook her head. 'I can't stand dogma.'

Mark offered his cigarette case. 'Smoke?'

'Thank you.' As she reached for the cigarette she became aware of her bitten nails. 'I've got so many bad habits,' she said.

'Haven't we all.' He struck a match, and she leaned across the table, squinting against the flame. For the first time that evening he caught the ripe smell of her body, but he did not draw back. It did not have to be excused, he told himself. It could be justified professionally, and it was not as distasteful as he had first thought. In fact, given the right time and place, he knew he could find it appetizing. A declaration of intent, Charlotte Bloom's manifesto. It was obvious why Louise Hoover disliked her so much.

He leafed through Ryman's notes and pushed one of the pages towards her. 'Did he show you this?'

She read the words silently, and then repeated them aloud. '*Post coitum omne animal triste*. After love all animals are sad. He was always quoting it.'

'He was quoting it wrong.'

'The original, or the translation?'

'Just the translation. *Animal* means spirit. The universal letdown.'

She smiled, and tapped the ash from her cigarette. 'Then it was Ryman's joke. We were all animals to him. Naked apes one and all. I know what he meant.'

'So do I.'

'Do you really?'

'Of course.' He looked at his watch, and groaned. 'Jesus, it's late. I've got to move.'

'Have a drink with me next time.'

'I've already done that.'

'I mean at my place.' She checked herself. 'Bring your wife. I'm bad about invitations. I've got out of the habit of asking people.'

They parted outside the club, and Mark trotted to the bottom of the hill. He would talk to Biddy about a car, he decided. Perhaps she could borrow the deposit from her mother. What was another couple of hundred on top of what they already owed? He was a good risk, or so the insurance companies thought who wanted to put him on their books. Two agents had written to him that week; there was a bush telegraph advising them of likely prospects. In a way it was flattering, an invitation to join the club. He was a man with a future. All hail to Proto, and sign on the dotted line.

As he topped the rise he saw a figure standing outside his house, and for a moment he thought, Ryman, and quickened his pace. Almost immediately, he realized he was mistaken. It was a girl, and she was carrying something, a bundle wrapped in white.

'Are you Dr Barrow?'

'That's right. Can I help you?'

'I didn't know whether to knock. My mum told me to come straight here.'

'Your *mum* told you?'

'That's right.' As she stepped forward a small sound leaked from the bundle in her arms. 'We had a falling-out, and she said I'd better come straight round.'

Mark looked at her stonily. 'What's that you're carrying?'

'Just the baby.'

'*What* baby?'

'It's mine,' said the girl. 'I'm Linda Gillis. I've come to work for you.'

The argument was well advanced when, two hours later, Louise called. Alec Bell hovered behind her on the garden path, twice taking his hat off, and twice putting it back on while information was exchanged.

'Your protegé is here,' Mark told Louise.

'Thank God for that.'

'A matter of opinion,' said Mark. 'The fact is, I don't want her.'

'But Biddy said you agreed to have her.'

'I changed my mind.'

'You can't do that. She has nowhere to go.'

'You'll find somewhere, I've no doubt.'

'I can't,' said Louise. 'Not tonight. There's been an accident. Francis is in hospital.'

Later, Mark saw that point of their dialogue as an act of demolition, shocking as though a pyramid of glasses which he had stacked with swift assurance had been felled by the removal of one tumbler. His anger with Louise disintegrated. Her misfortune was greater than his: scissors cut paper, stone blunts scissors. 'God, I'm sorry,' he said. 'What sort of accident? What happened?'

Alec Bell cleared his throat and rested his finger tips in the small of Louise's back. 'Perhaps we could come inside.'

'Yes, of course.' Mark let them in. He felt tremulous; with his anger drained away he was as holey as a sponge.

'Francis dropped a pot of coffee in his lap,' said Louise. 'The handle came off.'

'He's scalded?'

'Quite badly. But it's the shock . . .'

'At his age,' said Alec Bell, 'it's very distressing.'

'There's nothing more we can do at present,' said Louise. 'He's resting quite comfortably. He thinks he'll be out in a couple of days but it may be longer. We'll just have to wait and see.' She glanced round the hall. 'Where's Linda?'

'In the sitting room.' He opened the door, and they saw Linda Gillis and Biddy, poised attentively on opposite sides of the fire. It was like returning to the rehearsal of a play after an outside interruption, thought Mark. The scene was where he had left it, the lines waiting to be delivered, the outcome still to be resolved.

'I heard it all,' said Biddy to Louise. 'I'm sure he'll be all right.'

'I expect so.'

'And Linda will be staying. The argument is over.'

'What about Mark?'

'Mark was discourteous. I'm sorry about that.'

'Don't apologize for me,' said Mark, but his voice was hollow.

They were all looking at Biddy with profound respect. They recognized authority when they heard it. 'I'll go then,' said Louise. 'I'll give you a ring in the morning.'

Somehow, she avoided seeing Mark, but Alec Bell drew him to one side. 'Could you look in on me around ten? With Dr Hoover laid up you'd better let me know how the research stands.'

Mark nodded, too far gone for words. Upstairs, a child began to cry. Then the lament became a duet; first Baby, then James. They made a fine couple, he thought. He wondered why he had ever decided to leave America.

TEN

'Do you know an M.P. called Afton?' asked Lacey-Jones.

'Not personally,' said Alec Bell.

'You've heard of him, though?'

'Naturally.'

'The thing is,' said Lacey-Jones, 'I've had word that he's going to make a stink.'

It was the morning after Dr Hoover's accident, and Bell had moved into the Scientific Director's office. It was not strictly necessary, but Bell believed in exploiting every advantage, however briefly. He had told the switchboard that he would attend to all Dr Hoover's calls. He was hungry for information, but the filing system baffled him. None of the correspondence in the 'Pending' tray made sense. When Lacey-Jones came on the line he clutched at the straw and hung on.

'A stink?' he said tentatively.

'It's a follow-up to that newspaper enquiry,' said Lacey-Jones. 'Hoover must have mentioned it.'

Bell hummed into the receiver. 'In passing.'

'I tried to persuade him to play ball, but you know what he's like,' said Lacey-Jones. 'No visitors for the time being. Top security until there's something cut and dried. Anyway, some little bird's been chirping in Afton's ear that you're conducting fiendish experiments at Proto. He wants an enquiry.'

'That's ridiculous.'

'I hope so, but you know Afton.'

Alec Bell closed his eyes and tried to remember. The name was clear enough, but the image was blurred. 'Did he have something to do with television?'

Lacey-Jones laughed. 'Back in the dark ages.'

'He wore a bow tie?'

'Correct.'

'Horn-rimmed glasses?'

'Right again.'

'The Man of the People.'

'You've got him.'

Now it came back. Guy Afton, the TV Sage. The instant pundit – strong on feeling, short on information. Bell had always rather approved of him. Critics had called him reactionary, but, whatever his failings he was consistent. He stood for the old order; morality, the monarchy, Great Britain as opposed to Little England. He had entered politics, when – unaccountably to Bell – his television career had waned. As a legislator he had kindled no beacons, but his prejudices gave him fire power. Far to the right he volleyed and thundered: repatriate our coloured brethren, penalize strikers, make the students toe the line. Cartoonists drew him almost obsessively. He was newsworthy. Sound and fury followed in his wake. 'What sort of enquiry does he want?' asked Bell.

'He's not specified. It's not official yet. I should think a few visiting firemen would do the trick. Plus the press. He's bound to bring them along. He likes his headlines.'

'It's just the Contact research programme he's interested in, I suppose.'

'I imagine so,' said Lacey-Jones. 'You're not likely to have been maltreating a protein.' His voice became serious. 'I should really talk to Dr Hoover. I know how he feels about publicity, but he'll have to lay something on.'

Alec Bell cleared his throat. 'He's not available, I'm afraid. I've explained about the accident. It's most unfortunate, I can see that. But it could be weeks before he's up and about. Meanwhile, I'm in charge.'

'I'll have to get a statement prepared.'

'Of course, of course.' Bell made soothing noises. 'Has Mrs Deeley been informed?'

'Not yet.'

'Would you like me to do it?'

'I think that's my job.'

'I was merely trying to be helpful.'

'Naturally. Each in our separate ways.'

Not for the first time Bell reminded himself that Lacey-Jones was not a fool. He could, perhaps, be made use of. But his first loyalty was to Proto, and, of course, himself. If there was a plot he would not be cast in a role which did not give him good lines and a share of the action. Caution was advisable. 'How will Afton go about it?' he enquired.

'A question in the House, most likely. That way he's protected. Is the minister aware of public disquiet regarding experiments on live animals? etcetera, etcetera. We'll have to take him up on it right away. Show him round Proto. Get him photographed with a few friendly chimps – put them in rubber pants, if we want to be safe – and make damned sure there's nothing in sight to cause any upset. Actually, we could do very well out of it. There's nothing like being endorsed by an M.P.'

'And how soon is this likely to happen?'

'Fairly soon. Ten days or so. I think we should be prepared for a visitation by the end of the month.'

'I'll work to that estimate then. You'll keep me informed?'

'I'll make a point of it,' said Lacey-Jones. 'And you'll let me know about Dr Hoover.'

'As soon as I can,' said Alec Bell.

He put the receiver down gently, and laced his fingers over his stomach. He was curiously deficient in natural instincts, he realized; inhibited, as it were, by his awareness. It was not enough for him to see what needed to be done. What he lacked was the boldness, the very feeling for a situation, to proceed sure-footed across the minefield. He needed assistance, a guideline to take him from the wish to the deed. His first problem, though, was to define the wish. It was not to see Hoover destroyed, or even seriously discredited. All that he wanted, decided Alec Bell, was parity; an assurance that Hoover was merely mortal and subject to the same laws – economic and social – as the rest of the Proto establishment.

The difference between them had begun years before, he acknowledged. When he thought of Hoover emerging from the jungle, leading a gorilla by the hand, his spine crinkled. His sense of awe was practically superstitious. It was insane, he told himself. But it was the act of a man under divine protection. To strike him down now would be to invite retribution. But it was just conceivable that he, Alec Bell, was also a chosen instrument. God moved in a mysterious way, he reminded himself, and the wonders to be performed might well include the reorganization of Proto, with power and responsibility more equally divided. He closed his eyes for several seconds and uttered a silent prayer. When he opened them he saw clearly what he should do. He picked up the telephone and spoke to the operator. 'Get me the House of Commons,' he said. 'I want a personal call to Mr Guy Afton.'

As Mark walked to Charlotte Bloom's office he received a sudden mental image of his bowels, coil upon coil of intestine, gorged like a python, heavy as lead. Earlier that morning he had lowered himself on to the lavatory seat, confident of release. But at the critical moment the door knob turned, the bolt rattled, and a voice outside said 'Sorry'. Instantly, Mark had felt his guts contract, and his sphincter petrify into an iron rose.

It was beyond reason, beyond his control. Whatever mental drill he subjected himself to, his body ignored the briefing. He imagined sensors lodged in his viscera which flashed the message: strangers in the house. And, by instant reflex, all doors slammed shut. Security was complete. It was not Linda's fault, he reasoned. She and Baby were there by invitation. But as he walked along the corridor, the solids shifting within him like ballast, his irritation grew. Ahead of him he saw evenings with Ex-Lax, mornings with Liver Salts. Irrigation was, once again, to be his prime object in life. And Biddy was to blame.

They had slept in the same room, the same bed; but separately. Each had occupied an equal area of mattress. When, by accident, they touched, they apologized. Dressing, only an hour ago, had been an act of instant veiling, as though at all costs nakedness was to be avoided. At breakfast Biddy had used James as a chaperone, a bodyguard whose presence quelled conversation. When he left the house (a jerk of the head signalled goodbye) he felt he was making good his escape.

'Bad night?' asked Charlotte as he entered her office.

'Does it show?'

'A little line here, a little bag there.' She tilted his chin with her hand. 'Frankly,' she said, 'you look terrible.'

He sat down heavily. 'I feel it. I didn't sleep much.'

'Want some coffee?'

'If you're making it.'

She clicked her tongue. 'If I wasn't making it you couldn't have it. You English! You're not polite; you're obtuse.'

'Point taken.'

'Don't look so down.' She plugged in the kettle, and flicked the switch. 'Is this visit social or business?'

'A bit of both. You've heard about Hoover?'

'Just now. Is it serious?'

'I don't know. He'll be out of action for a while, and that means that Alec Bell's in charge.'

'He won't stop anything. He wouldn't dare.'

'That's not the problem. As far as I can gather Bell hasn't a clue what we're actually doing in Contact. Hoover kept him very much in the dark, partly because he's bloody-minded, partly because he thinks Bell is a natural enemy of research. I don't want to play games, but in this case I think Hoover's right. I don't propose telling him a thing about Otto.'

'What's so special about Otto?'

Mark raked his hair with stiff fingers. 'I don't know. I mean I can't be specific. But obviously he's a special case. Mrs Deeley says he betrayed her. He tore Ryman's arm off. He's far too old to learn new tricks, but he's at the end of every research programme that Hoover has launched. There's a pattern somewhere, but I can't see it.'

'Have you asked Hoover?'

'I've tried to. I've given him openings. But it's not easy to cross-examine God. I expect he'll tell me in his own good time, but I'm worried about what to do right now.'

She sat down beside him, and put her hand on his knee. 'I think you should push on. Full steam ahead. You know what Ryman was trying to do. What he may have *done*, in fact. Prove it to yourself, either way.'

'I'll need some help,' said Mark.

'I knew you were going to say that.' She poured boiling water into two mugs of coffee, and passed him the sugar bowl. As he took it his eyes rested for a moment on her belly, dented by the waistband of her slacks. Her smell was powerful but not unpleasant. He butted her softly with his forehead, earthing himself in her flesh. When he looked up she was smiling. 'That's where I've got to lose it.'

'Will you help?'

'If you like.'

'And say nothing to Alec Bell?'

'What do you think?' She raised her coffee cup in salute. 'To Otto,' she said. 'To our little secret.'

It was mid-morning, and the kitchen was yellow with sunlight. Linda Gillis hitched up her jumper and plugged Baby's mouth with her left nipple. On the other side of the table Biddy sat and watched. 'I couldn't do that,' she said. 'I didn't have enough milk.'

'I've got plenty.'

'So I see.'

A creamy rivulet ran down Baby's chin, and Linda dammed it with a napkin. 'She likes it better than a bottle. They tried her in hospital and she yelled bloody murder.' She put her hand to her mouth. 'Pardon.'

'It doesn't matter.'

'That matron said my language was terrible.'

'I'm sure she's heard worse.'

Baby made guzzling noises and burrowed into the swollen breast. Her eyes were closed and her small fists stirred against the bank of white skin. 'She's a greedy girl,' said Linda.

'She's lovely,' said Biddy.

She was not envious, she told herself. Baby belonged to Linda, and she had James. She was not deprived. She had every reason to be content. But the sight of the mother and child – united, unthinking – made her uneasy. She was not like that. For her it had been, and still was, hard work.

'Did you attend ante-natal clinic?' she asked.

Linda shook her head, and with her free hand plucked a cigarette from the packet on the table. 'I didn't bother. They wanted me to. Mrs Hoover kept on at me, but my mum said I had my rights like everyone else. They couldn't force me if I didn't want to.'

'They were only trying to help.'

'That's what they always say.' Linda lit the cigarette and blew three perfect smoke rings. 'They like to know what's going on. They like to keep tabs on you.'

Flakes of ash speckled the spun-silk head at her breast, and Biddy flicked them away. 'Do you think you ought to smoke while you feed her?'

'Why not? Will it get her into bad habits?'

'I don't think it's hygienic.'

'I don't suppose she minds.'

'I mind.' She was surprised by the sharpness of her own voice.

'All right then.' Linda took a last drag from the cigarette and stubbed it out in the ashtray.

'I'm not nagging,' said Biddy. 'I'm not being bossy either. But you're new to this. You've got to take advice.' She forced brightness into the words, smiling as she spoke.

'If you say so.'

'Not because I say so. Because it helps.'

'Are you going to go on at me like Mrs Hoover?'

'Nobody's going on at you. That's a silly thing to say.'

Linda rolled her eyes towards the ceiling, and tightened her embrace of the child so that her bare arm and the curve of Baby's cheek mirrored each other. 'She goes on at you too,' she said. 'It's her way.'

Thank God that Mark's not here, thought Biddy. 'Then you understand that it's not always important,' she said. 'We must make allowances.'

'She's an interfering old cow.'

'You mustn't say that.'

'It's what Mr Barrow thinks.'

'You've no idea what Mr Barrow thinks.'

Linda nodded deliberately. 'Oh yes I have. I know what men think. I've always known.'

'I don't think you've met anyone like my husband before this.'

'No? What makes him so different?' She hesitated, as though deliberating whether to reveal a secret. Then she shook her head. 'It's no use talking. But he's no different. They're all the same.'

It was not hostility that she sensed, thought Biddy, but resignation. Perhaps Linda was right. Perhaps conversation between them was impossible. But as she saw the doors closing snugly in their familiar sockets she longed for a phrase, a word even, to wedge them open, so that one channel would remain. 'Perhaps you're right,' she said.

End of dialogue. Ahead of them lay weeks and months of non-communication. It was like meeting the girl at the Social Centre. There was no common ground between them, or rather the shared experience was partitioned into compounds marked Us and Them. Trespassers would be ignored.

Linda shifted Baby from one breast to another, so smoothly that

the rhythm of the sucking barely faltered. Her jumper was rolled
up beneath her chin, and watching the transfer Biddy found herself
studying the tuck of fat over the red nylon pants, the shallow scoop
of the navel, and the abandoned nipple. It was tumescent, slick with
saliva, and – at its peak – pimpled with milk. Linda glanced down
and experimentally took hold of it between finger and thumb.
'There's still plenty there,' she said, and squeezed it. A thin,
cloudy jet sprang between them and splashed Biddy's cheek. For
a moment it hung suspended like an opaque tear, then rolled down
to the corner of her mouth.

'Christ, I'm sorry,' said Linda. 'I never meant to.'

Biddy smiled uncertainly, and then licked her lips. 'It's like
custard,' she said. 'Quite nice really.'

'Is it honestly?'

'Try it yourself.'

Linda squeezed a drop on to her finger, and put it in her mouth.
She cocked her head on one side. 'Nestlès milk,' she said. 'My
mum used to put it in her tea.'

'She put whisky in mine,' said Biddy.

'Did you like it?'

'Not much.'

'Dead common, my mum,' said Linda. 'Like me.' She grinned
over Baby's head and clasped Biddy's hand. 'Don't worry,' she said.
'You're not like Mrs Hoover. I reckon we'll get on all right.'

Mark unlocked the door of the cupboard in his office, and waved
Charlotte forward. 'For your eyes only.'

She studied the litter of books, and boxes, and equipment. On
one shelf there was an electric cattle prod, on another a gorilla
mask made of stretch rubber. There were Linguaphone records, a
tape recorder, a feathered head-dress, a carton of shelled peanuts.
'What is it all?' she asked.

'Ryman's bargain basement.'

'And where was it?'

'Here and there,' said Mark. 'Some of it in this office. Some in
the house. You wouldn't describe him as tidy-minded.'

'He said neatness was a mark of anal-eroticism.'

'Did he really?' Mark flipped the lid off a cardboard box and took
out a pack of playing cards. 'He had his little ways too.'

'He did indeed.' There were no conventional suits, no kings and queens, but couples and quartets, male and female, black and white, joined in impossible sexual congress. For several seconds Charlotte studied a photograph of a massively-breasted blonde advancing open-mouthed on a penis as thick as her wrist.

'Ambitious,' she said.

'Very.' Mark took the cards back, and put them in his pocket. 'I don't think they're a vital exhibit.'

'They don't upset me. Not like that, anyway. But it's like going through personal effects when someone's dead. All those dirty little secrets come out.' She shrugged her shoulders. 'We've all got something to hide.'

'Ryman had more than most, it seems.' Mark reached into the back of the cupboard. 'Did he ever show you this?'

It was an artificial snake, eighteen inches long, and brightly patterned with lozenges of yellow and black. Its tail was taped to a short cane, and its head was tethered to the same point by a length of cord. Mark moved the cane, and the snake swayed realistically, looping the cane, its glass eyes winking in the sunlight.

'I never saw it before,' said Charlotte.

Mark showed her the cattle prod. 'Or this?'

She shook her head. 'I don't think Hoover knew he had it either.'

Mark pressed the button, and the tip of the prod buzzed as though a swarm of bees was trapped within the filament. 'I believe it's quite painful,' he said. 'When I was in the States I saw cops use them for crowd control.' He smiled perfunctorily. 'A shocking business.'

'Current practice.'

'I thought only the English were addicted to puns.'

'And tea? And muffins?' Charlotte hitched up her slacks and smoothed her sweater. 'Bad habits are international, you know.' She took the prod and pressed the button. 'I suppose he used it on Otto.'

'As a last resort I should think. The snake would keep him away most of the time – chimps absolutely loathe them. But if he was working at close quarters the prod might be a comfort.'

'He didn't have it the day of the accident.'

'Obviously not.'

'That might have done it,' said Charlotte. 'You've read Ryman's notes. He wasn't a sadist, but he was quite prepared to use pain as a means to an end.' She winced in sympathy. 'If Otto saw him without the prod he wouldn't hesitate to move in.'

'Moral: stay clear.'

'Not necessarily.' She sat at his desk and spread her hands, palms upward. 'Because Otto attacked Ryman that doesn't mean that he'd go for you – or me.'

'He doesn't take too kindly to Mrs Deeley.'

'There may be another reason for that. How many people go near him now?'

'I'm not sure. There's a keeper of course, maybe more than one. The cage is kept clean. Someone has to make sure that Otto's out of the way when his food's brought in. But I doubt if there's any actual contact. He's not exactly a pet.'

'We don't even know if Ryman fixed anything in the cage. Lights, a tape recorder. What about the sleep-teaching with Lulu? What was it he said exactly?'

Her face was flushed, and as he pulled open a drawer of his desk Mark smelled the sharpness of her sweat. He moved upwind, and pointed to the file. 'It's near the end,' he said. 'The final entry I think.'

She turned the pages rapidly, then stopped. 'Here it is. Listen to this.' Her finger underlined the words as she read aloud. 'Lulu picked up cup this morning, and enunciated word clearly and correctly. No reward.' Her eyes skipped several lines, resting again on a block of capital letters. 'WOULD METHOD SUIT OTTO;' She threw herself back in the chair, damp patches darkening the wool beneath her arms. 'That's what Ryman was trying to find out,' she said. 'What we have to do is take it from there.'

'Ryman was round the bend.'

'You didn't know him.'

'I know what happened to him. I've no intention of going in that cage with Otto.'

Charlotte picked up the toy snake, and spun it once, twice round the cane. 'You don't have to,' she said. 'I'm volunteering.'

ELEVEN

'I can't let you,' said Mark.

'You can't stop me,' said Charlotte. 'And don't be so bloody silly. This isn't something on the telly. We're both in the business, and I'm better at it than you are. We're professionals.'

It was a lovely day, he thought irrelevantly. Fat, yellow clouds cruised through a sky of forget-me-not blue, and the bushes were loud with birdsong. The year was warming up. On their walk to Otto's enclosure they had passed girls in summer dresses, their arms bare, the ends of their hair tipped with light. Mark felt a mounting sense of desperation. In a canvas holdall he carried the snake and the cattle prod. Charlotte had not wanted him to bring them, but in a flash of precognition he had seen himself bounding towards the cage, his puny weapons at the ready. As they approached the cinder track he even remembered that he had not made out a will.

'We follow my rules,' said Charlotte. 'We say nothing. No verbal signals of any kind. I'll stay inside the arena for half an hour, then I'll come out.'

'If he'll let you.'

'Of course he'll let me. If not, I'll wait until he's ready. You're not to interfere.'

'But I'm responsible for what happens.'

'I'm responsible for myself.'

He was about to protest, but his argument seemed too weak to muster. If it came to the worst he knew he would be blamed. And rightly, he reminded himself. On his own initiative he had telephoned Administration and demanded the keys to Otto's enclosure. He had signed both a receipt and a document absolving Proto of responsibility should any accident befall him or Mrs Bloom (a standard form said the clerk, but not to be taken lightly). Furthermore, with Dr Hoover in hospital, and Alec Bell mysteriously absent – in London, said his secretary – he was the acting head of the Contact unit. Disaster, thought Mark, was the result of circumstances meshing too smoothly. On this occasion there had been no snag to provide a pause in which to reflect. Without a hitch he was speeding towards calamity.

The arena was empty when they arrived. Sparrows fought among the straw bales. There was a peaceful reek of stables. 'How do you want to go about it?' he whispered, unaware that he had dropped his voice until he heard the syllables hissing like steam from a leaky pipe.

Charlotte gestured towards the gate. 'Lock it.'

He did as he was told, and tiptoed back. 'Do you want me in here with you?'

She shook her head. 'There's an observation box by the tunnel. Open the door to the arena, then nip back quickly.'

He followed the direction in which she was pointing. The iron ribs of the tunnel led from the rear wall to the cage in the middle of the arena. At the wall end there was a heavy steel door, secured by bolts, top and bottom. From the observation box they could be slipped free with a long handling rod. 'Then what?' he asked.

'We wait.'

'For how long?'

'For as long as it takes. Let's check the cage first.'

They circled the iron box jutting into the arena like a landlocked pier. High in one corner there was a bracket holding a small spotlight. Facing it there was a loudspeaker. 'He really did get started with Otto,' said Charlotte. 'But did he get any results?'

'There's nothing written unless there's another notebook.'

'You'll have to ask him then.'

'I don't see him actually rushing forward to help.'

'It depends how you ask.'

'You know Ryman. I don't.'

'That's right,' said Charlotte. 'I know Ryman.'

In the blackness at the end of the tunnel something moved. They sensed, rather than heard the stir of air, the rasp of bare feet on concrete, and instinctively they moved closer together. Their hips collided, and in unison they turned and apologized. 'He's showing an interest,' said Charlotte. 'You'd better get in your box.'

'You're sure?'

'For Christ's sake,' she said, 'get moving.'

He obeyed her, ducking inside the steel cubicle – connected, he observed thankfully, to a passage which looped the perimeter – and rested the handling rod on the half-door. He slipped the bolts, top and bottom, hauled back the rod, and secured the observation grille. Twenty feet away Charlotte squatted on the ground, her legs crossed, her hands clasping her ankles. The lotus position, he thought; most unsuitable for a good Jewish girl. A handkerchief hung from her hip pocket, and there was a smudge of dirt on one cheek. Her lips moved silently, and he made a mental note to ask her, all in good time, what it was she was saying.

Out of the corner of his eye he saw something dark and shaggy fill the tunnel. It moved rapidly on all fours, straw sticking out of its fur. Mark leaned on the grille. A button chinked against metal, and the ape swung round, its eyes glinting under deeply-shelving brows. Its skull was almost bald, white whiskers frosted its slate-grey face. Automatically, Mark registered the colour of the skin. The books were right, he thought; the pale face darkened with age. He shrank back against the far wall, an inch at a time, allowing the shadows to absorb him. Otto continued to watch him for several seconds, then abruptly he turned to Charlotte.

She remained perfectly still; not even her lips now stirred. Hand over hand, Otto let himself down into the arena, and as he briefly stood erect Mark saw his true size. He was between four and five feet tall, bow-legged and dwarfish. But when he moved, propped on his knuckles, scooting forward on hairy crutches, he travelled like freight – a massive, compact bulk, braking suddenly on braced shoulders, funnelling his lips and hooting loudly, his mouth gaping to show red gums spiked on either side with yellow canines. He circled her, scuffing the ground with his flat feet, slapping it with his palms. The handkerchief caught his eye, and he tweaked it from her pocket, cramming it to his nose, dabbing it with his tongue, shredding it between his teeth. He bounced up and down, his head thudding into his chest. The hooting became more shrill. Charlotte's eyes were closed. She seemed asleep: a victim dozing at the stake. Reaching down into the holdall Mark felt for the cattle prod. He calculated the distance between them. Enter Dick Daring, he thought; but he was too late. The hooting stopped in mid-halloo; the clamour cancelled as if lopped by a knife. Otto sprang forward and clouted Charlotte on the back of her head. She pitched down, face in the dirt and craning over her Otto sniffed the length of her body, his nostrils flaring, his expression studious. His flattened face browsed over neck and armpits, belly and crotch. Slowly, he savoured each smell until satisfied he sat back on his haunches, forearms resting on his knees, calloused knuckles hanging limp.

Mark swallowed painfully. His throat was dry and his legs trembled. Peering through the grille he saw Charlotte's nose twitch, and he felt relief wash through him like water. She was unharmed, lying doggo. He would not have to go to her rescue. Otto picked up a straw and nibbled it, first one end, then the other. He scratched his head, prising loose a morsel of dead skin which he studied, then placed on his lower lip jutting out like a soup plate fringed with bristles.

The experiment had become a game, thought Mark. Variations on the theme of statues, with every rule in Otto's favour. He glanced at his watch and saw they had been in the arena for ten minutes. It seemed infinitely longer. The sparrows had returned, and one of them hopped over Otto's foot, grass trailing from its beak. He ignored it, even when it rummaged in his fur. A squad of ants marched in single file in front of him, vanishing down a crack in the concrete. He watched them steadily, and taking the straw from his mouth, inserted it into the fissure. The ants swarmed up the straw. When it was covered from top to bottom Otto ran it through his lips, wiping it clean of insects.

It was too much to bear, thought Mark. Primate toolmaking demonstrated by an adult chimpanzee, and not a camera in sight! There was no doubt about Otto's intelligence now. He dipped the straw into the hole once more. The ants clambered up it, beading the stem, and he picked them off one by one. A plane flew overhead and he watched it go from east to west. The sound of the jets ebbed away and he returned to the ants.

Slowly, in a fluid, continuous movement like rope uncoiling, Charlotte sat up. Her chin was daubed with grime, and her hair spiky with sweat, but she looked composed, and curiously at ease. She turned to face Otto, and with a courtesy which seemed entirely fitting she extended her right hand, palm downwards, the thumb and fingers tucked out of sight. It was almost, thought Mark, though she expected him to kiss it. They regarded each other gravely. The ants crawled between them – another safari returning home – and as if reminded of some antique ritual, Otto reached out and tapped the back of her hand with the tips of his fingers. Seconds ticked by, and without haste Charlotte rose to her feet and backed towards the observation box.

Otto watched her go, a frown bisecting his face. His own arm was still raised, and as she reached the door he lowered it gently. It was dreamlike, a ceremony conjured by sleep. Mark inched the door open, and drew Charlotte inside. He closed it again and she sagged against him, her sweater instantly damping his shirt. He was about to speak, but she put her finger to her lips. Through the grille they saw Otto climb smoothly back into the tunnel, and disappear. Mark slid the bolts home, and propped the rod in the corner.

'Well . . . ,' he began, and stopped when he saw her slumped against the wall, her face in her hands. 'Are you all right?' he asked.

She nodded violently. Her breath came and went in great gulps as though she was crying. 'Give me a minute.'

'As long as you like.'

She cleared her throat. 'Do you have a handkerchief? Otto took mine.'

'It's not too clean.'

'I don't care about that.' She wiped her face and blew her nose, then leaned back against the wall, her head tilted and her eyes closed.

'They'll never believe us,' said Mark. 'You were amazing.'

She smiled crookedly, and eased her clammy sweater from under her arms. 'I stink,' she said.

'It doesn't matter.'

'Not now, you mean.'

'Not at all.'

'You and Otto,' she said. 'At least you have one thing in common. You're not fussy.'

He leaned forward and kissed her, and saw her green eyes open as she pulled his head down and kissed him back.

TWELVE

'Rivers exert a powerful fascination,' said Guy Afton. 'The mighty Amazon, the greasy-green Limpopo, old father Thames.' He gestured over the parapet towards the torrent of mud which poured under Westminster Bridge. 'Sweet Thames, run softly till I end my song' he intoned, and closed his eyes. 'A gem for the ages.'

'As you say,' said Alec Bell.

Afton stared at him fiercely. 'Do you have time for poetry?'

'Very little I'm afraid.'

'A pity. I find it an endless source of inspiration. Endless. It refreshes me daily. Can you believe that?'

'Oh, yes,' said Bell.

'Milton, Shakespeare, Kipling. They're all friends who counsel me in moments of doubt.'

'Really.'

'English poets,' said Afton. 'Voices of the blood.' He cast around for a suitable quotation, failed to find one, and resolved to buy a companion volume to the *Garland of Verse* which had been sent to him by a constituent the previous Christmas. It had proved extraordinarily useful, he thought. A taste for literature went well with politics. He thought of Macmillan poring over his Trollope and Winston reciting the worst of Arthur Hugh Clough. One had to be careful not to overdo it. It was important not to be considered an intellectual. The correct impression to give was that of caring deeply and knowing a little, of being a passionate amateur. It was the natural stance of an Englishman among Englishmen. Afton's literary leanings were so slight as to keep him practically vertical, but he had the instinct to know which way to incline, having regard to the climate and the prevailing winds. He was, at heart, profoundly philistine; but he was also shrewd. His career – first as the TV sage, then as a politician – had been based on an understanding of public prejudice. It was his working capital, and he exploited it to the full.

He was also strong on sentiment. Whenever possible he had himself photographed with babies, young mothers, and old age pensioners. His campaign poster at the last election had shown him fondling a labrador – a dog which his researchers told him was regarded by eighty per cent of animal fanciers as the most lovable and trustworthy pet. And his interest in Proto was rooted in the same logic. People loved the chimpanzee – visitors to London Zoo had voted it their favourite animal. To champion its cause against the demon research was a simple but symbolical act. Afton had no objection to being called soppy, provided that the soppiness was on a grand scale. It showed that he had heart, and that it throbbed for creatures, great and small.

He had not yet made up his mind about Alec Bell. His telephone call had come as a surprise, and Afton's invitation to take tea on the Members' Terrace of the House of Commons was an opportunity for closer inspection. So far there had been no revelations. The poetry gambit had been received impassively. Obviously, Bell was not there to be charmed or impressed. In the pale sunlight he nibbled a cucumber sandwich, and shivered slightly as the breeze whipped off the river and ruffled his tonsure. No neck, Afton noted, and felt comforted. He held certain theories about physical types, and believed – for no clear reason – that the only danger came from men who looked lean and hungry. 'You only need to read Shakespeare,' he would say, when challenged. 'You can't argue with the Bard.'

'About our telephone conversation,' said Bell.

'Yes?'

'You are going to ask a question in the House.'

'I've already made that plain.'

'You know that Proto will offer you every facility to inspect what's going on?'

'Publicity will make certain of that.'

'Of course. But I was anticipating the demand.'

'I shall still ask the question.'

'Of course you will.'

Bell dabbed at his mouth with a paper napkin. 'Mind you, there's nothing to hide. At least, I hope not. It's a large organization. It's difficult to keep informed about all that goes on.'

'Surely you should know. You're the Director.'

'Not of the entire establishment.' Bell smiled apologetically.

'Contact – the unit that concerns you – is controlled by Dr Hoover, Dr Francis Hoover.'

'Are you here on his behalf?'

'Not exactly. We're colleagues, of course. But our responsibilities are separate. Dr Hoover is exceedingly independent.'

Afton watched a convoy of barges butt their way up-river. 'Does he know that you are here today?'

'He's in hospital. For the time being I'm in complete charge of the establishment.'

A gleam of light, fluttering like a candle at the end of a long passage, revealed itself. 'I understand your position,' said Afton.

'I hope so. In the absence of Dr Hoover I thought it my duty to tell you – as I have done – that you will be welcome to make an inspection.'

'In the public interest.'

'In everyone's interest.'

A seagull watched them attentively from the parapet, and Afton tossed the crust from his sandwich high in the air. The gull fluttered up and caught it, then returned for a second helping. 'Most responsible,' said Afton. 'I say that without prejudice, of course.'

'Naturally.'

'I take it that you would welcome members of the press?'

Bell nodded stiffly, bending from the waist like a pink thumb suited in grey flannel. 'A limited number.'

'I think it will be in about three weeks' time. Will Dr Hoover be back?'

'Probably. He was scalded in a rather stupid accident. No great damage done, but at his age there are sometimes complications.'

'Age?' invited Afton.

'Late sixties,' said Bell. 'Almost seventy, I believe. But I'm not suggesting he's senile. Far from it. He's very decisive, very positive.'

'Dictatorial?'

'Not exactly. But he hardly welcomes advice.'

Afton stroked the wings of his bow tie. It was a mannerism he had adopted in his days as a television interviewer, a small strategy designed to distract the interviewee before springing the lethal question. It was time now, he thought. 'Does Dr Hoover conduct inhumane experiments?'

'You must ask him.'

'To your knowledge?'

'I've already said: our responsibilities are separate. So is our work.' He hesitated. 'I do not think there should be this separation. It makes control virtually impossible. Situations like this should never arise.' He reached for another sandwich. 'As a matter of interest, how did it arise?'

'I beg your pardon?'

'Who told you something was wrong at Proto?'

The bluntness was shocking, thought Afton; chiefly because it was unexpected. It was like being savaged by a rabbit. His visitor needed to be reminded of the rules. 'I'm not at liberty to divulge that information,' he said, aware even as he spoke, that the formula was inadequate.

'I suppose it was Ryman.'

'I'm not able to comment.'

Bell popped the sandwich in his mouth and chewed it thoroughly. 'Mr Afton,' he said at last, 'we are not in conflict. We have a great deal in common. We should be able to dispense with secrets.'

The gull on the parapet flapped its wings, and Afton shooed it away. He watched it ride the wind, hovering above them until it was caught in an up-draught, and skimmed towards the City like a paper dart. 'We must be discreet,' he said.

'At all times.'

'And frank.'

'Wholeheartedly.'

'Very well.' Afton leaned across the table. 'It was Mr Ryman who got in touch with me.'

'I thought so.'

'And now perhaps you will answer some questions of mine . . .'

The man in the hospital bed was like a caricature of Dr Hoover, thought Mark. A nurse had combed his hair, and the usual tangle lay tamed and trim against the plump pillows. He was not wearing his spectacles, and the unframed eyes seemed curiously vulnerable in the parchment of his face. There was a bar of white skin across the bridge of his nose, and he pecked at it with his index finger as though trying to remove the ghost of a scab.

Mark sat on a hard wooden chair. 'How are you?'

'Restless.'

'But are you comfortable?'

The eyebrows arched like armpits. 'Have you ever been drenched in scalding coffee?'

'Never.'

'Then don't ask stupid questions. I'm covered in blisters and they hurt like hell.'

'I'm sorry.'

Dr Hoover raised his hand and let it fall limply back on to the sheet. 'They won't tell me what's happening. How long am I supposed to stay here?'

'A few more days I think. You had a severe shock.'

'That damned coffee pot! You know it was Bell who gave it to us. He's making good use of the time I suppose.'

'Just holding the fort.'

Dr Hoover raised himself on his elbows. 'Why is it that a sick person is invariably treated as an imbecile? Infirmity of the flesh does not mean frailty of the mind. I am entirely coherent and concerned. Do you believe me? Excellent. Now perhaps you will tell me what is going on.' He fell back on his pillow breathing heavily, his cheekbones pink with excitement.

'He's moved into your office,' said Mark. 'He's taking your calls. He has issued no instructions and made no requests.'

'So far.'

'There's no reason why he should. You'll be back soon.'

'Sooner than they think.'

'We're going ahead with Otto.'

Dr Hoover looked up sharply. 'What do you mean?'

Mark told him, at length. 'I think I should get in touch with Ryman,' he concluded.

'I would not advise it.'

'Why not?'

'He will be of no help. None whatever.'

'But Charlotte – Dr Bloom – can speak to him.'

Dr Hoover shook his head. 'Ryman is not reliable. He is a vengeful man.'

'He started the work. Surely he'd want to see it continue.'

'I doubt it.'

'But we need more information. I've been through the notes. There's not enough there.'

'You must make your own observations.'

Mark stood up abruptly. His chair capsized and clattered to the floor. 'There's not enough time. We're taking risks – real risks. And everyone's being so damned mysterious. What is it that's so special about Otto? Why is Mrs Deeley so interested? She told me that Otto had betrayed her.' He stood poised over Dr Hoover, inhaling disinfectant and the incense of old flesh; like confectionery, he thought, pink and white fondants in a cardboard box.

'Is that the word she used? Betrayed?'

'The exact word.'

'How curious.'

'Can you explain it?'

'I don't think I should.' Dr Hoover looked up into Mark's face and smiled. He touched his hand apologetically. 'You mustn't be angry. There's no need.'

'I'm not angry. Exasperated.'

'I understand.' He gestured towards the chair. 'Sit down for a minute.'

Mark did as he was told. 'I need some explanations.'

'Of course you do. So do we all. But they come in stages. Everyone contributes his tithe.'

Mark shook his head. 'No they don't. You've told me as little as you possibly can. You've made me guess. But the guessing's gone far enough. I want to know why we're working with an ape as adult as Otto. There's no mystery about the young ones and they're no danger. But you know what happened to Ryman. You should have seen what happened today. If we're to take chances I want to know why.'

Seconds passed, and Dr Hoover sighed. 'What would you say was the basic reason for establishing communication?'

'To exchange information.'

'And how do you set about that?'

'By asking questions.'

'Correct. And by receiving answers.'

Mark pushed his chair back impatiently. 'Well, of course . . .'

'There's no "of course" about it.'

'Am I to take it there is something we want to learn from Otto? Something specific?'

'You are.'

5

'Then what it is?'

Dr Hoover pulled the sheet up under his chin, stroking it smooth, and reaching at the same time for his bell-push. 'That is something you must ask Mrs Deeley. You have my permission.'

'Why Mrs Deeley?'

'Ask and ye shall find.' He closed his eyes, then re-opened them abruptly. 'She's coming tomorrow. Make her welcome.'

As he opened the front door the phone rang. He picked it up and heard the breathing. 'Mark Barrow here,' he said, 'Who's that?' Biddy came to the door of the kitchen and signalled to him. He covered the receiver with one hand. 'What's wrong?'

'It's being doing that all evening. No one answers.'

He spoke into the mouthpiece. 'Is it Ryman? I want to see you.'

He heard faint traffic noises, and the soft gravel of a man clearing his throat. 'Ryman,' he said, 'we have things to discuss. I need your help.'

'No help.' The voice was quite firm and controlled.

'Not for Proto. For me.'

'You work for Proto.'

'So did you.'

There was a long silence in which Mark found himsel f counting. He had reached eight when the abuse began. It was obscene, and comprehensive and delivered with a feeling for metre and invention which intrigued while it appalled him. He became aware that he was holding the phone several inches away from his ear, as if to avoid infection from the steady, almost prescribed flow of venom. 'Ryman,' he said sharply, 'listen to me. I'm not to blame for what's happened. It's not my fault.'

'. . . fucking, conniving, cancerous opportunists . . .'

'I'm trying to finish what you started. You'll get full credit.'

'. . . egotists full of their own shit . . .'

'Where can I reach you?'

The abuse stopped in mid-sentence and Ryman laughed with what sounded like genuine humour. 'You can't reach me,' he said. 'But I can reach you.' There was a click as the receiver was gently replaced, and then the purr of the dialling tone.

Mark shook his head. 'Hoover tried to warn me.'

'Does he sound dangerous?'

'He sounds out of his mind.'

Roll on tomorrow, he thought. Every hour brought another question for him to ask Mrs Deeley.

THIRTEEN

Charlotte Bloom tipped the sleeping tablets into the palm of her hand and dropped them singly and deliberately into the lavatory basin. They entered the water like miniature torpedoes, clustering together at the bottom until she pulled the chain. The cistern flushed, the tablets – half red, half blue – skimmed round the bowl, then plunged into the U-bend. She felt a pang seeing them go, but it was an act of faith. For a fortnight she had slept soundly without tablets, without dreams. All things were possible, she told herself. A relapse was always likely, but this morning she was ending the first of her bad habits. No more crutches, no more self-pity.

She cleaned her teeth and exchanged white smiles with her reflection. All over Proto, she thought, people were doing the same thing. The daily hello. Good morning self, and how's the world with you? Lately the exchange had become bearable. She no longer found herself hateful.

Almost unwillingly she looked for reasons. No letters from Johannesburg. No Ryman. No brushes with Louise Hoover. Progress at work. And, yes, she was forced to admit it, the advent of Mark Barrow. She rinsed her mouth and gargled. It was time to move. But as she made her bed and stacked the books on the night table she felt a twinge of doubt.

'Not again,' she said and noted that once more she was talking to herself. It was a habit (another bad one, she thought) which had developed since she had lived alone. In London, when she first arrived, she had carried on long debates with herself, acting out two distinct roles, dividing herself to present opposite points of view. In the street when she saw people's lips moving she shared their turmoil. Once, in a restaurant, she had watched a man – his table half-hidden by a partition – conduct an animated conversation across the bread sticks. He had smiled, gestured, listened sympathetically. But when she stood up to leave she saw that he had no companion. She had not yet reached that stage, but she was aware of the dangers.

In the kitchen she made coffee and drank it standing at the sink. Another habit noted. Even with time to spare solitaries always acted as though they had a train to catch, as though time spent sitting down forced them to assess their solitude. Ryman again, she thought: 'Create vacuum, i.e. boredom, to be filled with desired activity.' And recognizing its application she had argued with him, once bursting into angry tears, while his hands melted her body, drawing her to him and proving his point.

It was not going to be like that with Mark Barrow she told herself. The kiss had been a small cheer, a congratulation that she had succeeded with Otto. But as she drained her cup and rinsed it under the tap she knew that she was acknowledging only part of the truth. She recalled and recognized the sudden heat at the pit of her stomach, as though a pocket of gas had ignited in a wink of bright light. There was an attraction there, a creature she had to control.

When they had left the cage he had asked what it was she was reciting while she waited for Otto. At first she could not remember.

'Was it poetry?'

'I don't know any poetry.'

'You were saying *something*. Try and think.'

They had stopped for a moment, the light breeze chilly on her wet back. He had taken her arm and shaken it as if trying to crank an engine which would manufacture the required article, a charm, perhaps, an incantation. 'I don't recall.'

'Just try.'

And then she had remembered, and it was too silly to tell, and she had shaken her head, trembling with laughter.

'Tell me. I want to know.'

'It was the Apostles' Creed' she said. 'I believe in God the Father, maker of Heaven and Earth and in Jesus Christ his son, etcetera. Isn't that something?'

'Why that?'

'I've no idea. They made me learn it at school. My father complained. I was the only Jewish girl in the class, and they couldn't exclude me. They thought they were doing me a favour.'

'Maybe they were. It came in handy.' He had continued to

hold her arm until they reached the main road and then, gently, she had disengaged herself.

Perhaps that was the level at which she had to aim, a friendly, non-physical communion. Dear Miss Lonelyhearts, she extemporized, this is my problem. I am an intensely physical type, whose situation precludes any expression of same. If I get myself screwed, I get screwed up. What do you advise? It was one letter, thought Charlotte, which she would never write. Instead, she would take practical steps and invite both Mark and Biddy to tea. Or should it be coffee? Self-counsel was usually the best because it derived from self-knowledge. Ryman had been a dreadful warning, and she had (she thought, she hoped) taken it to heart.

'Abstention is the better part of valour,' she said and for once, excused herself for talking aloud.

Moving briskly, she tidied the flat, piling up newspapers, emptying ashtrays, packing bones and left-over vegetables into the waste disposal unit. It was therapy, she told herself, domestic massage to get the circulation going. But it was not to be despised because of that. It was necessary and only a fool rejected the way, whatever way, to survival. It solved nothing. But as she performed the chores, she received an image of her anxieties and apprehensions being drawn into a capsule, self-sealing and impermeable, which she could retain and examine as neatly as Goering's phial of cyanide. She was not ready for oblivion. She would carry the freight until she was ready to excrete it for good, or until it perished in store.

She was cheered by the thought. The day glinted through the venetian blinds, and she tugged the cord to adjust their slant. Two storeys down across the street a man looked up at the window. She let the cord go, stepped back and almost fell as she collided with the coffee table. When she looked again he had gone. She swallowed hard, keeping the capsule down. There was no cause for alarm, she told herself; no need to panic. At the same time she had to believe her eyes. She had not the slightest doubt that the man she had seen was Ryman.

There was a message to call Charlotte Bloom on Mark's desk when he arrived at the office. He glanced at his watch. Mrs Deeley was due in fifteen minutes, and he had to be there to meet her. He loosened his tie and dialled Charlotte's number. Engaged. He replaced the receiver and tried again with the same result. The call could wait, he decided. There was a clean dustcoat hanging behind the door, and he slipped it on. As Hoover's deputy he was uncertain how to present himself, but his instinct told him that a certain formality would be expected.

The day had begun well. He had been the first up. In the blessedly empty kitchen he had made tea, and taken his second cup to the lavatory where he had spent a fruitful ten minutes browsing through the Rupert Bear Annual while his bowels loosened and lightened. He even had time to shave and shower before Baby's early warning disturbed the peace.

'Morning,' he said to Linda as he passed her on the landing.

'Morning,' she said, hugging her breasts as they spilled from her yellow nightie.

Every situation, however bloody, had its compensations, thought Mark. It was the old principle of swings and roundabouts, and today he was ahead. Biddy stirred as he took his clothes from the wardrobe. She had thrown the blankets back during the night and the sheet moulded her body like a cerement. He kissed the back of her neck and she curled into a ball, clinging on to the last of sleep.

'Wake up,' he said.

'It's still dark.'

'Not really. The curtains are drawn.'

She rolled on to her back, her arm resting across her forehead, her eyes struggling to focus. 'You sound lively.'

'I am lively. It's D-Day.'

'What's that?'

'D for Deeley. Monica Deeley. Our patroness – God bless her.'

He whisked back the curtains and Biddy buried her face in the pillow. 'For God's sake,' she said. 'Slow down.'

'It's not the day for slowing down,' said Mark. 'It's the day of revelation.'

It was too much, he now acknowledged, especially at that early hour. But something of the excitement still lingered. He checked himself in the mirror. Zip fastened, hair presentable, eyes bright. He breathed deeply, and tightened his belt another notch. He was ready to go.

His timing was perfect. As he left reception with the keys to

Otto's enclosure, the Bentley drew up outside the door. A rear window slid down and in the dove-grey hull he saw the white loaf of Mrs Deeley's face. A cottage-loaf, he thought. That was the shape, but the colour was wrong. She did not move and, tactfully, he kept his hands behind his back. 'Good morning,' he said.

'I understand that Dr Hoover is indisposed.'

'He had an accident. He's in hospital.'

'Is he recovering?'

'I believe so.'

'I'm glad.'

She studied him impassively. 'You are to accompany me?'

'Dr Hoover thought I might.'

A slight pause and then she inclined her head. 'Very well. Get in.'

He was careful not to touch her. They sat rigidly side by side as the car drove slowly along the concrete ribbons, over the cinder track, and sighed to a halt outside the iron gate. Mark reached for the door handle, but Mrs Deeley raised a black-gloved finger. 'Wait.'

'But I have the keys.'

'I have my own keys.'

They sat in the car while the chauffeur unlocked the gate and unloaded a picnic basket and two canvas-backed chairs from the boot. He opened the door, and helped Mrs Deeley out. She peered at the sky and then at her watch. 'In three hours, I think.'

'Very well, madame.'

She turned to Mark. 'Come along then.'

He held open the gate and together they strolled towards the cage. Mrs Deeley looked neither to the left or to the right, nor did she trouble to look behind her. When she lowered herself, her chair was in place. The chauffeur saluted and withdrew. It was like a royal durbar, thought Mark; a lonely levee for the widow of Proto. But there were no festivities, no celebration. Mrs Deeley's eyes were fixed on the cage, although there was no sign of Otto.

'I was in here a couple of days ago' he said.

'Indeed?'

With Dr Bloom.'

The white face turned slowly towards him, revolving so smoothly that he imagined a ball-and-socket buried in the lard of her neck.

'She actually touched Otto. He touched her. They made contact.'

'Did he speak?'

'No, he didn't speak.'

'Do you think he will?'

He laughed nervously, converting it into a cough when he saw the intensity of her expression. 'There's no way of telling. I don't know what stage we're at.' He pointed towards the loudspeaker and the spotlight. 'We've only just discovered those. Ryman must have installed them just before the accident. I've tried to persuade him to tell me what else he knows – the stuff he didn't have time to put in his notes – but he's not rational. He hates Proto.'

'With reason, do you think?'

'Possibly.'

'It was my decision to treat him as we did.'

'I see.' His voice, hoped Mark, was completely neutral.

'Was I right?'

'I think you were harsh.'

She nodded slowly and with evident satisfaction. 'Yes, I was harsh. But he was an evil man. Dissolute.' She tweaked the folds of her coat, as though plucking off smuts. 'He was the wrong man for Otto.'

'You mean his methods were wrong?'

She stared straight ahead. 'I know nothing of his methods, only the man. He was immoral. I was informed.'

Spies now, thought Mark. 'But how would that affect his research?' he asked.

Mrs Deeley took a handkerchief from her sleeve and dabbed the sharp tip of her nose. 'Evil compounds evil.' She cocked her head to one side, and from within the tunnel Mark heard the faint scrape of Otto's feet. The shaggy form emerged and studied them, nostrils twitching, tufts of hair on his forearms fluttering like pennants. His upper lip wrinkled back, baring the teeth. The hooting, soft at first, rose to a crescendo, and a rain of straw and débris sprayed through the bars, falling just short of their chairs. 'We know each other, you see,' said Mrs Deeley. 'Otto knows that I am not deceived.'

'About what?'

'His nature. His abilities.' She watched the ape compose himself, squatting close to the bars, his eyes glinting within the linenfolds of hair. 'He could speak if he wanted to,' she said. 'I am convinced of it. He could tell me what I want to know.'

Mark took his time. With madness, he thought, you must never hurry. 'And what is that?' he asked.

Mrs Deeley shifted her hams slightly, the ritual movements of the storyteller preparing to tell a tale. 'Otto was our friend,' she said. 'My husband's and mine. When we started the business he was our mascot. He shared our home. When we went out we took him with us on a lead. He wore little pants, and a jacket in winter.' She smiled reminiscently, her white face creasing like dough. 'People warned us,' she went on. 'They said we'd have trouble when he grew bigger. But we didn't believe them. George – that was my husband – used to take him in the car. He always reckoned that, given time, Otto could learn to drive. He used to toot the horn. Toot-toot. Everyone knew it was him.'

She turned convulsively, as though pained by the memory. 'You should have seen him then.'

'I wish I had.'

'He was lovely,' she said. 'Really lovely. But he changed. My husband used to travel a lot and we had to shut Otto up. We told him why, we always told him why, but he wouldn't accept it. He became spiteful. One day he bit me and George said no more. He'd gone too far, he wasn't to be trusted. So we built him a little house and came to see him as often as we could. And George would go in and play with him and I'd sit and watch. But it wasn't the same. I always had forebodings.'

The ape stirred in his straw, and Mrs Deeley's head jerked up. 'One day he'll talk,' she said. 'One day I'll know.'

'You'll know what?'

'Everything,' said Mrs Deeley. And she told him.

Mark's forecast had been correct. It was a day of revelation. That afternoon Lacey-Jones telephoned him. 'How's the old man?'

'Mending,' said Mark. 'Not as fast as he wants to.'

'See if you can speed up the recovery. Get him on his feet.'

'What's the rush?'

'Bell's trying to carve him up, and it's being done behind my back. I don't like that.'

'I don't follow.'

'Nor did I.' Lacey-Jones explained about Afton, the forthcoming question in the House, and the visit to Proto. 'And the little bastard went to see him off his own bat,' he complained.

'I don't see how it can affect Hoover.'

Lacey-Jones sighed. 'To the pure all things are pure. There's no real shit for Afton to stir up. Right?'

'Almost right.'

'You can tell me about that later. Anyway, assuming there are no grounds for official censure quite a lot can be done unofficially. Proto's controlled by a board of directors. Mrs Deeley's the major shareholder, but she has to listen to complaints. If Afton raises doubts about how the place is run there are bound to be demands for reorganization. Bell's the man who goes by the book. Hoover's the oddball who listens to no one. Guess who'll be for the chop.'

'Hoover?'

'Indubitably.' There was an embarrassed pause. 'I rather liked him, you know.'

'So do I,' said Mark. 'I'll let him know.'

An hour later Charlotte came to see him. 'Ryman's around,' she said. 'I don't know where he is now, but this morning he was outside my flat.'

'He phoned me last night. He's off his head.'

They stared at each other in dismay. 'In fact,' said Mark, 'I'm beginning to think everyone's crazy.' Succinctly, he repeated Lacey-Jones's report: 'Also, I had the pleasure of Mrs Deeley's company this morning.'

'You took her to see Otto?'

'She took me.'

He hesitated before going on. The memory was still powerful, still vivid. But what he felt most strongly now was compassion. She had described Otto as she would have described a son. She had loved him; perhaps she still did. But he was evil, she insisted.

'Evil?'

He shrugged his shoulders. At second-hand the experience was bizarre; but remembering the set, white face, the matter-of-fact tone, the deliberate quenching of emotion, he felt the hairs on his neck rise. For a while he had believed. He still could not dismiss Mrs Deeley's belief.

She had opened the picnic basket, and served him ham and salad on a waxed plate. 'Oil and vinegar?'

'Just a drop.'

She had impaled a lettuce heart on her fork and crunched it reflectively. When she spoke her voice had been quite calm. 'Towards the end,' she said, 'it got so that only George could handle Otto. He had to wear leather leggings, and extra jumpers, and he'd still go in with him to give him exercise. Otto had a smaller cage then. We used to let him in through a sliding door, and George would be waiting, and they'd wrestle and roll about for ten or fifteen minutes, then George would say enough and the games would be over for that day. The trouble was that Otto never had enough, and sometimes he'd try and stop George from leaving. He'd set himself in front of the door and no one could get in or out.

'Everyone told us to leave him alone. But George said we'd raised him, and he was our responsibility, and he'd never hurt either of us. And then one day it happened, just as they'd warned us. George tried to leave the cage and Otto wouldn't let him go. George tried to coax him – he was very persuasive – and I thought what a nuisance, but it's just a matter of time. But while I sat there Otto looked me straight in the eye and took hold of my husband's head, and twisted it. He twisted it right round. I screamed and screamed, and I could see that George was dead, but Otto held on to him for an hour at least before they managed to get him away. They wanted to shoot him there and then, but I said no. And I carried on with the business and made some money, and I engaged Dr Hoover and we set up Contact. And, really, it's all to one end.'

Charlotte studied her bitten fingernails. 'Which is?'

'It's simple enough' said Mark. 'She wants Otto to tell us why he killed her husband.'

FOURTEEN

Biddy's father had been a regular soldier and her early childhood was spent in married quarters. Weekends at Proto reminded her of those days. There was the same sense of being surrounded by an institution, of being under surveillance and (her mother's phrase) of watching her social P's and Q's.

'Are you wearing those then?' asked Linda when she came downstairs in a pair of orange sailcloth jeans.

'Obviously I'm wearing them. D'you think I shouldn't?'

'Bit bright, aren't they?'

'I bought them in California. They go in for bright colours there.'

'I can see that.'

'Are they too much?'

'All right for the seaside. I don't know about here.'

But clearly, thought Biddy, she did know. Linda was Proto-born-and-bred and in her way she was the perfect arbiter. She did not give advice; she passed judgment. She was the voice of the market place and the market was where they were going.

It was not as rural as it sounded. In its wisdom Proto had built a shopping arcade abutting the Social Centre. There was a dry cleaners, a fried Chicken 'n Fish Bar, a stationer's and a small supermarket. There were also open stalls, manned by local farmers and smallholders. On Saturday mornings it was where the clans gathered. Linda had arranged to meet her mother and before she knew it, Biddy had been co-opted. So had Mark, and so had David Dempsey, car owner and innocent bystander.

'Why change?' enquired Mark, as Biddy peeled off the jeans and stepped into a skirt.

'Linda says they're too bloody bright.'

'Tell her to get knotted.'

'She's probably right. She's lived here.'

Mark brushed his hair and examined the whites of his eyes. 'I'm anaemic,' he said.

'You're no more anaemic than I am.'

'I'm intimidated,' he said. 'What am I supposed to be tagging along for this morning?'

'You're carrying the shopping.' She kissed him briefly on the cheek. 'And thank you.'

'We mustn't be too long. I want to see the old man.'

'Won't it keep till tomorrow?'

He thought for a moment. Perhaps he should give Hoover another day of recuperation before breaking the bad news. 'Perhaps it will.' He came up behind her as she inspected the skirt in the mirror.

'Hands off!'

'I can't hear you.' He gripped her thighs and felt them tighten against his palm. 'Lovely.'

She wriggled free. 'They'll be waiting.'

'You go ahead.' It was curious, he thought, how he was mellowed by the presence of women, how they actually made him feel better. Despite his initial resistance he was now reconciled to having Linda in the house. It was like having one's own harem, without the bonus of extra sex, but with the undeniable pleasure of seeing rooms and hallways padded – furnished, almost – with female flesh. The effect on Biddy had been unexpected too. It was as though she sensed competition and so made an effort to please. Stimulation all round, thought Mark, even at work, although the situation there could, at any time, prove perilous. It was part of its attraction, he realized. Charlotte was an antidote to Biddy at her most antiseptic. Also, he admired her as a colleague. But there was a recklessness about her, a whiff of old scandal which gave their relationship an extra relish. In his mind's eye he saw it developing like a comic strip, but he had no desire to skim through to the end. There was still some way to go before the vital frame.

The car hooted, and he trotted downstairs. He opened the front door and saw Dempseys, large and small, with their faces pressed to the car windows.

'Sorry,' said Dempsey. 'We're going to be a bit squashed.'

Mark smiled bleakly. 'It's perfectly all right.'

'The thing is,' said Dempsey, 'we'll have to do a bit of arranging.

Biddy in front with me and the two babes. You and Linda in the back with my pair.'

'What about the springs?'

'They've put up with it before.'

'Isn't Peg coming?' asked Biddy.

Mark threw up his hands. 'For God's sake, woman, where would we put her?'

At the same, he told himself as they drove away, thighs jammed together, elbows gouging armpits, a family outing had its points. Its normality, even its discomforts, made a refreshing contrast to the Proto pattern. In his more sentimental moments he thought of domesticity as an old song, something to hum mindlessly while life went on. Quite possibly, he admitted, he was wrong. Ideally, it should not be an accompaniment, but the measure to which husband and wife walked or danced according to their mood. He and Biddy had not yet reached that state of equilibrium. But he saw it as a prospect, within reach, and greatly to be desired.

'What's the drill?' asked Dempsey.

'I'm meeting my mum,' said Linda. 'She wants to see Baby.'

'I'm shopping,' said Biddy. 'Perhaps we could meet for a drink when I'm finished.'

'At the centre?'

She pulled James's hand from the gear lever. 'If you like. Give me an hour.'

Rarely had he seen her look so happy, thought Mark. 'And I'm the beast of burden,' he said.

The smaller Dempsey squirmed on his lap. 'What sort of beast?'

'I don't know. What sort do you think?'

'A camel.'

His brother shouted him down. 'No, an elephant.'

'Steady,' said Dempsey, slamming on the brakes as a pack of Proto dogs sauntered across the road.

'I really don't mind,' said Mark. 'Today I'll be any beast you like, so long as it's not a chimp.'

In the supermarket James reached out from his carry-chair resting on Biddy's hip and with no apparent effort pulled down a pyramid of baked bean tins. Mark turned in time to see them sway and lunged forward to catch them. He was too late. The tins tumbled, bounced, and ricochetted in all directions.

'Oh God,' said Biddy, as the assistants picked them up, 'I'm terribly sorry.'

They looked up from their hands and knees and smiled reassuringly. Not her fault, they said. Not the kiddie's fault either. Only natural to want to touch. Bless him.

'It's Disneyland,' said Mark as they paid up and left.

'They simply accept children.'

'Proto tradition?'

'Village tradition. They just behave naturally.'

He propped the carrier bag between his feet and looked about him. No one within reach, he thought, gave a damn whether Bell toppled Hoover, or Otto talked, or Mrs Deeley received an answer to her question. They were all Proto people and, as Biddy had said, they were behaving naturally, with a selfishness that was almost sublime. They had a union, shop stewards, and a worker's council. But there was no real dialogue between them and the Proto management. Perhaps there had once been when George Deeley was in the chair. Even that was doubtful. Deeley was an idealist. Everything pointed to it from the model estates to his treatment of Otto. He had faith in the best of all possible worlds; not in its existence but in its eventual creation. And that would have made people uneasy. In England, thought Mark, visionaries were treated like the village idiot; sometimes abused, more often ignored.

All the same, he had done a good job, a decent job. The supermarket buzzed behind him. The scent of frying batter billowed from the Chicken 'n Fish Bar. There was a distant thunder of rock music from the record shop. Spring flowers starred the pavement. Small pleasures, but not to be despised. A community existed. Its needs were being met. And the reason for its continued existence, he thought, was one woman's obsession. 'All to one end,' Mrs Deeley had told him. Perhaps it was better that each side kept its own counsel. A little ignorance could be a comforting thing.

They entered the Social Centre. 'GRAND DANCE, SATURDAY NEXT 8 p.m.' advertised St Francis. 'How about it?' he said.

'If you like.'

'It's bound to be just a hop.'

'I like hops.'

He squeezed her arm. 'All right then. It's a date.'

In an annexe to the bar they ordered coffee for themselves and orange juice for James. There was no sign of Linda or the Dempseys, but bee-lining through the obstacle course of blue-topped tables he saw Alec and Kitty Bell. There was no escape.

'Say nothing about the Hoover business,' hissed Mark.

Alec Bell wore his weekend uniform of baggy grey slacks and a blue barathea blazer. There was an RAF crest on the breast pocket and he wore a service tie. Mark stood up and smiled his Borgia smile. 'Have some coffee,' he said.

Kitty Bell wore a dull pink dress, the colour of a cinder glowing through wood ash. She held out a finger to James who ignored it. 'Isn't he sweet,' she said. 'A dear little chap.'

James extended a pudgy hand and took hold of Mrs Bell's beads. Gently, Biddy tried to disengage him, but he held on. He tugged once and the thread broke, showering the table with plastic cubes. 'I'm terribly sorry,' said Biddy.

It was the reason, she told Mark, why she agreed to attend the Sunday meeting at the Bells' house the following morning. 'It was all those bloody beads,' she said. 'There were so many. I'd have said yes to anything rather than pick up any more of them.'

But not Mark. 'Will you come too?' Kitty Bell asked him.

'Sorry,' he said.

'It's non-denominational. Everyone's welcome.'

'It's kind of you. But no thanks.'

'We'll pick you up if you have no car,' she offered.

Alec Bell covered her hand with his own pink paw. 'I'm sure that Mark has other things to do.'

'I have, actually.'

'That's it, then,' said Bell. 'We don't feel slighted. Another time.'

Mark sipped his coffee, and made a mental reservation to avoid it in future. 'I doubt it,' he said. 'I'm an atheist.'

'I see,' said Kitty Bell. She stood up and several beads exploded underfoot. 'We look forward to seeing *you*,' she told Biddy. 'Alec will call for you around ten.'

'Thank you.'

They watched them steer a straight course for the exit and Mark grinned across the table. 'Brush up on your hymns Ancient and Modern.'

'You bastard.'

'Stand your ground,' he said. 'It's your own fault if you're lumbered.'

'I'm not making a habit of it.'

'Wait till she asks you again.'

As they drove back, threading their way through shoppers and cyclists, Dempsey slowed down to avoid what appeared to Mark to be the same pack of Proto dogs they had met on their way in. He counted fifteen.

'Are there always so many dogs about?'

'Dogs?' said Dempsey vaguely. 'I suppose so. I've never noticed really.'

'They're everywhere.'

'I suppose they are now you mention it.' He whistled through his teeth. 'Funny thing,' he said. 'Just as we were coming into the centre I saw something else peculiar. There was this chap across the road. I could have sworn it was Ryman.'

In the afternoon they went for a walk, and in the evening they made love. It was the first time since the night he had agreed to Linda's coming, Mark recalled.

He turned Biddy over on to her stomach and wobbled her bottom with one hand. 'Jelly on a plate,' he said.

'Mmm.'

'Do you like it?'

'Love it.'

'Why, what's so special?'

She hesitated. 'It's so . . . friendly.'

'Not sexy?'

'That too. But it's not something you'd ask a lover to do. Not any old lover. You'd have to know him pretty well.'

'And how many old lovers do you know?'

'Hundreds.'

'How many?' he said. 'Seriously.'

She pulled the pillow over her head so that her voice was muffled. 'Two. Two and a half perhaps.'

'Who's the half?'

'The first one. We never did it properly. We were hopeless.'

Mark pushed the pillow away. 'You never told me about him. What went wrong?'

'Don't be so inquisitive! I don't ask you to tell me things.'

'I'll tell you anything you like.'

'Really?' She sat up in bed, and smoothed back her hair. 'Anything at all?'

'Within reason.'

'That's no good.'

'It's ninety per cent good. I reserve the right to protect my marriage. There are some things you wouldn't want to know.' He pulled her into the crook of his arm. 'What if I fancied little boys? Would you want to know about that?'

'Do you?'

'What do you think?'

She reached down and felt between his legs. 'I think you prefer married ladies.'

'Only married ladies?'

'Married ladies and Linda.'

'I don't fancy Linda.'

She blew into his ear. 'Come on. I've seen you look at her yellow nightie.'

'The fall-out, you mean. That's a reflex action. There's nothing personal. It's merely glandular.'

'Louise Hoover, then.'

'Too bossy.'

'Peg Dempsey?'

'Too stringy.'

'Charlotte Bloom?'

'You've never met Charlotte Bloom.'

'I've heard about her.' Her fingers gripped him tightly.

'Careful,' he said. 'It's the only one I've got.'

'What about Charlotte Bloom?'

'I work with her,' said Mark. 'I don't fancy her.' He arched his back to relieve the strain.

'She had an affair with Ryman.'

'I suppose Peg Dempsey told you that. The old wives' association.'

'It's true, isn't it?'

'True enough,' said Mark. 'If it matters.'

'It matters that you didn't tell me.'

'I didn't think it was important.'

'Has it anything to do with him phoning here, that call the other night?'

'For God's sake,' said Mark, 'of course not.' At least, he thought, as her hand began to move rhythmically, and he heard himself groan with pleasure, I honestly and truly hope not.

The next morning at eleven-thirty, Biddy sat on the edge of a straightbacked chair in the Bell's sitting room and balanced a cup of coffee on her knee. Soon, she told herself, she would have to start cutting out sugar. God knows how many calories she absorbed in a normal Proto week.

'A biscuit?' said Alec Bell. 'Wholemeal or Garibaldi.'

'No thank you.'

'No sweet tooth?'

'I'm thinking of lunch. It's not long to go.'

He bobbed his head several times, and she realized that he was signifying his agreement. It was like something from the Mikado she thought, or a wind-up doll going through its tiny repertoire.

'Did you enjoy the meeting?' he asked.

'Very much.'

'I want you to know that I understand about Mark. You mustn't feel awkward.'

'I don't.'

'Good, good.' He bobbed some more.

'We make our own decisions. Neither of us has to excuse the other.'

'That's as it should be.'

'It was kind of you to ask me though.'

'You must come again.'

Never, thought Biddy. The meeting had been sixty minutes of pure embarrassment. For one thing, the room in which they met was too small to contain such a volume of sincerity. She felt gummy with goodwill, battered by fellow feeling. Twenty people had shaken her hand. Twenty smiles had flashed a welcome. Kitty Bell had played the harmonium, and she had played it badly. Alec Bell had read from the Bible, and another man wearing a shiny blue mohair suit had told anecdotes of such withering cuteness that she guessed their source before spotting the magazine tucked beneath his hymnal. Full marks, she told herself when she saw the title. The *Reader's Digest* strikes again.

The noise, too, had been deafening. Everyone sang with heart and voice. 'Fight the good fight', 'Jesu, lover of my soul', 'From Greenland's icy mountains'; she knew them all, several were her favourites. But the renderings were so vehement, the performances so unsparing that she imagined consciences being shaken like dusters, and sins bolting through the window on ladders of air.

She recalled some of the faces from the party given by Dr Hoover. All of them, she thought, were members of Alec Bell's team. A middleaged woman with protruding teeth, whose grey stockings toned morbidly with her greying hair took the adjacent seat. 'Where did you last pray?' she enquired.

'I beg your pardon.'

'Which church did you attend?'

'I didn't,' said Biddy. 'Not regularly. Not since I was a girl.'

Five minutes more, she told herself, and then she was off. Most likely Mark would be home by that time. He and David Dempsey had driven to the hospital to see Dr Hoover, and although the visiting hours could be bent to suit the convenience of the Scientific Director visitors were not encouraged to stay too long.

'We have a Bible class for tinies,' said the woman. 'Would you like to bring your little boy?'

Biddy looked for somewhere to leave her coffee cup. 'He's much too young,' she said.

'No one is too young to be blessed. It's a matter of creating the right atmosphere. They have no need to comprehend, only to imbibe.'

Briefly, Biddy had a vision of a sterile igloo, flushed through and through with the odour of sanctity. Alec Bell, she thought, could probably make the stuff in his laboratories, packing it in cylinders like oxygen.

'He's too young,' she repeated. 'He's only a year old.'

Across the room she saw Kitty Bell raise the coffee pot, and she shook her head, more violently than she had intended. Between her and the door there was a wall of bodies. She felt a sudden surge of panic. She had to get out. She would walk home if necessary. And then the door opened, and framed in a halo of yellow varnish she saw Mark's fair hair and the tangled crown of Dr Hoover.

Twenty heads turned as one, presenting her with a plantation of buns, braids, and shaven necks. She heard Alec Bell clear his throat, the chime of a spoon striking a saucer, the gurgle of her neighbour's stomach; then silence.

'Good morning all,' said Dr Hoover, his smile radiant, his spectacles striking fire in the pale sunlight. 'The patient is recovered. The prodigal has returned.'

FIFTEEN

'I couldn't stop him,' Mark told Charlotte. 'The minute he heard about Bell's little scheme he was out of bed and bellowing for his clothes. The personal appearance was a gift. He said it would confound the enemy.'

'Smiting them hip and thigh.'

'Smiling as he did it.' Mark shook his head reminiscently. 'He was bloody marvellous.'

'But is he really better?'

He picked up the oil-can, and pulled the pin from the nozzle. 'Psychologically, he's fine. Bell's put him on his mettle. But the scalding shook him up. He needs looking after.'

'He looked good this morning.'

They had met for a briefing at nine o'clock. Enthroned at his desk, Hoover had welcomed them in. As usual, the windows were half open, and a steady breeze ruffled typescripts, newspaper cuttings and Hoover's gunmetal curls. He demanded progress reports, news of Otto, an account of Mark's meeting with Mrs Deeley.

At the end of it, he spread his arms. 'As I foretold. Stage by stage, little by little, we learn what we want to know.'

'You could have told me at the beginning,' said Mark.

'But would you have been ready? Would you have been responsive? An adult chimpanzee, and an eccentric lady who wants to talk to him. Would you have taken that seriously for a single moment?'

'Not eccentric,' said Mark. 'Mad.'

'Are you certain?'

'Aren't you?'

Dr Hoover wagged a warning finger. 'Mrs Deeley has known Otto for most of his life. To her he is not an object of research. He is an individual. She may have observed more, divined more, understood more than any of us. I accept the fact that she is eccentric. I have no evidence that she is mad.'

'Do you believe that Otto can talk?'

'My dear boy,' said Dr Hoover, 'that is what we are here to discover.'

He had agreed, still sceptical, still resenting Hoover's tactics, but persuaded that it was better to go forward than dawdle and be snapped up by the opposition. 'We must put on a show,' Hoover had said. 'I will consult that agreeable young man. What was his name?'

'Lacey-Jones.'

'Of course, Lacey-Jones. He should be able to advise on our presentation.'

'He'd love that. And what about us, Charlotte and myself? Where do we concentrate?'

Dr Hoover had reached out and squeezed Charlotte's hand. 'My congratulations. Belated, but heartfelt. I would like you to continue. Give Ryman's method a try. Sleep-teaching, wasn't it? Yes, sleep-teaching.'

And again, thought Mark, they had been beguiled. Stooped inside the observation box he wrestled with a wall plate, gouging at dirt that clogged the groove along which it was meant to slide. Behind him Charlotte traced a complex of wires which veined the walls and ceiling to their parent plugs and sockets behind the door.

'This is where he played the tapes,' she said. 'Some of the good old good ones.'

'And this is where he watched Otto. Night observation post.' The plate jolted to one side, revealing an oval of reinforced glass. Mark rubbed it clean, and peering through saw a concrete shelf piled high with straw. The straw heaved, and Otto's head emerged, seeded with husks as though he had just attended a wedding. He raked together more straw and twined it round himself, binding his body like a hot water pipe.

Mark pointed to the far corner of the ceiling. 'There's the speaker. The light must be over here.' He stared out into the compound. 'Why did he put them in the outside cage as well?'

'Twenty-four hour service. That's Ryman for you. He never let up.'

'Does he worry you?'

'Certainly he worries me. I don't like to think I'm being watched.'

Mark jerked his head towards the window. 'It doesn't worry Otto.'

'Otto doesn't go much on Mrs Deeley. And I know how he feels. It makes my skin crawl.' She chafed her arms as though the irritation was there and Mark pushed the door open so that the box was flooded with light.

'Look, no Ryman,' he said.

'I didn't imagine him. He's real.'

'I know he's real.' He put his hand on her shoulder. 'David Dempsey saw him too.'

'When was that? Where?'

'On Saturday near the centre. I told Hoover.'

'There you are,' said Charlotte. 'He means trouble.'

Mark laughed quietly; a small, self-satisfied sound. 'Biddy thinks it's because of you. She asked me if I fancied you.'

He was not prepared for the reaction. Charlotte's head snapped round. 'What a ghastly expression. Fancied!'

'She didn't mean it like that.'

'I'm quite sure that she did.' She took two steps forward and stood against him, her breasts lodged against his chest. 'A little of what you fancy,' she said, barging him softly. 'Is that it? Do you fancy me?'

'I like you,' he said.

'That's not the same thing. Not the same at all.' She pushed harder, using herself as a weapon, until he was forced back. 'A passing fancy,' she said. 'How bloody insulting.'

She was frightened, thought Mark, not angry. He took her face in his hands, covering her mouth, aware that she was trembling. 'It's merely a word,' he said. 'It doesn't apply to you.'

She nodded her head, and he felt his fingers skid on her teeth. Definitions! he thought. Distinctions! But she was right. 'Fancy' was wholly appropriate. What he felt was not love; it was not even desire. A brief but intense attraction, flaring like anger; a sweet itch that would recur again and again, however promptly he scratched it. He acknowledged the diagnosis, and repeated the lie.

Her eyes softened and he felt her body relax. She was not deceived, but the bad moment was past. She dropped her head, and stepped back so that his fingers grazed her neck. 'We know,' she said, 'both of us. Not that it's worth discussing. Not that there's time.'

She rapped on the glass of the spy-hole. 'Wake him up,' she said. 'Get him out of there. We've got work to do.'

'What I want to know,' said Biddy, 'is how the instant coffee habit caught on.' She reviewed the selection of tins lining the kitchen dresser. 'Dextrose,' she said, reading from a label. 'What's that got to do with coffee?'

'I can't imagine.' Louise Hoover pushed forward her glass and Biddy refilled it with sherry.

She was a little drunk, she thought, but not noticeably so. 'Do you like it?' she enquired.

'Very much.'

'I decided yesterday. No more coffee. It's practically a vice here. Everyone gives you coffee and it's so awful.' She re-corked the bottle and set it between them. It was mid-morning and through the window she could see the washing-line. Bibs, small vests and sleeping suits flapped in the breeze. 'How's Dr Hoover?' she asked.

'Better.' Louise put down her glass. 'I think he left hospital too soon. I wanted him to stay till the end of the week.'

'So did Alec Bell I should think.'

'It must have been dreadful yesterday.'

'Not a bit.' Biddy giggled. 'It was splendid, really. I could have hugged him.'

'I should have been there.'

'You'd have enjoyed it.'

'I don't think so.' She leaned across the table. 'He has to be careful. There's a lot at stake.'

Biddy straightened her face. 'I know.'

'I introduced him to Mrs Deeley and he's worked so hard. All these years we've been here. The things we've tried to do. The things I want to do still.'

'You'll do them.'

'I hope so.'

Was it the sherry talking? Biddy wondered. She fingered the cord, but Louise shook her head. 'You've heard about this question in the House? The visit by this ridiculous M.P.?'

'Mark told me.'

'It's got to be handled properly. We've got to impress them in the right way. But Francis treats it like a game.'

'So long as he wins it.'

'You're wrong. Wrong!'

She thumped the table with her clenched fists, and Biddy looked up in alarm. On the line the vests arranged themselves like naval flags, 'Proto expects . . . ' and she bowed her head. Message received. 'Mark knows how important it is,' she said.

'Does he?' demanded Louise. 'Does he really?'

'I'm certain he does.'

She sat back in her chair. 'That's what I wanted to know.'

'If that's all, you needn't worry.' She was slurring the words a little but she had made the point. It was something to her credit. For reassuring Louise Hoover: ten marks out of ten.

'Then there's this Ryman business,' said Louise. 'Francis told me there'd been some unpleasantness.'

It was as though she had been ducked in cold water. A dirty trick, thought Biddy, sneaking in with that stuff about being worried about the visit and then coming up with Ryman. 'Just a phone call,' she said precisely. 'He called the other night.'

'I've had a word with our security people, and they'll be watching out for him,' said Louise, 'but you'll lock up carefully, won't you. I don't think we should take any chances.'

Biddy felt sick, but she drained her glass. 'Why don't we get the police?'

'Think,' said Louise. 'Think of the visit. We don't want to draw attention to anything else.'

'I suppose not,' said Biddy.

'I'm sure there's no need to worry.'

The bibs danced on the line, blue and white against thunder-clouds and she thought of James upstairs. Urgently, she wanted to hold him and to guard his body with her own.

'It's keep-fit tomorrow,' said Louise. 'Shall I see you there?'

'I'm not sure.'

'It's important to keep at it.' She laughed gaily. 'We've got to chase the inches.'

'I'll let you know,' said Biddy, willing her to be gone. She felt threatened, unable to explain why.

Lacey-Jones arrived after lunch, a brown paper parcel on the passenger seat of the Morgan. 'I'm returning your clothes,' he told Mark, 'many thanks for the loan.'

'Thanks for remembering.'

'I've got a good memory,' he said, 'basic equipment for the job. I liked the sweater, by the way. Very stylish.'

'Bloomingdale's basement. Very cheap.' He held open the car door as Lacey-Jones clambered out. 'Sorry about last time.'

'Not to worry. We're on the same side now I gather.'

'We always were.'

'Hardly, old boy. Hardly.' He sniffed the air and looked about him. 'Incidentally, they've fixed the date for Afton's visit. The end of this week. May the tenth. How does that strike you?'

'With a dull thud,' said Mark. He had been at Proto for nearly two months, he realized. 'When does he put the question in the House?'

'That's tomorrow.' Lacey-Jones took hold of Mark's elbow as they walked side by side. 'You're bound to get press enquiries. Don't try to handle them. Put them on to me.'

'I'll tell the switchboard.'

'Excellent. And now you can tell me everything I ought to know about Proto. The unexpurgated version.'

'I didn't leave much out last time.'

'Tell me about Otto,' said Lacey-Jones.

'Hoover phoned you?'

'He was on the blower for hours.' He opened a notebook and unsheathed his ballpoint. 'From the beginning,' he said.

The story took an hour to tell. In Charlotte's office they finished the last of the vodka. 'What I don't understand,' said Lacey-Jones, 'is why no one filled me in on this before. Can't they see – can't Hoover see – what the press could make of it?' He sketched head-lines in the air: ' "I was gagged," says man who taught ape to talk'.

'He didn't,' said Charlotte. 'Not as far as we know.'

'Jealousy charge by sacked scientist.'

'No one was jealous,' said Mark.

Lacey-Jones tilted his chair back and put his feet on the desk. 'Anticipate the worst. First step in the campaign.'

'What about the rest of the work?' said Charlotte. 'Surely that's good for something.'

'Certainly. But there's one rule in life that you ignore at your peril – if you're in PR, that is. Bad news is more interesting than good news. There's no comparison.' He flicked dust from one dazzling toe cap, and clasped his hands behind his head. 'Still, better look on the bright side. I'll get a photographer down tomorrow. I want two sets of pictures. One lot scientific, and one for the mums and dads. Tell me what's possible and we'll work out a shooting script.'

'They won't perform to order.'

Lacey-Jones glanced at him sharply. 'The only one I know performed without orders. Which reminds me. Rubber pants for any chimp that's likely to be picked up.'

'We don't want too much of that,' said Mark. 'They also bite.'

'Find me one that doesn't.'

'I'll try.' He doodled on the message pad. 'What about Otto?' he asked.

'What do you mean "what about Otto?" '

'Are we putting him on show?'

'Of course we are.' Lacey-Jones sat up straight in his chair. 'Do you suppose for one minute we're going to conceal anything? This is an official visit. We've actually invited the buggers to come and look round. They've got to be given *carte blanche*.'

'Do we tell them about Mrs Deeley?'

Lacey-Jones heaved a sigh. 'Are you really good at your job?' he enquired.

'Reasonably.'

'I'm glad about that. You'd be a disaster in public relations.' He hitched his chair forward. 'Always tell the truth whenever possible. Never volunteer information you can't expand. Only lie as a last resort, but when you do – do it from the heart.'

'In other words, Otto's just part of the programme.'

'Exactly.'

'No mention of Mrs Deeley.'

'Right again.'

'And what about Ryman?'

'Full credit. But emphasize the team effort. You and Charlotte, especially Charlotte.' He peered across the desk. 'Can you do anything about your face?'

'Such as?'

'Astringent pack, eye-liner, lipstick. I'll send you some down.'
He smiled apologetically. 'Nothing personal. It's for the photographers. Do you use perfume?'

'Not while I'm working. It destroys contact.'

'I see. Ah well, can't be helped. You'll have to use natural charm.'

It was amazing, thought Mark. Without a tremor Lacey-Jones
waltzed in where others had feared to tread. What he was watching,
he realized, was a professional at work. They were on the same side
and to take offence would be foolish. They were being projected
and Charlotte had understood without any preliminary softening
up. He had no idea what Lacey-Jones was paid, probably a great
deal. But he earned every penny. He gave value for money.

'You've not seen Otto yet,' he said.

'I was coming to that.'

'We could go over now,' Mark offered. 'We checked the lights
this morning, and set up the tape recorder. You could see how it
looks.'

'Right you are. Then we can sort out the programme. What to
show Afton's lot, from A to Z.'

The gate to the arena was shut but not locked. Otto was in his
cage, and from the roof dangled the remains of the spotlight and
the speaker. Through the spy-hole in the observation box they saw
the same havoc in his sleeping quarters. The tape recorder was
smashed, and the tapes themselves littered the floor like seaweed.

Lacey-Jones put his hands on his hips. 'Jesus Christ,' he said.
'What's been going on here?'

'Sabotage,' said Mark.

'You mean Otto? Did he do this?'

'Not Otto.'

'It was Ryman,' said Charlotte.

'That was what I meant to tell you,' said Mark. 'Ryman's back.'

SIXTEEN

In the courtyard outside the main office Francis Hoover reviewed his troops. His curls squirmed from beneath an ARP helmet and a truncheon was looped round his right wrist. At six o'clock that evening they had told him of the sabotage. At six-thirty he had called for volunteers to reinforce Proto's security patrol. An hour later they had reported for duty; a dozen men – clerks, cleaners, and laboratory assistants – with Mark, and David Dempsey standing sheepishly at the end of the line. Neither of them had served in the forces. Their youth and then the end of conscription had saved them from several wars. But they were in the company of old sweats.

There was Malloy from stores, a former sergeant in the Iniskilling Fusiliers; Dennison and Matlock, 8th Army veterans, who manned the cleaning vans; Butler from personnel, who had fought in Korea; and Lofting, from correspondence, who had survived the street battles of Cyprus. Mark sucked in his stomach, and stood tall. The wind whipped through the birches at the end of the yard, and he shivered.

The security men stood apart in their peaked caps and uniforms of blue serge. Three of them were dog handlers. Their Alsatians lay grinning at their feet. The wind dropped and the pine walls of the office block exhaled the scent of resin. It was eerie, thought Mark. The camp atmosphere was very strong. There were no prisoners, no guards, but he felt the same unease he had experienced when he had first read through Ryman's notes.

Dr Hoover positioned himself under the lamp above the notice board. Moths danced over his head and small beetles pinged off his helmet. 'Just a few words,' he said. 'First I'd like to thank you for turning out. I've not called in the police because this is a family affair. But it's in everyone's interest to catch this chap before he does any more mischief.' His truncheon glinted in the light as he whacked it into the palm of his free hand.

'Some of you know him,' he said. 'He had a nasty accident and we think he's a bit unbalanced. So no rough stuff. On the other hand he may be violent, so take no chances.' He turned to the map pinned on the notice board. 'I want you to go in pairs. Divide the area between you. Look where you think someone could be hiding. Flush him out if you can.'

'I'll flush the sod out,' hissed Malloy. 'Just give me one of those dogs.'

'If you are successful,' said Dr Hoover, 'telephone for assistance immediately. That is all. And thank you.'

'Is he really round the bend?' asked Malloy.

Mark tugged at the tag of his anorak. 'There's not much doubt about that.'

A strand of wool was caught between the teeth of the zip, and it refused to open or close. Malloy took out his clasp knife and picked it free. 'I'd cut the bugger's throat if he messed with anyone of mine,' he said. 'I stuck three Jerries with this, and I'd do it again.'

Mark swallowed audibly. 'Are we going out together?'

'Why?' asked Malloy. 'Do you fancy me?' He whooped with laughter and cast round for an audience. 'Did you hear that?' he demanded. 'This feller fancies me.'

Like hell I do, thought Mark. What he felt was certainly not love; it was not even like. In this case the word did not apply. He made a mental note to tell Charlotte in the morning. 'What area have we drawn?' he asked.

'Hereabouts,' said Malloy, his index finger – saffron to the first knuckle – pointing beyond the Social Centre.

'He won't be there.'

'We'll make bloody sure of that. He's not a mate of yours is he?'

'I've never met him.'

'It's just as well. I wouldn't like to think I was sticking your blood brother.'

'You heard Dr Hoover,' said Mark. 'There'll be no rough stuff. He's a nuisance, but he's a sick man.'

'Yes, sir. Certainly, sir.' Malloy threw an exaggerated salute. 'Mind you,' he said, 'we have to defend ourselves.'

'Within reason.' Mark felt the camp closing in again. The dog handlers slipped the muzzles off the Alsatians, and their teeth shone like peeled twigs. As they loped past the volunteers, one man bent to pat a brindled head. There was a warning snarl, and the handler hauled on the choke chain.

'You do realize, don't you,' he said conversationally, 'you nearly got your hand bitten off.'

'I'm sorry,' said the dog-lover.

'You would have been, mate, I promise you.'

'Did you see that?' said Malloy. 'He nearly had him.' He was jigging about from foot to foot as though his bladder was paining him.

Mark studied him carefully. 'Do you want a pee before we go?'

'I've just had one.'

'Eager to be off, then.'

'Ready when you are.'

They climbed into the security van, four on each side, a dog on the floor, its head resting on its paws. It was dusk and every colour seemed to be deepened, enriched. There was something by Byron about that, thought Mark. 'And on the sea a deeper blue, And on the leaf a richer hue,' he said aloud.

Malloy turned his head. 'What was that?'

'Nothing.'

Nothing was right, he told himself. He was unable to pass on the experience. Malloy would laugh and he would be embarrassed. It was not the language that was at fault. There were no inadequacies there; no – what was the word? – shortfall. What was lacking was habit, shared custom, affection. He thought of Otto – prodded by goads, menaced by paper snakes – all in the name of communication. He had nothing to say to his tormentors. If Mrs Deeley was right he did not choose to talk to them. His language was violence. The interrogation was useless.

The van stopped, the rear door swung open, and the men piled out. They were behind the supermarket, he realized. The sky had an electric glow, a yellow shine that washed up from the façade. Three blocks of tower flats marched away to the west. On each landing hung a small blue light that seemed to wax and wane in brilliance like a star.

'Gather round,' said the driver, spreading a street map on the bonnet. 'You're in four pairs. You go in four separate directions, starting from the square.' He numbered them off and pointed out their routes. 'Check all sheds, all lock-up garages, all lean-to's.

6

Those of you who go by the flats' – he motioned at Mark and Malloy – 'take a look in the basements. If you see anything suspicious remember what Dr Hoover said. No violence. Ring for assistance.' He looked round the circle. 'Any questions?'

'How long do we go on looking?'

'Each patrol lasts two hours. You cover the route twice in that time. Then you report back here.' He issued them with black rubber torches, eighteen inches long, and heavy in the hand. 'Off you go then. Back here at ten.'

Mark checked his watch. Within a radius of five miles, he thought, other patrols were setting off, three at least, to comb through the streets and slopes of Proto. George Deeley would have been appalled. He saw Malloy's boots striking fire from the pavements and hurried after him.

Dr Hoover did not feel well. He cut a square inch of steak into smaller pieces and picked them singly from his plate. The exhilaration of the evening was beginning to wear off. He felt a steady ebb as though small holes had been made in his veins. Not pin pricks; incisions big enough to admit drainage tubes through which his energy seeped away.

Louise poured him another glass of wine. 'You look exhausted.'

'I'm not,' he said. 'It's just the first day back. There's been a lot to do.'

'Too much.'

'Probably.' He chewed the meat doggedly. 'It's too much to think of. It's not the physical effort. It's trying to deal with everything at once.' He swallowed some wine, and pushed his plate away. 'I ought to get back,' he said.

'They know where to reach you if anything happens.'

'That's true.' Calling for volunteers he had obeyed an impulse and wearing the helmet had been an act of bravado. Theatrical, he thought; most likely he had looked absurd. 'I'll leave the helmet behind,' he said. 'I'd forgotten how heavy it is.'

'You don't need it.'

'I know I don't need it.' It was astonishing how obtuse Louise could be. He had not worn it for protection. In a way it was fancy dress; the costume for a part. He remembered the war: searchlights over Regents Park, shrapnel tinkling down and the wolves howling.

He had worn it then and foolishly he had tried to revive the sensation of being in command of guarding his flock.

'The blisters hurt,' he said.

'I'll have a look at them.'

'Later.' He was dismayed by his own body. His lower belly and thighs were peeling. New, pink flesh showed in patches beneath the rags of yellow skin. At first, he had been cheered. He was merely in moult. The rooster would crow again. The thought had excited him and for the first time in years he had been awakened by sexual dreams.

He had rung for the night nurse, a West Indian, whose uniform billowed over mammy breasts and massive thighs. As she changed his dressing he had felt himself stir and she had shaken her head and patted him where he ached. 'Poor old fellow,' she said. 'Poor old man been in the wars.'

She pitied him, he thought; but not as a man. His age unsexed him. He was still troubled by dreams, but their nature had changed. He was no longer a lucky tumbler, rutting at will, but a casualty. He saw himself walking down a long loft. The floorboards vanished into infinity. On either side there were bedclothes heaped on the floor, frozen in the act of being flung aside, like mountains of egg white. He was naked, but from his navel to the middle of his thighs there was a hole, blue-black and bottomless. In it revolved constellations, suns, all wasting themselves in space. He ached with loneliness and even when he awoke the feeling of desolation remained within him like a bruise.

He had tried to ignore it. He had read books, listened to the radio. Once the matron called in to protest when he had sung Fidelio, all the parts, at the top of his voice when the opera was broadcast at two in the morning by a continental station. On the face of it he was recovering. He had impressed everyone by discharging himself from hospital. There had been an instant response to his call for volunteers. No one questioned his drive, his virility, his leadership. But they were deluded, thought Hoover. He had made his own examination, arrived at his own conclusions.

In terms of animal behaviour his to-ing and fro-ing could be categorized as displacement activity, a determined whirl devised to avoid – or displace – what was imminent and unpleasant. If he was obviously busy he could be excused for failing to notice that the industry was to no avail. Hoover sighed and drank the last of the wine.

'If you're really going out again I should see to your dressing,' said Louise.

'Very well. In a minute.'

'Now!'

'If you like.' He walked stiffly upstairs wondering whether Louise would behave any differently from the nurse if he showed signs of sexual arousal. Quite possibly, he thought, but not in any way that would benefit him. She would not pity his pathetic hard-on; she would ignore it. Already she saw him as he appeared in his dream. The eye of the beholder, he thought, unzipping his fly and exposing the void.

Behind the Chicken 'n Fish Bar cats excavated the dustbins. A pile of cartons toppled to the ground and Malloy flashed his torch, zig-zagging the beam over yellow brick walls and clumps of sodden paper. A boy and a girl standing in an alcove flinched from the light. The girl's coat was undone and Mark saw the long, yearning line of her throat.

Malloy kept the beam steady. 'Want some help,' he called.

'Piss off!'

'Leave them alone,' said Mark.

Malloy ignored him. 'Get it in there,' he shouted. 'It's your birthday.'

The boy came towards them, screwing up his eyes, attempting to swagger. 'What's up with you then?' He had a small, sad moustache and there were pimples round his mouth.

'Up?' said Malloy. 'Who's talking about up?'

'I am.'

'You want to watch your language, sonny.'

'Piss off.'

Mark took hold of Malloy's arm. 'Come on,' he said. 'It's none of our business.' It was the search, he thought, the way it had been organized, which turned citizens into vigilantes, licensed bully-boys questing for trouble.

'Bloody kid,' said Malloy.

'He wasn't doing anything.'

'You want your eyes tested. Didn't you see what he was doing?'

'It's not our concern.'

The boy still faced them, his thumbs hooked in his belt. 'Take your girl friend home,' said Mark. 'There may be trouble round here tonight.'

'What sort of trouble?'

'We're looking for a nutter,' said Malloy. 'He's been smashing things up.' He turned the beam of the torch in a slow arc, like a wire slicing cheese.

'Come on,' said the girl. 'I want to go.'

Malloy swung the torch, and the cats scattered. 'Go now,' said Mark. 'Go on home.' He stepped in front of Malloy and pointed ahead. 'We go that way.'

For several seconds no one moved, and then Malloy threw another of his mock salutes. 'Yes, *sir*! Certainly, *sir*!' He about turned, stamping his feet on the concrete and marched off smartly. A dozen paces away he stopped. 'You'd best be gone when we come back,' he said. 'I don't want to catch you round here again.'

The square was empty. In a window of the arcade a girl in a velvet playsuit danced across three rows of television screens. Her long, blonde hair flogged her shoulders and the camera lights burned on her pelvis. She was not unlike Linda, thought Mark; slimmer, but with the same centre of gravity. When she thrust her belly forward, jerking in time to the unheard music, the invitation was unmistakeable. 'Very fair,' said Malloy.

'Are you married?'

'Have been for fifteen years. Just after I came here.' He stared through the window, and sucked the end of his torch. 'Look at that,' he said. 'That's the propaganda. That's how they get you.'

'Not always.'

'Always, mate. That's how it's done. And it's all lies.'

They passed the Social Centre. Behind the glass doors St Francis stretched out his plaster hands. 'Everyone's at it,' said Malloy. 'Patron bloody saint.' He spat in the gutter.

'Don't you like it here?'

'Like it?' He broke step and looked Mark in the face. 'I'm not here because I like it. I just work here.'

'It could be worse.'

'Oh yes.' He chuckled, without humour. 'I know about Proto. I know how it all started. They've got a guide book. St Francis and

St George Deeley. They're on the same shelf. But it's all balls. It's all propaganda.'

Composed, most likely, by Lacey-Jones, thought Mark. 'But you're working for Proto now,' he said. 'You didn't have to come out. You volunteered.'

'I came to please myself.'

The odour of good works, long gone and long resented, hung in the air like mist from a fly spray. The chances were that Malloy no longer noticed it, but he was not immune. The antibody he had produced unknowingly for years was active now. Whatever he found, whoever he hurt – the blow was aimed at Proto. 'I came to please myself,' he had said.

'I believe you,' said Mark.

Charlotte Bloom received two telephone calls that evening. Shortly before nine Ryman called. 'Guess who . . . ' he began.

'I can guess.'

'I want to see you.'

'Leave me alone.' Her door, she saw thankfully, was locked; the safety chain in position. 'They're looking for you,' she said. 'If you come here they'll catch you.'

'I've done nothing.'

'You broke Otto's equipment. I saw it. I was there.'

'With Barrow.'

'Yes, with Barrow.' She remembered what Mark had told her. 'It's his project now,' she said. 'He wanted your advice.'

'Too late. Much too late.'

'We're giving you credit. Nobody's trying to cheat you.'

'Everyone tries to cheat me.' He whispered into the mouthpiece: 'Is he there now?'

'Is who here? Who do you mean?'

'Is Barrow with you?'

'Of course not.' Biddy was right, she thought. That was what he suspected. 'He's never here,' she said.

'Lying bitch,' said Ryman. 'Is he good at it? Is he better than me?'

'I won't discuss it.'

'Does he make you scream?'

'Be quiet!'

'I made you scream. When you came you screamed for me.'

'I'm ringing off,' said Charlotte.

'You loved me,' he said.

'No, no.'

'You loved me,' he repeated. 'And I put up with your stink.'

Numbly, she replaced the receiver and sat down. One winter, when she first lived in London, a water pipe had burst in her bedroom. She had seen the pool beneath the basin and reached for the power point to check that the switch was off. As she touched the wall she felt a shock, an enormous blow, as though the air had turned into a sandbag which struck her in all parts of her body – violently, simultaneously, and without warning.

Ryman's call had the same effect. Her chest ached. Her breathing was shallow. She sat quite still, afraid to move in case the blow was repeated, and watched the telephone, willing it to remain silent. When it rang again she ignored it for as long as she could bear, and when at last she picked it up she held it away from one ear so that the voice of the operator reached her distantly like a soprano on an old recording.

'Is that Mrs Bloom?'

'It is,' she admitted.

'Mrs Charlotte Bloom?'

'That's right.'

'I have a person-to-person call from Mr Gerald Bloom in Johannesburg.'

'Very well.'

She had no time to prepare herself. Still groggy, she received and returned greetings. And then, concise as ever, Gerald came to the point. 'I'm sorry to be the one to tell you,' he said, 'but your mother has cancer. The hospital gives her two more weeks.'

At ten o'clock the volunteers reported back to Dr Hoover. No one had seen Ryman. Lovers had been routed; a drunk helped home; an adulterer observed as he sneaked out of a back door. A normal sort of evening, said Malloy.

'Unusual for me,' said Mark.

'How's that?'

'I feel I've been on a guided tour.'

'How the other half lives, you mean.'

'Not exactly. But I've been given a sense of the place.'

Unnervingly so, he thought. Walking through the neat rows of terrace houses, and the canyons of the tower blocks he had been made unremittingly aware of how Proto, great and small, had imposed itself on the country. Over the years it had developed; even matured. But it had not been assimilated. It remained a concept, a working model.

They had stopped outside Malloy's house. 'Fancy a cup of char?'

'I wouldn't mind.'

They had drunk it in the kitchen, sitting at a table covered with a yellow cloth. 'It's big enough for the two of us,' Malloy had said. 'There's even a spare bedroom, but the wife keeps going on about improvements.'

'The firm does the maintenance, surely.'

'Over and above that. She wants double glazing.'

'Why not? It's easy to install.'

'You don't understand.' Malloy had taken the cups, and put them on the draining board. 'It's not as if it was ours. We're not here permanently.'

'You've been here fifteen years.'

'That's not permanent.'

And neither was the place itself, thought Mark. It was a posting station in his life and the lives of everyone who worked there. They merely rested on the roots. They were travellers and the camp could be broken more easily than any of them realized.

'See you around,' he told Malloy as he handed in his torch.

'I expect so.'

'You didn't need the knife,' he said, making light of it.

'I still might. You never know.'

Back at the rallying point Dr Hoover was listening to reports of non-success. 'We'll repair the equipment tomorrow,' Hoover said. 'I've told the joiner and the electricians. They'll meet you there in the morning.'

'Is someone there now?'

'Two patrols are watching all the animals.'

'You look exhausted,' said Mark. 'You should go home.'

Dr Hoover nodded, the entire length of his body sagging and then hauling itself upright, like a doll strung on slack wires. 'I'm going,' he said. 'There's nothing more that I can do now.' He sat in the front of Dempsey's car, his head thrown back, his hands clasped in his lap. 'Ridiculous,' he said.

Dempsey glanced round at Mark. 'What's ridiculous?'

'Everything.'

'Yesterday wasn't ridiculous,' said Mark. 'You settled Alec Bell.'

'I doubt it.' Hoover sighed deeply. 'I have an overwhelming sense of futility. We are not writing history; we are scribbling on walls.'

'It's just a setback,' said Mark. 'You're used to those.'

They topped the rise, and saw the houses encircling the green. Hoover stared at the road ahead. 'Ten years here, and I miscalculated. I should have handled Ryman differently. He should not have been dismissed.'

'We're bound to find him,' said Dempsey.

The car pulled up outside Dr Hoover's house, and they walked with him to the front door. On the path their feet crunched on the broken bodies of the gnomes from beneath the apple tree. On the doorstep lay the head of the ornamental crane.

Louise opened the door and the light that spilled out from the hall showed uprooted flower beds, torn bushes, an overturned sundial. 'You see,' said Dr Hoover. 'A gross miscalculation. The damage has already been done.'

SEVENTEEN

At breakfast James gulped his orange juice and eyed Mark over the rim of his mug. 'He'll be helping himself soon,' said Linda. 'Meat and two veg next month.'

'Little hog,' said Mark, offering his finger.

'Little love,' said Linda. 'He's Linda's little love.' She swooped on James from behind, cushioning his head on her chest. 'You don't know about kids,' she said. 'All you know about are those old monkeys.'

Mark waved his butter knife in ritual protest. 'Not monkeys. Apes.'

'Apes then. You still don't know about kids.'

True enough, thought Mark, spooning marmalade on to his plate. Children were a mystery, but he was learning to live with it. He was no longer exasperated by the standard mealtime prattle. He had learned to expect a disturbed night and to be thankful when he was allowed to sleep. In several ways, he decided, life as a parent was like living through a war. One got used to anything.

'Where's the Oxford marmalade?' he demanded. 'I can't bear this lemony stuff.'

'Mrs Barrow said they were sold out at the supermarket.'

'And where, come to think of it, is Mrs Barrow?'

'She's having a lie-in,' said Linda.

'When I left her she was getting up.'

'She changed her mind. I've taken her a cup of tea.'

'It's all right for some,' said Mark. 'I never get that treatment.'

'You could if you wanted. All you've got to do is ask.'

A warning bell, distant but clear, rang at the back of his skull. This was how it started: I fancy, you fancy, we fancy. He conjugated the verb as Linda swabbed his son's face with a flannel. It was like walking wires, or presenting a radio programme; to some people it came naturally. The old rhyme answered itself. Fancy was bred in the heart, never in the head.

But it could also be set aside, he thought. Not stifled, but shelved; a nest egg which could be added to and never spent. 'My wants are small,' he said.

'Tell me another.'

'It's the secret of happiness,' said Mark. 'Didn't they teach you that at school? We had hundreds of them. Never a borrower, nor a lender be. Many hands make light work. Men won't make passes at girls who wear glasses.'

'Go on,' she said. 'They never taught you that.'

'They did. I went to a very progressive school.' He could not imagine why he felt so cheerful. Ryman was still at large. Hoover was on the verge of collapse. Afton was putting his question to the House. And Bell was waiting in the wings. He was walking through a mine field, but he was unworried, sure of his footing.

Was it, he wondered, a case of rising to the occasion? He remembered his friend Alvin Berg, a surgeon in Los Angeles, whose wife decided to combat his new affair by draining him sexually. She failed. For two or three days Alvin walked like a zombie, but at the end of a week he had found his second wind. 'I can't believe it,' he told Mark. 'She woke me up at five this morning, and I screwed her three times. This afternoon it was the other one. Three more times. And I feel great. I'm operating in the morning.'

No one died under Alvin's knife, thought Mark. He had rare stamina, for sure. But the phenomenon he illustrated was fairly general. He watched Linda clear the table. She wore a blue denim dress with big white buttons, easy to fumble, easy to undo. Beneath it, he was certain, she wore very little.

I could cope, he thought. Physically I could cope. But the emotional hangups would make it impossible. He pushed back his chair and dabbed his mouth with a napkin. 'I'll see what she's doing,' he said.

The bedroom was still dusky, the curtains half-drawn. Scum had formed on the cup of tea and at first he thought that Biddy was asleep. 'Hello,' he said tentatively.

'Hello.'

'Are you getting up?'

'Later.' She was propped up in bed, staring at the window.

'Do you feel all right?'

'I'm frightened.'

When he had come home the previous night he had told her of the damage to Hoover's garden, but she had not seemed unduly alarmed. He had gone to sleep in the middle of describing Malloy, her head on his chest, their legs twined. Somewhere between then and now he felt he had missed an instalment. 'When did this come on?' he asked.

'It's been there all the time. It's just got worse.'

He sat on the edge of the bed and put his arm round her shoulders. 'There's nothing to be afraid of. Everyone's watching out for him. He'll be picked up today, I'm sure.'

'Everyone was looking for him last night,' she said. 'And he was here on the hill. Just a few houses away.'

'He won't come back.'

'Not there,' she said. 'Next time he'll come here.'

Mark stroked the back of her head, sliding his fingers over the knobs of her vertebrae. 'You've got Linda. You've got a chain on the door. You can tell him to go away.'

'It sounds so bloody easy,' she said.

'Not easy, but you can do it.'

She fell forward, burying her face in the blankets. 'I can't,' she said. 'I really can't. You don't know how I feel. You don't care.'

'Of course I care.'

'No you don't. You wouldn't ask me to stay.'

Mark pulled her upright. 'What do you mean "ask you to stay"? The question hasn't come up.'

'It has now.' She sat very straight, her hands folded in her lap. Tears scored her cheeks and there was a drop at the end of her nose. 'I want to go away until all this is over.'

'Go where?'

'Anywhere.'

'Back to mummy.'

'Yes. Back to mummy.'

'Christ Almighty!' He wrenched the curtains apart, and glared through the nylon net. The pack of Proto dogs trotted across the green. He counted them; fifteen again. 'When do you want to go?'

'Today. I'll ask David to drive me to the station.'

'I should think he's bloody tired of being our chauffeur.'

Biddy blew her nose. 'I suppose he is.'

'You can ask mummy about a car. Maybe she'll come across.'

She threw back the bedclothes and went into the bathroom. 'I've got to go,' said Mark, his face against the door. The lavatory flushed. He heard water running. 'Did you hear me?'

'Yes, I heard you.'

'Ring me when you get there.'

'I'll ring this evening.' She came out, naked.

He watched her step into a pair of pants. Her body and the inside of her thighs were peppered with talc. 'What about James?' he asked.

'I'll take him with me, naturally.'

'Naturally. And what about Linda?'

'She can stay here, or go to her mother. It's up to her.'

He sat down. 'It's all decided then.'

'Yes, it is.'

'Marvellous. The power of positive thinking. And you intend to stay until I give you the all clear?'

Biddy paused in the act of fastening her bra. 'I'm sorry,' she said. 'I didn't plan it like this. But I can't stay.' She slipped the catch through the elastic loop and settled the straps.

'Give the old bag my love,' said Mark.

'Not if you don't mean it.'

'I don't know what I mean.' He put his arms round her, and kissed her nursery-smelling neck. Ryman, Hoover, Afton and now this he thought. He hoped he could rise to the occasion.

The joiner and the electrician were waiting for him at Otto's cage. There was no sign of Charlotte. 'I don't think we need the speaker outside,' he said.

'Dr Hoover told us to make good.'

'Make good?' It sounded like a father's injunction to a son.

'Do all necessary repairs,' said the joiner.

'I see.'

Otto was still in his den. The sparrows rummaged in the straw and scraps of paper blew about the arena. It was a bit squalid for visiting firemen, thought Mark. 'Do you think you could tidy up a bit?' he asked.

'Not our job, mate,' said the electrician.

'All it needs is a broom.'

'You want the cleaning department. Get them on the blower.'

'Thanks very much.'

'He's safe in there, is he?' asked the joiner. 'He won't get out?'

Mark indicated the steel shutter sealing off the den. 'That's controlled from the observation box. He's perfectly safe.'

'Right then.' The joiner climbed into the cage. 'Bit niffy,' he said.

'Home from home,' said the electrician. He gripped the bars, and jumped up and down. 'Give us a cokernut,' he called.

He was graceless, thought Mark; completely unlike Otto. There was no indication of that fund of energy which drove the ape from floor to ceiling, daemonic but controlled. Instead of fury there was facetiousness. Not only clothes made the man. Evolution had a lot to answer for. And yet, from a distance, there were similarities. Movement became ritualized. Bending over their tools the workmen's stoop was simian. It was a family occasion, he thought. Cousins a thousand times removed were putting Otto's house in order.

In the observation box he gathered up the loops of tape. The wires, he saw, had been wrenched from the wall and severed in half a dozen places. The tape recorder was in ruins. The metal frame was bent grotesquely out of shape as though it had been lifted high in the air, and smashed on the concrete. Fragments of plastic were stamped with the marks of rubber soles. A feeling of spent violence, like the hush following an explosion, still lingered. He heard a sound behind him and swung round, his heart thudding.

'Sorry I'm late,' said Charlotte.

'Christ, you startled me!'

'It's so quiet in here. Like a tomb.'

He shivered theatrically. 'Watch your language. You're right though. It's the grave of something. Hopes. Ambitions. Someone's career.' He prodded the tape recorder with his toe. 'Look at that. Three hundred quid gone for a burton. I hope he got his money's worth.'

'I expect he did.'

'He turned Hoover's garden over too.'

'So I heard. And he telephoned me.'

'He's going the rounds.' Mark tilted her chin. 'Are you all right?'

'It's hard to say. I had a call from South Africa too. My mother's dying.'

'That's terrible.' He pushed her towards a canvas chair and obediently she sat down. 'I'm very sorry,' he said. 'If there's anything I can do . . . '

'There's nothing.'

'Do you think you should work today?'

'I'll go out of my mind if I don't.'

'I understand.' He squatted down beside her. 'Are you very close? I mean you and your mother.'

'Not at all. We can't stand each other. But that's not the point. She brought me up. She's my only blood relative. I know what's expected.' She lit a cigarette and watched the smoke stream through the open door. 'She knows they'll send for me and she knows I'll go. It doesn't matter whether we're close or not. We don't need to talk about it.' She poked her finger through a smoke ring, and watched it buckle and dissolve. 'In our family,' she said, 'we see each other off.'

'When?'

'I'll go next week.'

'So you'll be here for Afton's little lot.'

'Certainly I will.' They heard hammering from the cage and she smiled. 'After all,' she said, 'I want to know how it works out.'

Guy Afton put his question to the House at three o'clock precisely. 'Is the Minister aware,' he enquired, 'of certain experiments being conducted at the animal food manufacturing establishment known as Proto? My information is that operations have been performed on chimpanzees – live chimpanzees, I should say – which are both shocking and inhumane.'

In the public gallery Lacey-Jones coughed delicately behind his hand, and paid attention. Afton was pitching it a bit strong, he thought; and needlessly. An agreement had been reached. For all his interfering, Alec Bell had given the necessary guarantees. Proto would be open to inspection and Afton would reap the desired publicity. His performance now was dressing on the salad.

Already he had given a press conference. News editors had been informed, reporters had attended. It was like a ballet, thought Lacey-Jones; everyone went through their paces and the fact that the steps were familiar made no difference. Afton had become an institution, a bad national habit in which everyone indulged.

In fact, there was little about the man that was endearing. Lacey-Jones had known his first wife, Cynthia. There had been rumours of an attempted suicide and a minor scandal when she had run away with Afton's assistant, a television researcher named Draper. His name, saw Lacey-Jones, was missing from the press list submitted for the visit to Proto. It was just as well he thought. No further aggravation was needed. He had enough to be going on with.

He had been up until the small hours preparing the press kits; a run-down on Contact, a profile of Dr Hoover, notes on Mark Barrow and Charlotte Bloom, a glowing mention of Ryman. The last item had been the most bothersome. It was like tossing scraps to a starving wolf, but the gesture had to be made. Afton was unlikely to name him as the instigator of the enquiry, but it was possible that Ryman himself had talked to any number of journalists.

After fifteen minutes Afton was still on his feet. The Speaker studied his watch. On the Opposition benches several members yawned and Lacey-Jones felt his own eyelids droop. It was time for the wind-up, he thought.

'As one of a nation of animal lovers,' said Afton, 'I feel there is cause – if not for alarm – then for an enquiry.' He sat down abruptly, and scooped his papers together. Most of them, guessed Lacey-Jones, were blank sheets, but bumf in bulk always looked impressive.

He sidled out as the Minister made his formal reply. What he said was unimportant. The wheels were already in motion. The route and the destination had been decided. All that he had to ensure was that there were no diversions, no mystery trips. He caught up with Afton in the lobby. 'Lacey-Jones,' he said. 'We've spoken on the phone.'

'I remember.' Afton dug one hand in his trouser pocket and scratched his groin. 'Did you hear me?' he asked. 'Were you in the House?'

'I heard you,' said Lacey-Jones. 'Very pungent.'

'Pungent? Yes, I suppose it was, I like to deliver it hot and strong.'

'I came to confirm the details of the visit. The times, and so on.'
'They're as we agreed?'

'Absolutely. The car will call at ten. You'll be there by eleven. A quick drink. Photographs – I know the evening papers have to catch an edition – then lunch. After that, the place is yours. Go where you like, ask what you like. I think you'll find it very interesting.'

'I've no doubt.' Afton glanced at him suspiciously. 'In the first instance I was approached by Dr Bell. Does he know what the arrangements are?'

'He does indeed.' Lacey-Jones wore his most candid smile. 'He's been most helpful. But I'm happy to say that Dr Hoover has recovered. He's looking forward to meeting you, I know.'

'He's already running things again?'

'There's no stopping him. He's a dedicated man.'

'Autocratic, I've heard.'

'Really?' Lacey-Jones raised both eyebrows – a grimace which his friends would have recognized as self-parody. 'I've always found him perfectly charming. Brilliant, of course. But always approachable, always ready to explain his work. I don't think it's going too far to describe him as a genius. A good many people say that he is. And that may be the difficulty. Great men have their moods. I'm sure you've had experience of that.'

Lacey-Jones held his breath. In his experience, the grosser the flattery, the greater its chance of success. As a television interviewer, Afton had interrogated many distinguished men; one or two of them could possibly be called great. But he chose another way of interpreting Lacey-Jones's final remark.

'Speaking personally,' he said. 'I have my valleys and my peaks; my ups and my downs. But I try to remain stable. I endeavour to stay on an even keel.'

Behind a poker face Lacey-Jones uttered three hearty cheers. In taking the bait Afton had acknowledged Hoover and abandoned Bell. Public relations was an awful profession, he reflected, but it did offer certain compensations. At no time did he actually have to soil his hands. He could be sure that others would do the dirty work. One bastard could always be relied upon to polish off another.

'That's it then,' said the joiner, 'good as new.' He stepped down from the ladder and admired the day's work. The spotlights and speakers had been restored, the wiring replaced, a new tape recorder installed. 'You want to keep your eye on it this time,' he said.

'Right you are,' said Mark. Another formula uttered, he thought. Conversation on this level was like swapping coloured tokens, a kind of linguistic barter. At first he had been derisive, but lately he had found himself collecting banalities to trade. 'Nice weather for ducks' and 'It'll get worse before it gets better'; he was becoming used to serving them with a flourish.

The time, he saw, was almost four o'clock. He checked the bolts on the cage and raised the steel shutter. Otto seemed to relish the last hours of daylight. Once Mark had observed him actually watching the sunset. When it dipped below the wall of the arena he had climbed the bars to see the last of it and when the final trace of red was snuffed out by cloud he had lowered himself to the ground and returned to his den.

He was intrigued by the workmen, not angered, but interested in their equipment and the traces of themselves they had left behind. He turned a paper bag inside out, pasting the crumbs on to the flap of his lower lip. He dismantled a cigarette packet, gently separating the tissue from the silver paper. He sucked thoughtfully at a tomato and then swung himself up to the roof to inspect the spotlight and the amplifier.

'He could have smashed them up himself,' said the joiner.

'But he didn't,' said Mark. 'There was the tape recorder and the wires in the observation box. Anyway, just look at him now.'

Otto swarmed across to the amplifier and sniffed it – front, back, top and bottom. He did the same to the spotlight, and then felt it with his lips, committing to memory the pattern of belts, swivel and bracket. He seemed satisfied and lowered himself on to a straw bale where he sat sucking the tomato, savouring each pip and occasionally jutting out his lip to inspect the meal in progress.

'He didn't do the damage,' said Mark again.

'I reckon you're right.'

'He's a good old boy,' said the electrician. 'What do you call him?'

'Otto.'

'Good old Otto,' said the electrician. 'Have another tomato.' He opened his lunch tin and before Mark could restrain him, put his hand through the bars of the cage. Otto lunged forward, and the electrician threw himself back. His face was white. The pulped tomato oozed through his fingers. 'Christ,' he said, 'he almost had me.'

'You were trespassing,' said Mark. 'You were going into his cage, his territory. He was simply defending it.' He made a mental note to keep Afton and company at least three or four feet away. 'I'm sorry,' he said. 'I should have warned you.'

'Good job you weren't in there with him,' said the joiner. 'He'd have your guts for garters.'

The electrician buttoned his jacket. 'He's bloody lethal,' he said. He picked up his bag of tools and headed for the waiting van. The joiner followed him.

'How about you?' Mark asked Charlotte. 'If you're going back they could give you a lift.'

'What are you doing?'

'I'm staying here tonight. Biddy's away, and I want to keep an eye on things.'

'Where will you sleep?'

'There's a camp bed in the keeper's room and the security people are bringing me some food.' He motioned towards the observation box. 'I thought I might give Ryman's method a try. Just for the record.' The van started up, and the driver tooted the horn. 'They're waiting,' he said.

'I know they are.' She turned and waved. 'Would you mind if I came back later?'

'Not a bit.'

'You're sure?'

'Certain.'

'I'll see you then. Around nine.'

He watched them drive away, the wheels crunching the cinders, the horn sounding a cheery farewell. Otto was watching too, he realized. 'You've got company tonight,' he said. 'Make us feel welcome.'

EIGHTEEN

Mrs Antrobus – Biddy's mother – passed a copy of the evening paper across the table. On the front page there was a photograph of Guy Afton beneath a headline reading 'MP ALLEGES CRUELTY TO CHIMPS'.

'Where there's smoke there's fire,' said Mrs Antrobus.

'Not necessarily,' said Biddy.

Mrs Antrobus tweaked her nose with a handkerchief. 'That's loyalty speaking,' she said. 'But a Member of Parliament doesn't get his facts wrong.'

It's a good job that Mark's not here, thought Biddy. Her mother's pronouncements along with her laying claim to the lavatory, drove him to a state of fury which he relieved by muttered abuse, sufficiently vehement to penetrate locked doors and bedroom walls.

She was a hen, he said; a Rhode Island Red, beady-eyed, bird-brained and egg-bound. He impersonated her, crooking his arms and flapping his elbows. It was cruel, but not inaccurate. Her mother had a habit of emphasizing a remark by aiming a backhanded slap at the person sitting next to her. Her aim was haphazard and her hand had been known to strike face, breast, and belly with equal impartiality. 'Cluck! Cluck!' Mark would say, hopping towards Biddy over the bed. 'Cluck! Cluck! Flap! Flap!'

Already she missed him. He had seen her off on the train to London and she had hung out of the carriage window, waving goodbye until a bend in the track cancelled him out. Her mother had been at the station to meet her. In the taxi she had insisted on holding James and he had cried until they reached the flat and Biddy had taken over. There was no danger here, she thought. There were hall porters and lift operators and waiters from the ground floor restaurant to turn away any intruder. The rent was astronomical, but security – said the landlords – was absolute.

Biddy walked to the window, slapping her thigh with the paper. They were on the sixth floor and below her lay Hampstead, Chalk

Farm and the rest of London, lapped by the spring twilight. The flat in which she had lived with Mark was not far away. If she could pick out the canal, she thought, she could place it exactly.

'How long are you staying?' asked her mother.

'Not long.'

'What was the rumpus?'

'There was no rumpus. I just wanted a change for a few days. I thought you'd like to see your grandson.'

'I always like to see my grandson. And my daughter.'

No mention of Mark, thought Biddy. 'I want to do some shopping,' she said. 'There's not much selection up there.'

'I'm not surprised.' She tweaked her nose again with the handkerchief. No one, to Biddy's knowledge, had ever seen her blow it.

'We're not in the wilds, you know. It's simply like being in the provinces.'

Mrs Antrobus tucked her handkerchief in her sleeve. 'It wouldn't suit me,' she said.

The darkness outside the window deepened. The horizon was purple, blue-black. At home, she thought, Mark will be pouring himself a drink before eating his meal. She longed to hear his voice, but when she telephoned it was Linda who answered.

'He's up at that ape's cage,' she said.

'You mean Otto?'

'I expect so,' said Linda. 'He said he wanted to keep an eye on things.'

Biddy's disappointment was intense. When she put the phone down she felt her eyes sting and water and she turned her back so that her mother would not see the tears.

'Is he out?' asked Mrs Antrobus.

'He's still working.'

'He must have known you were going to call.'

'Most likely he'll ring himself.'

Up went the elbows (Cluck! bloody Cluck! thought Biddy). 'If he remembers,' said Mrs Antrobus.

Poor Mrs Barrow, thought Linda, leafing through a rack of Biddy's clothes. Always so nervy, always so anxious; what she did was put people off. She took a blue silk shirt from its hanger and held it against her chest. It was a pity their colouring was different; if she lost a few pounds she could wear most of these clothes. She laid out a selection on the bed; dresses, beach pyjamas, a gown that jangled like chain mail. Linda enjoyed dressing up, and she looked forward to an evening of uninterrupted pleasure.

She picked through the perfumes on the dressing table. None of the names were familiar. She removed the stoppers and dabbed a selection on the insides of both arms. Lovely, she thought. It was a pity that none of the boys she knew were on the phone. She imagined opening the door and welcoming them in with a billow of scent. The back of the van had smelled of old rubber and oil. Some of it had dirtied the back of her skirt and she remembered being worried about it getting in her hair.

The odd thing was that she had forgotten their faces. Five of them, she thought, one after the other and all she could recall was the scratch of a hangnail on her thigh and the circle of cigarette ends glowing as they hung over her, waiting for their turn. Ian Emery had been first, then Terry Payne. She had forgotten the rest.

Mrs Hoover had made a big thing of it. She had even wanted to send her to a psychiatrist, but her mum had put her foot down and quite right too. The result of it all had been Baby, who was asleep down the corridor and a nice job in a nice house and what was so bad about that? It was better than working in the factory, or the supermarket and it was better than living at home with mum and her legs, and grandpa with his chest and dad on night shift forever going on about the radio being too loud.

Linda took out her slides and combed her hair. Everyone made too much fuss, she thought. Dr Barrow went on about his apes and Mrs Barrow went on about James. She had heard them quarrelling, not shouting like her mum and dad shouted, but nagging at each other, scoring points, refusing to let well alone. She liked them, though. Mrs Barrow was kind, and Dr Barrow was quite good-looking and in the mornings she knew that his eyes, if not his hands, were everywhere and it was nice to be noticed.

She applied eye-liner and painted her lips with a camel-hair brush and squeezed a blackhead on her nose. So many bottles, she thought; astringents and lotions and complexion milk. It was like a medicine chest with remedies for complaints she'd never heard of. There were several mirrors too, including one which magnified the pores of her face so that they looked like craters. She pushed it to one side. There was no point in brooding over what she would normally not know about.

She unbuttoned her dress and tossed it over a chair. First the gown, she decided; tight over the hips and bust, but beautiful, like last year's Christmas tree at the Social Centre. She switched on the bedside radio and danced to the music, admiring the way that the plastic scales shimmered in the light, trembling when she moved, clashing softly, insisting that she was the one, the intended wearer.

The music stopped and she took it off, brushing it down with her hand, replacing it on the hanger. One day, she thought, Mrs Barrow might give it to her. Already she had presented her with two sweaters, a blue and a red one, and a packet of disposable paper pants which Linda had not yet nerved herself to wear.

There was a peal of thunder and she clapped her hands to her ears. She was afraid of storms. At school they had made jokes about King Kong moving his piano, but she was still uneasy. The curtains were open and she ran to close them, shutting out the night. Again the music played and she moved in time, singing the words, her toes crisping on the pile of the carpet.

Outside, her voice carried faintly to the man standing in the shadow of the hedge. He cocked his head, straining to hear the tune, and then recognizing it, whistled softly to himself. When it began to rain he pulled up the collar of his coat, but he did not move. There was nowhere else he wanted to be.

In his den the ape slept soundly and Mark and Charlotte watched him through the spy-hole. He was cradled in straw, with another handful thatching his head.

'We'll give him a bit longer,' said Mark. 'There's no rush.'

He had eaten his supper – braised heart, mashed potato and cabbage – the least popular item on Tuesday's canteen menu, he surmised. The security men who brought it – tepid under aluminium lids – had refused a drink. 'Not while we're on duty,' said the dog handler, as though he had made an improper suggestion.

He had raised his own glass. 'Cheers, then.'

Solemnly, they had watched him sip and swallow, then they had gone. He was glad to see the back of them. They brought with them the atmosphere of the camp, an amalgam of drabness, authority, and bullying. It was like boarding school, he realized, and even now he felt that whisky in hand he was breaking the rules.

He knew that he was being irrational and in any case, he had performed his set task. He had followed Ryman's procedure faithfully, setting a plastic cup on a box in Otto's den with the beam of the spotlight illuminating it like a trophy in a display case. When Otto picked it up, transferring it from hand to hand, he had played the tape. 'Cup,' his own voice repeated. 'Cup,' he said, as Otto nibbled the plastic. He had dimmed the lights and reduced the volume as Ryman prescribed and in the gloom he had seen Otto prepare for bed, replacing the cup on the box and heaving himself on to the pile of straw.

'I'll wake him in half an hour,' he told Charlotte. 'Come and inspect the rest of the estate.'

The keeper's room lay off the corridor that ringed the arena. It was painted in mustard yellow and there was matting on the concrete floor. In one corner there was a sink and a gas ring. In another there was a camp bed. There was one chair and a reading light.

'Just the place for a dirty weekend,' he said.

She looked at him sharply and pursed her lips. 'I'd choose somewhere different.'

'Where, for instance?'

'I don't know. By the sea.'

'Very traditional. The English go to Brighton.'

'I've never been there.'

'There you are then.' He leaned forward and sniffed her hair. 'You've washed it.'

'Just before I came out. The ends are still damp.'

'I like it.' She had bathed, too, he decided, but the spice was still there. The glands were still humming, distilling their musk. In the cheerless room it was like taking the lid from a casserole and inhaling the smell of home cooking. Not his own home, he thought, but another place; somewhere foreign where the stock was rich and the gravy shone with pebbles of oil.

'I've asked Hoover for leave of absence,' she said.

'And he's agreed?'

'Oh, yes, he agreed. I think he'd have lent me the fare.'

'Will you be able to manage?'

'Easily, thanks.' She sat on the armchair and wriggled from side to side. 'The springs are gone,' she said.

'Will you come back?'

'I'm not sure. I certainly won't stay there.'

'Biddy's gone to her mother,' said Mark.

'Not for good?'

He laughed. 'I don't think so. Just for the emergency, I imagine. She thinks of it like wartime. Mummy's the safe area. Boring as hell, but safe.'

'I can understand that.'

'So can I.' He prodded the camp bed with his toe and the bolts securing it sighed. 'It's not just Ryman,' he said. 'It's the place itself. We can all feel it. It's like the end of empire. Another noble experiment up the spout.'

'We've done good work here,' said Charlotte.

'I know you've done good work, but the whole thing's falling apart. There are too many factions. The energy's going in the wrong directions.'

'You'd run it differently?'

'I'd bloody well try,' he said, and she looked at him curiously.

'I think you mean it.'

'I suppose I do.' He spread his hands and shrugged. 'I'd change the name for a start. Or try to live up to it.'

'Which name?'

'Contact,' he said. 'It's pathetic. God knows how many people work here, and there's not even a common language. We're supposed to be talking to chimps but we can't even talk to each other. I tried it the other night. Useless.'

'No more whisky,' said Charlotte. 'You're making speeches.'

'Am I? I'm sorry.'

'It doesn't matter.' She stood up and tugged her sweater over her hips. 'Let's go and see Otto.'

Inside the observation box the air was damp. It was like being underground, thought Mark; the Fuehrer's bunker, or a concrete pill box guarding a home counties crossroads. He remembered one near his own home. Tramps slept there and he had groped his first girl against the rough walls, his feet sliding on rubble and empty bottles.

He looked through the spy-hole. 'He's still asleep.'

The straw had slipped from Otto's head and he lay on his side, his knees tucked up against his chest, the fingers of one hand in his mouth. Mark pressed the switch and the spotlight shone on the plastic cup. Otto tugged the straw over his head and retreated further into sleep.

The light brightened and the speaker buzzed. 'Cup,' said Mark's voice. 'Cup,' he repeated. The tape revolved smoothly and he turned up the volume. Otto opened his eyes and brushed the straw to one side. 'Cup,' said Mark again.

The spotlight dazzled and he switched it off. Otto heaved himself on to his haunches and in the gloom they saw him listening intently, his head turning from left to right, his nostrils flexing like moist buds. He scratched his head and lay down, tucking the straw beneath his arms. 'Cup,' said Mark, turning up the light and Otto raised his head slightly to study the speaker, fixed in the far corner.

'It won't work,' said Charlotte.

'How long do you suppose Ryman kept it up?'

'Hours, probably.'

'Then we'll keep at it.'

He turned the light to maximum brightness and the den was bleached to a pale primrose, without shadows, a cell from which the only way of escape was to repeat the formula. 'Cup,' said Mark. 'Cup,' he said, as Otto covered his eyes.

The den was equipped with a sprinkler system and microphones had been wired to the two nozzles set into the ceiling. They heard Otto's breathing, an angry snuffle punctuated by low grunts. It was the sound of bewilderment, a drowsy irritation which continued when the light snapped off again.

'I wish to God I could have talked to Ryman,' said Mark. 'We have no idea if he got anywhere.'

Charlotte pointed through the spy-hole. 'Look at him now.'

Hunched in the corner, Otto stared at the cup in the middle of the room. With his left hand he scratched his groin. With his right hand he manipulated his lips, plucking them like elastic, clamping them together between the thumb and forefinger. 'What sound would that make?' asked Charlotte.

Mark experimented with his own mouth. 'Pip,' he said hopefully. 'Puff.'

'Just the consonant.'

'Pee?'

She held up three fingers, one after the other, spelling out the letters. 'C.U.P.'

'You really think so?'

'It's possible.'

Mark turned up the light and Otto's hand dropped into his lap. His lips peeled back, exposing his freckled gums and suddenly he sprang forward and swept the cup off the box. It bounced on the floor and he picked it up and threw it against the wall.

'End of performance,' said Mark. 'No more tonight.'

Charlotte peered over his shoulder. 'Turn the light out then. Let him go to sleep.'

They watched him bury himself in the straw, turning round and round until the nest was rifled like a gun barrel. His eye glinted and then closed. 'He certainly told us what he thought,' said Mark.

'Contact established.'

'In a way.'

'Positively and unmistakeably.'

She craned forward and he felt her breasts poulticing his back. 'Shall we try him again later?' he asked.

'That's why we're here.'

'Not entirely,' said Mark.

He turned and put his arms around her. For a moment she resisted, stiffening her body and pushing him away. Then she relaxed and he felt her flow against him. It was like the slow creep of honey across a plate, he thought; a smooth, advancing tide which glued them together, filling every space, every crevice between their limbs. Her mouth was tacky, as though it, too, had been rinsed with syrup. She was heavy, molten; a wave of sweet mercury breaking irresistibly without surf, drowning them both.

'Did you know this was going to happen?' he asked.

She nodded, her head against his chest. 'I suppose so.'

'Did you want it to?'

'Not really.'

'I did,' he said.

'You're just a fancier.'

'You make it sound trivial.'

'Isn't it?'

He laughed. 'No, it's not. It's accepting the inevitable.'

'Choosing from the trolley as it comes by.'

'Not that,' said Mark. 'Not like that at all.'

It was too urban, he thought; too civilized. What he felt for Charlotte was older, simpler. He had followed his nose like any other animal, tracking the drops of her sweat, the flavour of her body, the sudden thermals reaching up from her crotch. His response had nothing to do with love; even the fact that he liked her was incidental. He imagined their relationship drawn as a diagram; the two separate tracks entering the frame, coming closer, progressing jointly, merging briefly and leaving singly. The pattern was classic, but he found himself resenting it. It had been imposed by circumstance and he was conforming to it. Like Otto, he was obeying an impulse. He was not considering the alternatives.

He turned her body, pressing her against the wall and reached down with one hand, sliding his fingers between her belly and the waistband of her jeans. He felt hair and then a sudden wetness as if the skin of a peach had burst and she sighed and thrust forward, and her mouth smeared against his neck.

'Come to bed,' he murmured, but she shook her head, and dragged on his arms like an anchor.

'We don't have to,' she said.

'I want to.'

'Not enough.'

The blood knocked in his head and briefly he saw himself and Charlotte joined in a wild, slippery ride in which he was both participant and spectator. There was no joy in it. He was the appalled occupant of a private carriage which careered behind the locomotive, dancing and skidding across the tracks. The landscape was black and desolate and small cinders whizzed by the window. He took a deep breath and withdrew his hand. The speed lessened, the cinders flew back into the night and the carriage stopped.

'That's better,' she said.

He laughed shakily, and pressed his forehead against hers. 'Don't move. Not just yet.'

'I won't.'

They leaned together, face to face. 'What was that saying of Ryman's?' he asked. 'The one he got wrong.'

'All animals are sad.'

'That's only half of it.'

'The other half doesn't apply.'

He kissed her on the one cheek, then the other. 'A matter of choice,' he said.

Through the speaker they heard Otto stir in his den. There was a rustle of straw, and then a whisper, so faint that at first Mark thought he had imagined it. He squeezed Charlotte's arm. 'Listen.'

The straw rustled once more and then came a voice, husky and untried, like an invalid begging for attention. 'Cup,' it said. 'Cup,' it said again.

NINETEEN

Lacey-Jones made a firm, approving tick on his clipboard and raised his glass of pink gin to the light. 'Not bad at all,' he said, 'not at all bad.'

The approach of zero hour always inspired him. As the hours wore away he felt the familiar surge of adrenalin through his veins and found himself actually looking forward to the moment of confrontation. The Afton visit had put him on his mettle and he welcomed the opportunity of showing what he could do. The Proto account was important, but his concern was not measured in terms of cash. Lacey-Jones enjoyed the game, if not entirely for its own sake, then for the tonic effect it had on his liver. With problems to solve and converts to make he felt fitter, stronger, more resolute. The Proto image, he told himself, was firm; proof against shits like Bell and lunatics like Ryman. That part of the business was untidy, but every excess weakened the case for the opposition. He had no doubt that Hoover (walking wounded and therefore a sympathy-getter) would convince all visiting members of the press that he was – as they had so often depicted him – a Grand Old Man. So, the suggestions of cruelty and professional jealousy would fade away. The wrecking of the equipment (Lacey-Jones planned to leak the information, with the tip that Ryman was clearly round the bend) would strengthen the Proto case. And the double-act of Mark and Charlotte ('toilet-water' he noted on his clipboard) would round off the programme of positive thinking. Often, Lacey-Jones had pondered the old saw which said that truth lay at the bottom of a well. In his case it was not so. Truth lay all around in a thousand guises and sizes. The skill lay not in finding it, but in sticking it together. The composition he had moulded over the past few days was an object of which Lacey-Jones had reason to feel proud.

He had even co-opted Louise Hoover in such a way that, while she had done nothing to influence the shape of the grand design, she had speeded its assembly, applying oil here, tightening a bolt there. It was she who had suggested making use of the Social Centre rather than the canteen to entertain the guests.

'We'll do without the Musak,' she said.

'Naturally.'

'And I decided against champagne. We mustn't make it seem festive.'

'There's no danger of that,' said Lacey-Jones. 'Journalists are serious drinkers.'

She was a handsome woman, he thought, but not to be considered, even briefly, as a sexual object. He tipped more tonic into her glass and raised his own in salute. By marrying Hoover she had caught the big fish. But she had been unable to creep inside his skin, so that now she swam fretfully within a small pond, unable to summon up the salmon leap which would propel her into deeper waters, wider streams.

'You must find it rather monotonous here at times,' he suggested.

'There's plenty to do.'

'I'm sure there is. But there's a difference between intensity and variety.'

'Very profound.' Ice clinked against her teeth and she dabbed her lips with a handkerchief. 'What you fail to understand,' she said, 'what Proto itself fails to understand is the nature of this community. In a sense, we govern it.'

'We?'

'Francis. The administrators. Whoever accepts responsibility for the people's welfare.'

'You do an excellent job.'

Louise shook her head. 'You've never considered it. You don't know what sort of job we do.'

'It all goes very smoothly.'

'And that's what matters.' She laughed shortly. 'They don't like us, you know. They resent us.' She leaned across the table, and Lacey-Jones noted her centre-parting, as vivid as a scar. 'When all our garden furniture was broken up the other night . . .'

'Furniture?'

'The gnomes,' said Louise. 'Francis's gnomes. When they were smashed up, some people were actually pleased. I saw them smiling in the street. Behind their hands, of course.'

'I can't believe that.'

'Behind their hands,' said Louise. 'It used to worry me, that sort of thing, but I've grown used to it. I still resent it, I suppose, but it's the nature of the beast. I've learned to set it on one side, to get on with what matters. After all, we're not here to be thanked.'

'It's nice if we are now and again.'

She shook her head. 'Expect nothing, and you won't be disappointed.' She pointed at the clipboard. 'Did I give you the names of the workers I thought we should introduce to Mr Afton?'

'Yes, you did. Mrs Bream and Mr Lycett.'

'Very civil, both of them. They're used to meeting people.'

Unofficial greeters, thought Lacey-Jones; forelock tuggers most likely. They had their uses, of course and boosting the ego of Guy Afton, M.P., was one of them. 'You've been a great help,' he said.

Louise drained her glass and set it carefully on the mat in front of her. She pulled on her gloves and smoothed the black kid over each finger. 'Not a great help. But some help.'

Lacey-Jones smiled as warmly as he knew how. 'A great help,' he repeated.

She led the way to the staircase. 'Perhaps if the board knew I was prepared to take a more active role . . .' she said.

'You mean here, of course.'

'I mean within the company.'

He looked down on to the head of St Francis. Squirrels and small rodents seemed to spill out of his ears. 'I can mention it if you like,' he said.

'Tactfully.'

'Of course.'

'I would be most grateful.'

Lacey-Jones thought of Dr Hoover, suddenly frail, an encumbrance rather than a launching pad. It was not his business, he decided, but he felt a twinge of compassion for the old man. 'Mind you,' he said, 'I hardly think this is the moment to suggest any major innovation.'

'The sooner the better,' said Louise.

They went out through the swing doors and into the street. As they headed for his car a woman caught hold of Louise's sleeve. 'I want to talk to you about my Linda,' she said.

Her legs were bandaged, Lacey-Jones observed, and she wore carpet slippers. She stood in the middle of the pavement, and passers-

by were forced into the gutter. She ignored them, her back brawny
in a braided grey coat a wedding band winking on the hand that
gripped Louise's sleeve. There was something African in her posture,
he thought; something tribal. She was a suppliant by right; a
woman accustomed to demanding favours, confident that they would
be granted. He produced his smile again and backed away: 'I'll wait
for you in the car.'

The woman ignored him; her business was with Louise. 'Mrs
Barrow's gone off,' she said, her voice drilling through the noise
of the crowd. 'My Linda's all alone with a married man, and it's
not right.'

Lacey-Jones increased his pace. As Louise had said, he did not
understand the nature of the community and he was thankful for
small mercies.

In the observation box, Mark played the tape for the hundredth
time. He had gone home to breakfast and changed his shirt, but the
total turn-round had taken him no more than an hour.

'Mrs Barrow phoned,' Linda told him when he arrived.

'What did she have to say?'

'Nothing really. She wanted to talk to you.'

'I'll ring her later.'

'Will you be back tonight?'

'I'm not sure. I'm in the middle of some work.'

'Oh, yes?' said Linda. 'My mum doesn't think it's right, me
being here alone with you.'

'You haven't been alone with me.'

'I know. But when I saw her I thought I was going to be.'

Mark sipped his coffee, stifling his impatience. 'Why did you
mention it at all?'

'I dunno.' Linda giggled. 'I took Baby for a walk and my mum
asked me when I had to be back and I said there was no hurry and
that's how it came out.'

'Tell her I'm a night worker.'

'She knows better than that.'

'Tell her she's got a dirty mind.'

'I wouldn't dare.'

'Tell her I'm too busy.'

'That's more like it,' said Linda. 'I don't mind telling her that.'

'It's her professional pride,' Mark explained to Charlotte. 'She doesn't like being overlooked. She has a reputation to think of.'

'So I gather.' Charlotte nodded towards the tape. 'What are we going to do about this?'

'Nothing. Not yet. It's too soon. We don't know what we've got.'

'I know and so do you.'

Mark shook his head. 'One word, or what sounds like a word, isn't enough. We need more than that.' He looked through the spy-hole and as he did so raised the hatch giving Otto access to the outside cage. For several minutes the ape did not move, but sat swathed in his straw, resting on his knees, unkempt as an armchair whose upholstery had burst.

'I wonder if Mrs Deeley's right,' said Charlotte. 'What if he does understand what he's done? What if he's got some sort of conscience?'

'I'll pretend I didn't hear that.'

'Is it really impossible?'

'Unlikely.'

'I wonder,' said Charlotte. 'We're so bloody strict with ourselves. We're afraid to speculate.'

Otto shuffled forward to the cage door, blinking as daylight washed over the planes of his face. The overhang of his brow cast a deep shadow. His nose twitched and beads of moisture sparkled like dew on the whiskers fringing his lips. Mark scuffed his feet and the ape looked round sharply. There was no change of expression, but the eyes were keen like those of a poker player appraising the state of the game.

'He could do more than say "cup",' said Charlotte. 'Do you doubt it?'

'No, I don't doubt it.'

'That's good enough then. I just want to know you have an open mind.'

'Parting words,' said Mark. 'And so we bid farewell to the great unknown.' He put his arm round Charlotte's shoulders. 'I'll miss you.'

'I'll be back.'

'For sure?'

'Some time, yes. Not right away though.'

'I'm glad we didn't do it,' said Mark.

'I'm glad you wanted to.'

They were silent for several moments, and then Mark picked up his brief case. 'The cleaner's due any minute. We'd better go and see Hoover. Not a word about last night. The experiments continue. Nothing for anyone to get worked up about.'

Charlotte nodded. 'Just as you say.'

'I'm coming back this afternoon. Most likely I'll sleep here tonight. I want someone here all the time; for the time being at least.'

'Ryman?'

'Ryman and Otto. They both need watching,' said Mark.

In Dr Hoover's office Lacey-Jones ran through the itinerary once again. 'Eleven hundred hours, reception at the Proto Social Centre,' he announced, waving his clipboard in the direction of Louise. 'That was Mrs Hoover's suggestion. We'll have the photographers there and perhaps we could have one or two of the more amenable apes in attendance.' He paused significantly. 'Suitably dressed I trust.'

Dr Hoover stirred in his chair. 'We're not running a circus.'

'Of course not, nothing like that. But we have to consider the eventualities. We don't want any accidents.'

Dr Hoover fed himself snuff. 'Go on.'

'A statement of policy by you. We introduce Dr Barrow and Dr Bloom, not forgetting the chimps. Then questions and photographs.' He raised his ballpoint like a conductor's baton. 'A point which just occurred to me. I wonder if any of your employees have small children, girls preferably. Something to demonstrate that the chimps are manageable animals . . .' His voice trailed off as Dr Hoover buried his face in a red bandana. 'You take my point?'

'I reject it,' said Dr Hoover. 'I understand the need to ingratiate but I refuse to become maudlin.' He waved the bandana. 'Proceed.'

'No children then,' said Lacey-Jones, not at all cast down. He had expected objections; it was part of his technique to include two or three outrageous proposals in a programme which was otherwise unexceptionable. Tossing out the worst items gave the client the illusion of participation. 'What is important,' he said, 'is to explain things so clearly to the journalists and especially to Mr Afton that they feel informed without being patronized.' He tapped a pile of bright yellow folders. 'The press kits will take care of the journalists. The story practically writes itself in any case and I doubt if we'll have many experts with us. As for Mr Afton, we'll all have to make him very welcome.' He turned to Louise: 'I suggest that you act as his chaperone.'

'Gladly.'

'Mrs Deeley and the rest of the executives will join us for lunch. After which there'll be a tour of inspection, with demonstrations laid on wherever appropriate.'

'Including Otto,' said Mark.

Lacey-Jones nodded agreeably. 'Including Otto.' He folded his arms and sat back in his chair. 'Are there any questions?'

There was a clearing of throats and a general swivelling of heads towards Dr Hoover. It was as though a button had been pressed which rotated everyone present by remote control, thought Mark. He excluded himself. He had been watching Hoover from the start and he was shocked by what he saw. Superficially, the doctor was unchanged. His half-moon spectacles were still lodged midway down his nose. His hair still sprang from his head as if arrested in flight. The suit was as hairy as ever; trout flies still clustered on his lapels. The bulk was the same; there had been no corporal shrinkage. But he sat inertly as though, somewhere, a fuse had been doused. His protests had been perfunctory. He looked resigned, thought Mark, and the word reverberated like a bad pun; a man who had left something, who was about to leave.

'Dr Hoover,' he said 'are there any aspects of Contact that you'd like us to emphasize?'

He made an effort; hoisting himself upright, shoving his spectacles towards the tangle of his eyebrows, throwing back his head as if he was about to launch into an aria. But his voice, when it emerged, was vague. The singer was indifferent to the song. 'No particular aspect,' he said. 'Promise no miracles. Dignify your work.' He spread his hands and smiled. 'You know the expression: blind them with science.'

'I thought we were to do the opposite.'

'As I see it,' said Dr Hoover, 'the object of the exercise is to impress. Enlighten wherever possible. But always entertain.' He addressed Lacey-Jones: 'Would you agree?'

'More or less.'

'You see,' said Dr Hoover, 'we have the advice of experts. On this occasion we must be advised.'

He saw their puzzled faces and longed to apologize. I have betrayed them, he thought, but he could not explain. His body ached. From the navel down his flesh dreamed of its mortal wound. He crossed his legs and folded his hands over his belly. His fingers stroked the leather buttons of his cardigan and he pulled it closer, guarding the injury. Louise stared at him across the room and he nodded his acknowledgment. Her hands had applied the dressing. She knew what was wrong. For the time being it was their secret; but not, he thought, for long. He closed his eyes and saw the void between his thighs, a cavity vast enough to engulf worlds.

That morning in Regents Park a man tried to pick Biddy up.

She had left James with her mother and travelled by bus to the corner of the road where she had lived with Mark in the summer before their marriage. Half the houses in the row had been demolished. A crane swung a massive steel ball against the façade of what had been a grocer's shop and as she watched, the wall dissolved in a cloud of yellow dust. It settled on her coat like pollen and when she licked her lips there was grit on her tongue.

She walked slowly past their old flat. There were new cards against the door bells. In the pub no one recognized her and the landlord hesitated with his hand on the water jug when she addressed him by name.

'You don't remember me?' she asked.

'The face is familiar.' He tilted the jug. 'Say when.'

'I used to live next door,' said Biddy.

'When was that?'

'Four years ago. We had the first floor flat. The lions used to keep us awake.'

'Really? They're still at it.' He poured water into her whisky. 'Enough?'

She nodded. 'It's all changed. They're knocking everything down.'

'Development,' said the landlord. 'They're building a luxury block. Penthouses and all. Might do us a bit of good.' He folded a towel and draped it on the bar. 'Just visiting?'

'Just passing.'

'It's not like it was. Mind you, you don't expect things to stay the same. Nothing stands still.'

'How true,' said Biddy. She drained her glass and slid off the stool. 'My name's Barrow,' she said. 'Not that it matters.'

She walked past the zoo and turned into the park. Crocuses gaped beneath the trees and squirrels scuttled along the branches overhead. She sat on a branch and one inched towards her. Its tail twitched and bristled as though electric currents were passing through it and three feet away it sat on its haunches and pawed the air. 'I've nothing for you,' she said. 'I'm sorry.'

A man sat down beside her and the squirrel scampered away. 'He'll be back,' said the man.

'I let him down,' said Biddy. 'I brought no food.'

'They get too much. They're not really wild.'

'I used to feed them when I lived here.'

'They expect it.'

He moved closer and Biddy smelled his after-shave, lemony and unfamiliar. 'This is really my garden,' he said. 'This time of year it's quite private.' Their thighs touched and she braced herself. 'The reason is,' he said, 'it's quite chilly. Would you like a drink to warm you?'

'I've just had one.'

'Have another.'

'I'm married,' said Biddy.

'So am I.'

'Then go away.'

'You don't mean that.'

'I most certainly do.'

'All I did was offer you a drink,' he said. 'Is that so terrible?'

'Not terrible,' said Biddy. 'Corny.' She looked at him attentively. He was middleaged, with dark, polished hair and a small razor nick on his chin. He wore a blue overcoat and what she privately termed a commuter's scarf – silk on one side, alpaca on the reverse. He looked a decent man, she thought. She did not want to hurt his feelings. 'The fact is, I'm a faithful wife,' she said. 'That's corny too.'

'Not very,' he said. 'Uncommon really.'

'You pick people up here all the time?'

'It's been known.'

'I believe you,' she said. 'But not today.'

He stood up and held out his hand. 'My misfortune,' he said, and bowed.

She watched him walk away, his stomach tucked in, his back held straight, and she felt herself smiling. I must tell Mark, she thought, and she ran to find a taxi.

He was in his office when she telephoned. 'Are you feeling better?' he asked.

'Much better.'

'Are you still frightened?'

'When I think about it.'

'There's no need to be.'

'Yes, there is,' said Biddy. 'But tomorrow I'm coming back. I love you.'

At tea-time Linda played hostess. In Biddy's wardrobe she found a blue mandarin gown and black silk slippers which pinched her toes and forced her to take tiny, mincing steps as she wheeled the trolley into the sitting room.

Baby lay in a nest of cushions, wedged into a corner of the settee. Bubbles like seed pearls dripped from her lips and Linda dabbed them dry with a tissue. 'Your feed comes later,' she said.

The fire was warm on her back and she struck poses, feeling the silk tight across her buttocks and smooth against her calves. Baby watched her as she held a tea cup at arm's length and turned to greet an imaginary guest. 'You'll take tea, of course. With milk or lemon?' It was lovely, she thought. There was no one to tell her what to do, no one to say she was being silly. She lit a cigarette and smoked it graciously, tossing it away when there was still over an inch left. The windows rattled and she drew the curtains, shutting out the dusk.

At home she had rarely been alone. There was always Mum slopping up and down the stairs in her carpet slippers, or Dad coughing his heart out in the next room. She liked the Barrows, but they hardly knew they were born. They had no idea what true luxury was. She held Baby in her arms and rocked her from side to side. Luxury was here and now. It was warmth and cuddles and the certainty that no one would bother you. It was bliss. 'Bliss,' she said aloud and nuzzled Baby's neck, smelling talc, and flesh, and clean wool. The house was hers for hours, possibly days. Dr Barrow was busy with his chimps and Mrs Barrow was still in London. There was no telling when they would be back. Her mum had gone on about her being alone with a man, but her concern, thought Linda, came a little late in the day. The business in the lorry had settled all that. There was nothing here to be afraid of; nothing she could not manage.

She lifted Baby from the settee and laid her on the hearthrug. 'Time to change your nappy,' she said. Baby goggled at the fire, her fingers and toes paddling the air. Linda wiped her dry and as she did so, felt a draught behind her. 'Cover up botty,' she said, and slid a napkin beneath Baby's buttocks. She snapped the poppers and pulled up the plastic pants. The draught persisted and she turned to see where it was coming from.

In the open doorway stood a man wearing a fawn trenchcoat. It was speckled with rain, and one empty sleeve was tucked into the belt. Linda put Baby back on the settee and wedged cushions on either side. 'All right,' she said, 'what is it you want?'

'What have you got?' asked Ryman.

TWENTY

Lacey-Jones had sent the Rolls to collect Guy Afton. It was not, he admitted, the symbol of sleek self-confidence that it had once been, but at the same time it was no company runabout. It signified probity and substance; two vital elements in the Proto image.

Afton, however, was in no mood to be impressed. He had overslept and consequently he had been forced to bolt his breakfast. The bacon had been so overdone that it had splintered when he touched it with his fork and his morning mail, containing two final demands, had not increased his equanimity. There was a letter from his ex-wife, Cynthia, reminding him that he had not yet returned to her a small drawing by Samuel Palmer (he had, in fact, sold it eight months previously). And to compound his aggravation there was an airgraph from his present wife on holiday in Morocco. She intended to remain there for a further two weeks, she wrote. The weather was perfect.

'Delighted to see you again,' said Lacey-Jones, opening the car door with a flourish. 'Everyone's gathered.'

'Who is everyone?'

'Dr Hoover, Dr Bloom, Dr Barrow, Dr Bell . . .'

'I mean which papers?'

'Let me see.' Lacey-Jones scanned his clipboard. 'So far we've got the *Standard*, the *Guardian*, the *Mirror*, the *Express*, the *Sunday Times*, the BBC – sound and television, ITV, and *Fur and Feather*.'

'No agencies?'

'The Press Association's coming.'

'Anyone else?'

'Someone from the *Observer* telephoned, but they were very vague.'

'They always are.'

Lacey-Jones snickered politely. It was not his policy to pick sides. Friends were friends wherever they could be found, and

Afton's old feuds were not his affair. 'There's coffee upstairs,' he said.

'Lead the way,' said Afton.

There were three flights of stairs to climb to the bar of the Social Centre, giving him adequate time to decide on his face for the day. He dismissed the morning's quota of bad news. None of it was urgent and the immediate situation required his complete attention. There were three points to consider. First: he had come to Proto as the Champion of Our Dumb Friends ('Was that a statue of St Francis as we came in?' he asked Lacey-Jones. 'It was? Good.') Second: he must appear to be impartial, interested and progressive. Third: without obvious grandstanding he must present the gentlemen of the press with a newsworthy story – above all, an attitude – which would satisfy brows both high and low.

Lacey-Jones pushed open the swing doors and Guy Afton's dilemma was at an end. A small chimpanzee wearing pink pants toddled forward to meet him. Afton extended his hand. The chimp took it. And the cameras clicked.

'Her name is Rosie,' said Francis Hoover. 'On behalf of Proto she bids you welcome.'

Waitresses, hand-picked by Lacey-Jones, dispensed coffee. Two waiters circulated with trays of sherry. There was no mingling yet. A nucleus had formed around Rosie, who sat on Charlotte's knee sipping a mug of milk. But the Proto staff remained on one side, while journalists hovered on the other. Lacey-Jones raised his glass to the man from the *Sunday Times*. 'Cheers, Bryan,' he said.

'When are we getting started?'

'Any minute now.' There was a time, thought Lacey-Jones, when science correspondents looked like boffins instead of Tudor princelings with shoulder-length hair. But his, he recalled, was not to reason why. 'I'll get the old man to say his piece very soon,' he promised.

Easing his way towards Dr Hoover, he jogged the arm of a pink-faced man wearing a grey check suit. 'A positively baroque turn of phrase,' he was saying, 'words which were never savoured by the human tongue.' Lacey-Jones lingered. It was impossible to guess the topic of conversation. The speaker was the host of a radio breakfast programme, a role he performed with some distinction, and a testiness which had become his trade mark. His style was a unique blend of courtesy and choler. 'And when,' he asked Lacey-Jones, 'is all to be revealed?'

'Soon, Bob,' he promised (noting the twitch of disapproval as he spoke the Christian name), 'very soon.'

'The Tablets have been brought down from the Mount?'

'They have indeed,' he said, groping for the reference.

'Then I shall try to contain myself.' He sipped his sherry. 'For a brief period.'

Lacey-Jones attempted to catch Dr Hoover's eye. 'Five minutes,' he mouthed, semaphoring with his fingers. There was no sign of Louise, but Afton was lecturing David Dempsey, who was offering him – Lacey-Jones saw with horror – a tray heaped with Proto biscuits. Afton popped two or three into his mouth and continued his monologue. Dempsey tried to interrupt, but Lacey-Jones was at his side before he could speak.

'I think we should press on,' he said.

Dempsey pushed his tray forward. 'I was about to tell Mr Afton about the biscuits.'

'Later.'

'But I'm sure he'd be interested . . .'

'Not now,' said Lacey-Jones. 'Some of these gentlemen have deadlines.'

'But I wanted to tell him what they were . . .'

Lacey-Jones lurched into the tray, glaring indignantly over his shoulder as he did so. The biscuits scattered and the tray gonged softly on to the red carpet. 'Terrible crush,' he said, 'better get people sitting down.'

He had taken pains over the seating plan. Too often, he thought, a press conference was reminiscent of the Last Supper, with the guests of honour flanking whoever spoke like unwilling disciples. His own arrangement created pools of interest, with Afton to one side of Dr Hoover and Louise (whenever she arrived, he thought savagely), and Mark and Charlotte placed in the body of the audience, with the chimp in the centre of the arena.

He steered Afton to his place, and grabbed Mark's elbow as he came by. 'Everything O.K.?' he hissed.

'As far as I know. I spent the night with Otto. I've not been home yet.' He fingered his collar. 'Does the shirt look all right?'

'Perfectly.' Lacey-Jones counted heads. 'I think most people are here. Have you seen Mrs Hoover?'

'She was going to call on our home help. Her mother's been playing up.'

'She had to do it *today*?'

'All part of the service. Proto never sleeps.'

'She was supposed to take care of Afton.'

'She'll be here.'

'She'd better be,' said Lacey-Jones. He patted a passing journalist on the shoulder. 'How's it going, Peter? Have a refill before they get started.'

The man from the *Express* grinned broadly and brandished his glass of tonic water. 'I'm off the booze,' he said. 'Not a drop for the past two months.' He plucked at the waistband of his trousers. 'A stone and a half down. High protein diet, and squash every morning. How about a game?'

'In the morning, you say?'

'Eight-thirty sharp.'

Lacey-Jones shuddered slightly. 'I'll call you,' he promised.

'Good for the liver.'

'I believe you.' Once upon a time, he thought, contacts were maintained over civilized games of golf. The prospect of a dawn caper round a squash court filled him with profound gloom. His head jerked up as the far door opened and a squat woman in black entered. She was followed by a uniformed chauffeur who carried a picnic basket under one arm and a canvas chair beneath the other.

Lacey-Jones took a deep breath. Mrs Deeley had arrived. It was time for the circus to begin.

Louise Hoover left home at half-past nine. Afton was arriving at eleven, and she had promised Lacey-Jones to be there to greet him. It gave her ample time, she reasoned, to see Linda Gillis and keep the peace with her monstrous mother.

This was the last of her crusades, she told herself. If there was a future with Proto, it was away from the kitchen sink. Social work was the job of a social worker. In any case, she decided, it was time for a change; indeed, a change had already come about. Since the scalding Francis had been a different man. He had suffered severe shock; anyone could see that. But in another, less apparent way, he was depleted. There was a loss of force, of heat almost. He was no longer dominant. Somewhere a vacuum had been created and her own nature impelled her to fill the vacant space.

'I have some things to attend to,' she told him, purposely vague, as he drank his lemon juice. 'I'll see you at the Centre.' Lacey-Jones would collect him, she thought; or David Dempsey. The transport arrangements at Proto were no longer her concern.

She left the car in the garage and walked across the green. The verges had been clipped and the scent of grass mingled with the smell of sap from the chestnuts that banded the fields. During the past week their colour had lightened. The bursting buds showed lips of white and new leaves surrounded each branch like sparks from a firework. Rooks clambered among the tops of the elms, hunched like jockeys as the wind blew. The year was turning, thought Louise, and she should go with it.

Rain had fallen during the night and her heels drilled small sockets in the turf. She would have to change her shoes before going on to meet Afton, but there was no hurry. A ribbon of smoke streamed from the chimney of the Dempseys' house, but none was coming from the Barrows'. Louise frowned slightly. Perhaps Linda was still asleep. She opened the gate and marched up the path. Laziness, she thought, and rang the bell. Somewhere in the house she heard movement. She rang the bell again and rattled the letter box. 'Linda,' she called, 'it's me, Mrs Hoover.'

Out of the corner of her eye she saw the Proto dogs on their morning patrol. She turned to watch them go by and the front door swung open. She felt a hand grip her wrist, and she was jerked into the hall. 'Good morning, Mrs Hoover,' said Ryman.

Her heart almost stopped, and then began to bounce uncontrollably against her lungs so that she sobbed as she drew breath. 'What are you doing here?' she whispered.

Ryman cocked his head on one side and studied her. 'Checking up, are you?'

She swallowed hard. 'Of course not.'

'Paying a social call?'

'It's my job.'

'Seeing that the staff are keeping up to scratch?'

'Not at all.'

'Oh, yes,' said Ryman. 'Seeing that they're not getting up to mischief.'

'I don't know what you mean.'

'No carrying-on. Proto doesn't like it.'

'I never judged you,' said Louise. 'I never blamed you for anything.'

'Indeed?'

She shook her head. 'It was nothing to do with me.'

'What a liar you are,' said Ryman.

'They treated you badly. I always said so.'

'To whom?'

'My husband,' said Louise. 'He thought very highly of you.' She saw Linda come from the kitchen. She was pale and the house-coat she was wearing was held together by only one button. When she stepped forward, Louise could see her bare breasts and a long scratch across her belly. 'Are you all right?' she asked.

Ryman jerked his head. 'Tell her.'

'I'm all right.'

'Has he hurt you?'

'He didn't hurt me.'

'But what did he *do*?' Louise insisted.

Ryman laughed. 'Nothing she wasn't used to.'

'Baby's safe,' said Linda. 'He promised not to touch her.'

A clock chimed the quarter hour and Louise glanced at her wrist watch. It was nine forty-five. Only fifteen minutes earlier she had been in her own home. 'They've been looking for you,' she said.

'I know they have,' said Ryman, 'but I saw them first.'

He shoved her quite gently towards the living room and when she was in front of him brought up his hand like an axe between her legs so that she screamed in surprise as much as in pain. He put a finger to his lips. 'Hush,' he said.

Louise backed away. 'They know I'm here.'

'That doesn't matter.'

'They're picking me up.'

'Are they really?'

She heard David Dempsey's car drive away from the front of the house. To collect Francis most likely, she thought. 'Not *that* car then,' said Ryman.

'Someone else,' she said. 'The public relations man, Lacey-Jones. You don't know him.'

He sat down and tucked his empty sleeve more securely into his jacket pocket. 'Get undressed.'

'Why?'

'Because I say so.'

'Are you going to rape me?'

'Don't flatter yourself,' said Ryman. He snapped his fingers. 'Get on with it. Don't waste time.'

'I don't understand.'

'Think about it,' he said. 'Think about it while you take them off.'

Her fingers were clumsy with the buttons of her coat, and when it slipped from her shoulders she shivered although the room was warm. 'Why me?' she asked.

'It doesn't matter that it's you.'

She thought of the smashed garden ornaments, the damage to Otto's cage, the telephone calls, the charges that led to Afton's visit. There was no sense to any of them. They were like obscene scribbles on the walls of a building, on the walls of the institution that was Proto. With a fearful clarity she read their meaning. The impulse was to deface and defile. As Francis Hoover's wife she was part of the establishment which had given offence and what she had helped to nurture was now being humiliated. She paused as she unzipped her dress, reminded suddenly of a time when a house belonging to friends was burgled. Little of value had been stolen, but bottles of scent, and pots of face cream had been trodden into the carpet, the bath taps had been left running and in the centre of a Persian rug in the living room they had found a configuration of turds ('a monumental stool' Francis had called it), layered like a ziggurat, a token of such contempt and hostility that – even hearing of it at secondhand – she had gasped with outrage. And now it was her turn. She stepped out of her dress, and folded it deliberately. She had to be careful not to give him fresh initiative.

'You're fat,' said Ryman. 'Look at that belly.' He leaned forward and prodded her below the navel.

'I can't help that,' she said.

Upstairs Baby began to cry and involuntarily Linda took a step towards the door. 'Stay where you are,' said Ryman.

'She needs me.'

'Not for a while' he said. 'I want you to see the show.'

'I don't want to see it.'

He stood up and pressed her against the wall, his hand spanning her throat. 'Do as you're told,' he said.

For a moment his back was turned, and Louise noticed – as if seeing the detail in a flashlight photograph – the scurf on his collar and the grease-stains on his jacket. She groped for an ashtray, solid as a glass brick, on the table beside her and as his grip tightened, blanching the flesh beneath each finger, she swung it at the base of his skull. The impact stung her hand. Ryman staggered but he did not go down. He released Linda and felt his head.

'Look at that,' he said, showing her the blood that streaked his hand. 'Look at what you've done.'

He caught her wrist as she raised the ashtray again and wrenched it so that she stumbled to her knees. A trickle of red wormed slowly round his neck and soaked into his shirt collar and as he stooped over her his empty sleeve swung loose from his pocket.

Beneath it, she thought, lay the injury inflicted by them all. 'I'm sorry,' she said.

'Sorry?' said Ryman, and his fist blotted out the light.

'Where do you think she's got to?' Lacey-Jones asked Mark.

'I've no idea. She's got her own car.'

'Perhaps it's broken down.'

'Possibly.'

'Do you think I should go and look?'

'She'd have phoned if anything was wrong.'

'I suppose so.' He was not convinced, but there were other matters to attend to. The reception was going well. Hoover had done his stuff like a TV uncle, making the obvious intriguing, the obscure lucid, recounting ten years' work like a suspense story with the final revelation expected at any moment. The experiments, he assured them, involved no cruelty. They would see for themselves.

Rosie sat on his knee like a ventriloquist's doll, permitting him to pinch her lips into the desired position. 'Papa,' he mouthed silently.

'Pa-pa,' she whispered back.

Hoover lowered his head and she rummaged in his hair while,

at the same time, he tickled beneath her arms. The affection was mutual and obvious. The speech, or what passed for speech, was most likely mimicry, thought Lacey-Jones. But one thing was quite apparent. Rosie had never been ill-treated.

There was a flutter of applause and Guy Afton joined in, while preserving his interested-but-impartial face. At least, he was not declaring himself for the opposition and Lacey-Jones offered up a silent prayer of thanks.

The *Sunday Times* reporter held up his hand. 'Dr Hoover,' he asked. 'Do you think that any of us could obtain the same result?'

Hoover peered at the press list, and then patted the chair beside him. 'Come and try, Mr Silcock,' he said. 'Rosie has never met a journalist before today.' He perched her on the reporter's lap and nodded amiably. 'Proceed,' he said.

'Papa,' said Silcock, staring into the chimpanzee's brown eyes. 'Ma-ma,' said Rosie, tugging out his tie.

The applause was instant, and Hoover seemed to conduct it, spreading his arms in mock dismay. 'My apologies,' he said. 'Unisex is everywhere.'

'You mentioned experiments with an adult ape,' said Silcock, cutting through the laughter. 'Were these conducted by you, or by . . .' he consulted his press kit 'Dr Ryman?'

'Dr Ryman conducted the experiments under my supervision.'

'He's not here today?'

'Unfortunately not. Dr Ryman received injuries in an accident and he is still convalescent.' Hoover raised his right hand and plucked silence from the air. 'But let me pay grateful tribute to the work he began. It is now being continued by Dr Barrow and no doubt he can answer any questions regarding its progress.'

It was a neat stroke, thought Lacey-Jones – an apology, a compliment, and a come-on delivered in one heart-warming package. But Silcock had not finished. 'Was Dr Ryman injured in the course of his work?' he asked.

'He was, yes.'

'Is he still a member of your staff?'

'Not at present.' Hoover shrugged sadly. 'He's not fit.'

'Do you mean physically? Or professionally?'

'Physically, of course. I have the highest regard for Dr Ryman's work.'

Lacey-Jones held his breath. The reporter was clearly following up a tip which, without doubt, had been passed to more than one paper. Now he had put his questions and Hoover had answered them. There had been nothing shifty in his manner. He had not tried to dazzle them with his sincerity. The chances were, thought Lacey-Jones, that he was going to get away with it.

'Would you welcome him back?' asked Silcock.

'I would welcome any recruit who increased the sum of our knowledge.'

'Including Dr Ryman?'

'I make no exceptions,' said Francis Hoover.

Seated on his right, Guy Afton cleared his throat. 'Provided, of course, that he, she, whoever the recruit might be, worked under your direction.'

'Precisely.'

'As Dr Ryman did not always do . . . ?'

'He was sometimes over-zealous.'

'But you tried to contain his zeal.'

Hoover nodded gravely. 'I did indeed. Too late to save him injury. But he was the only one who suffered.'

Lacey-Jones hooked both thumbs into the pockets of his waist-coat and hummed a little tune. Get on with it, he thought. On the face of it Guy Afton may have appeared to have been lending support, but his interjection was really a reminder that he expected his own turn to come soon.

There was more applause when Hoover sat down and Mark allowed time for it to subside before taking the floor. Lacey-Jones tapped the face of his wristwatch. 'Five minutes,' he hissed. After Mark came Charlotte and after Charlotte came lunch. He did not want to strain Afton's patience too far.

He looked hopefully round the room, but there was still no sign of Louise Hoover. Silly bitch, he thought, as Mark began to speak. She was missing her chance and there was nothing he could do about it. It was peculiar, though; she had seemed keen enough at the time.

Ryman walked slowly down the garden path. The road was empty except for the Proto dogs shunting each other, nose to tail, across the concrete and on to the grass. It was like the old days, he thought;

before the bloody accident. But it was increasingly difficult to remember any detail. Memory lived beyond an interval of pain, a gulf as deep and fissured as the Grand Canyon. The bottom was too far down to see and on the far side the rocks and shrubs were enveloped in a haze like tobacco smoke. He had worked (he visualized himself as a manikin performing tiny tasks) in a place with bars and padlocks, conversing – if that was the word – with an ape. That was Otto. He remembered the name. That was who he was going to see.

He could no longer recall why he was going. He understood only the simplest of actions; the cause and effect. His head ached and his collar was stiff with dried blood. Someone had struck him and he had struck back. There were no complications there. He paused in mid-stride and tried to think what had gone before. It was too confused. The images flickered and jerked like actors in an old film, jumpy in their movements, mugging and grimacing in frantic silence. Ryman stood and watched the show. The woman on her knees was pleading for mercy. Or was she screaming for help? Another woman tried to lift her up, but she was thrown aside. He saw shoes denting flesh; liquid on leather. The screen within his skull went blank and he blinked hard to regain his vision. Colour seeped back. He saw worm casts and grass ruffled by the wind. He raised his arm and saw the bruised knuckles on his fist, red turning to blue. He looked down at his shoes and saw the brown toecaps dyed black. He touched them and his finger came away rusty. Only connect, he thought (turning the phrase in his mind like a coin found in the pocket of an old suit); but he did not know how to begin.

In the distance he heard factory hooters and he had an impression of people wearing overalls, jostling along narrow paths, their conversation flocking above their heads like birds. He did not want to go there; what they were saying did not concern him. Somewhere, in the opposite direction, there was a simpler dialogue which he wanted to continue. Correction: which he wanted to end. The pain in his head was intense. He saw it rather than felt it, like a white sheet, or a magnesium flare fired behind his eyeballs. For seconds it hung there, drifting away to the west, the whiteness ebbing, colour seeping gingerly back as it finally dropped out of sight.

It was like a reprieve. He had been granted time (not long, he thought) to conclude his business. The sunlight sparkled on the grass, enamelling the green. Smoke streamed from the chimneys. The dogs trooped away in procession, their backs – black, brown, and white – jogging like segments in a dragon dance. Ryman turned left and followed them. Otto, he told himself. It was Otto he had to see.

TWENTY-ONE

'For what we are about to receive may the Lord make us truly thankful. Amen,' said Guy Afton and sat down promptly while the rest of the company remained standing with their eyes closed. The old one-two, he thought; instant devoutness and no hanging about. It was a combination punch which had felled giants. He beamed up at the waiter who filled his glass. 'Thank you.'

The chair on his right was empty and he leaned over to read the place card. 'Mrs Hoover.'

'I'm afraid she's not here,' said Lacey-Jones. 'She must have been called away on some urgent business.'

Afton nodded. 'No doubt.'

'She never stops,' said Francis Hoover. 'She's always busy. It's a great pity, though. I know that she wanted to meet you.'

He looked exhausted, thought Afton. The skin of his face was transparent as though his blood was too tired to struggle through the capillaries and lend it colour. His manner, too, was absent. He had spoken for almost an hour – making points, answering questions – and he had performed well. But the morning had taken its toll.

Afton nudged the glass towards his hand. 'Have a drink,' he said. 'You've earned it.'

'Good of you to say so.'

'Not at all.' He was curious about Hoover. It was perfectly plain that Bell had attempted to engineer a *coup* and just as evident that it had failed. But something was still amiss. 'Do you feel all right?' he asked.

'A little tired.' Hoover sipped his wine and sat up straight. 'They tell me I'm supposed to be convalescent. I keep forgetting.'

'You must take care,' said Afton. He was totally sincere. He remembered the time he had been invited to crown Miss Great Britain, a mere month before his official adoption as Parliamentary candidate. Surrounded by press and television cameras he had posed obediently, clutching the gilt and rhinestone hoop, calculating how many column inches his picture would occupy when, disconcertingly, the girl had pitched forward and he had been left standing there while journalists swarmed around the fallen beauty queen, angling their shots to take in yards of thigh and breasts like burial mounds.

'It was the excitement,' she explained later. 'I felt faint.'

'Get well soon,' snapped Afton, wishing her dead.

The pictures had all been of her, except one which showed several inches of his trouser leg. All the same, it had given him a valuable lesson. He had learned to beware of frailty. It was entirely on the cards that some of the morning's photographs – ostensibly of Rosie sitting on his knee – would be trimmed by picture editors to favour the chimpanzee. But, on balance, he could expect a decent showing. If, on the other hand, Francis Hoover chose to collapse in public view he could say goodbye to page one. He beckoned to the wine waiter. 'I could do with a drop more,' he said. 'So could Dr Hoover.'

Seated at the next table, Lacey-Jones beamed his approval. The occasion was not meant to be festive (Louise Hoover had said that, he recalled) but there was no harm done in dispensing lubricants as liberally as possible. Every little helped. For a moment he had quailed when Mrs Deeley refused to join them for lunch. But she had intended no offence.

'You see,' she said, patting her picnic basket. 'I have come prepared.'

'But what about Mr Afton . . . ?'

'You can introduce me later.'

He had felt Mark dig him in the ribs and he had raised no further objection. Eccentricity was not, perhaps, devoutly to be wished. But it was permitted when the eccentric was also his employer. He leaned towards Afton's table and tapped the BBC shoulder to his right. 'Are they looking after you?' he enquired.

'Tolerably.'

'Another drink?'

'Gracious, no. My temples are pounding.'

Not for the first time Lacey-Jones noted how the presenter's conversation was flecked with quotation marks. Somehow he made every exchange, however casual, sound like a passage from a

Victorian novel. What was more, his manner bred formality where none had existed. 'Do you seek to interview Mr Afton?' he heard himself say.

'I doubt it.'

'Dr Hoover?'

'That sounds more likely.'

'Just give me the nod when you're ready.'

'That would be unwise,' said the presenter. 'People might get the wrong idea.'

A joke, thought Lacey-Jones jubilantly. 'I take the point,' he said.

On the far side of the room Alec Bell stirred his soup. 'Have you spoken to him yet?' hissed his wife.

'Not yet.' He had, in fact, made several attempts to catch Afton's eye, but so far he had failed to make contact. Twice, Lacey-Jones had interposed himself, blotting out Bell's field of vision with his pin-striped back. Twice, Afton had seemed about to acknowledge him, but at the last second it was as though a screen of invisible plastic had been lowered from the ceiling and Afton's answering smile had been deflected. Bell had watched it spin at a tangent over his head and he had felt despair.

He drank from his glass and frowned at the unfamiliar taste. His wife tugged at his sleeve. 'What on earth are you doing?'

'Doing?'

'You've let them give you wine.'

Bell spat into his napkin and dabbed his lips. Past generations of Rechabites stared at him reproachfully. The day was past redemption, he thought. Afton had ignored him and now he had broken the pledge. It was not his fault, but no one – especially Kitty – was interested in excuses. He had let them both down. He did not expect to be forgiven.

'Did you see that?' asked Mark.

'Did I see what?'

'Alec Bell was drinking wine.'

'I don't believe it,' said Charlotte. When she brushed against him he felt her warmth, as though her dress was a cornet filled to the brim and susceptible to any sudden movement. At the same time there was a gravity about her, a sense of composure which was entirely new. Soon she was going away to attend a death. She was

performing a duty and her acceptance was somehow soothing. It
defined their roles, clarified their relationship.

'Kitty's furious.'

'My heart bleeds.'

'Does it really?'

She shook her head. 'Not so you'd notice.'

Lacey-Jones winked across the cutlery and he smiled in reply.
'Cheers,' he said, raising his glass. It was too soon to gloat, but he
felt his anxieties lifting. Perhaps, after all, they would have something
to celebrate.

Approaching the arena, Ryman avoided the cinder path and walked
on the grass verge. The stains on his shoes worried him. Specks of
grit adhered to the toecaps and he was reminded of his least
favourite sweetmeat, a small plug of liquorice dusted with red,
white and blue beads. It was like eating a regimental brooch, he
thought. Disgusting.

He watched one foot lead the other forward and marvelled at
their confidence. There was no hesitation. His feet knew the way.
He enjoyed the sensation of walking, of being transported. Distantly
(in his mind's eye he saw a tower whose top storey dwindled into the
clouds) his head ached. He did not know why he could not remember. The sunlight hurt his eyes, but he was aware how it picked out
colours in the grass. There were snowdrops under the hedge and
dabs of yellow where the coltsfoot was in flower. He spoke the
names as if he was reading them from seed packets. They came from
far away; relics from another country, another time.

A car was parked at the end of the path, but there was no sign of
the driver. Ryman hesitated. He had seen the car before and the
recollection – vague though it was – troubled him. He walked on to
meet his reflection in the hub cap. His feet were enormous and his
body tapered away like the tower he had thought of earlier. He bent
his head to the open window and smelled leather and wool carpeting.
Someone laughed, and he ducked down and backed away to the
ditch by the perimeter wall. He flattened himself to the ground and
eased himself into the depression. Water struck coldly through his
trousers and a thorn lanced into his knee, but he made no sound.

A man in a grey uniform came out of the arena carrying a wicker
basket. 'She's all set then,' he said. 'Communing with the spirits.'

'When do the rest of them get here?' There were two others, Ryman saw, dressed in blue with peaked caps.

'About an hour I reckon. When they've got a skinful.'

'Bloody coach party,' said one of the men in blue.

'Bloody M.P.s,' said the other. He lit a cigarette and through the fringe of grass that bearded the ditch Ryman saw the smoke swirl away, expanding and dissolving in the sunlight. He dug his chin into the bank and breathed the scent of wet earth. His fingers were sheathed in mud and he licked them clean.

'Time for a jar?' said the man in grey.

'We're supposed to stay here.'

'She'll be all right. All she cares about's that monkey.'

'Ten minutes then.'

'Right you are, there and back.'

Ryman heard the car doors open and close. The engine roared and exhaust fumes snorted across the turf. He kept his head down as the tyres crunched over the cinders and raised it to see the number plate vanish round the corner. The wind blew gently through a clump of nettles growing beside him and closer to the track the coltsfoot tugged at its leathery mooring. There was no other sound. Nothing moved except the grass and the clouds. He clambered out of the ditch and pulled the thorn from his knee. His shoes were soaked an all-over black that disguised the stains on the toecaps and he smiled his satisfaction. The grit that sugared them had been washed away and when he moved water squelched over the uppers.

It was not important, he thought. Wet or dry, his feet knew the way. He followed them to the gate of the arena and turned the handle. The gate swung open and he stepped inside. Carefully he closed the gate behind him and rested for several seconds as waves of pain fluttered behind his eyes. He blinked hard to dispel them and saw a woman sitting in front of the cage with her back to him. She was talking to Otto, but her voice was low and insistent, and he could not distinguish the words.

Ryman stepped forward and Otto saw him. He flung himself against the bars, hooting loudly. Beneath the overhang of his forehead his eyes gleamed and he stamped on the floor of his cage. The woman turned round, her face tight with anger. 'What are you doing here?' she demanded. 'This is private property.'

Ryman shook his head. 'I belong here.'

'Don't be absurd.' She looked at him more closely. 'I know who you are. I dismissed you.'

Ryman shook his head again. The words may once have had meaning but now they were irrelevant. 'I came to see Otto,' he said.

She stood in front of him, clutching her handbag, her breast bumping his belly like the fender on a boat. 'I forbid it,' she said, 'go away.'

Ryman pushed her aside and touched the bars of the cage. The ape grunted nervously, but did not move. 'Hello, Otto,' he said. It was difficult to remember why he had come. It was like arriving at a conference only to find he had forgotten the subject he had to discuss. He felt embarrassed.

'He's wicked,' said Mrs Deeley. 'You're both wicked.'

'Not wicked,' he said, remembering. That had been the start of it, the first madness. All the pain had proceeded from that point. He could not go back. He was too weary even to explain and there was no one who would understand.

The ape watched him intently, tweaking the hairs on his upper lip. He scratched his right ear, frayed at the top, and Ryman was aware of their matching shabbiness. With a sudden cruel lucidity he thought of Charlotte and the accident and his dismissal, and the ways in which he had tried to get back at them and the awful aching futility of it all. When he stared through the bars it was like looking into a mirror. 'You and me,' he said. 'Bloody animals.' He found the handling tool and pulled back the top bolt on the cage door.

'What are you doing?' demanded Mrs Deeley.

He slipped the bottom bolt and jerked the door open. 'Ask Otto,' he said.

There were no speeches at the end of the lunch; Lacey-Jones saw to that. 'You lose goodwill if people go on gassing,' he told Mark. 'Get them up and away before the brandy evaporates.'

Several photographers were still present and while the light held it was important to let them dispose of any outdoor shots. 'I thought we might start with Otto,' he suggested.

Francis Hoover pushed his glasses up to the bridge of his nose. 'If you think so,' he said. 'Let us proceed.'

Lacey-Jones followed him to the door. 'There's still no sign of Mrs Hoover.'

'So I've noticed.'

'Shall I get someone to look for her?'

Hoover shook his curly head. 'No need for that.' He offered his snuff box to Afton. 'Reduce the tax on this stuff,' he said. 'You'd cut your hospital bills in no time.'

'I doubt it,' said Afton, smiling fiercely. The moment was approaching, he thought, when he would have to assume control of the operation. He had, after all, engineered it, and while he had no objection to Proto making capital of the occasion he had assigned the star role to himself. 'About these allegations of cruelty . . . ' he said, and noted with satisfaction, an all-round ripple of interest.

'Absurd,' said Hoover, 'as you will see.'

Afton made soothing noises and ignored the slither of notebooks as they descended the stairs. 'It's a matter of public confidence,' he said. 'I'm sure you appreciate that it's your job to allay any fears.'

'Certainly I do.'

' . . . and that I and these gentlemen are here to report what we see with complete impartiality.'

'That's why we invited you.'

Afton paused on the bottom step. 'I thought, perhaps, that we should remind ourselves of the fact. No more.' He saw several reporters making notes and walked on. Years ago he had learned that while there was a scant profit in merely stating the obvious there were surprising benefits to be gained by repeating it firmly and often. Everyone liked to be reminded of what he already knew.

'The cars are waiting,' said Lacey-Jones, steering them past the statue of St Francis. He was not put out by Afton's performance, but he thought it advisable to lead his flock on to the next attraction without delay. One sensation cancelled out another.

They drove in convoy towards the arena with Lacey-Jones and Mark leading the column, the Rolls following closely behind and the press cars bringing up the rear.

Charlotte was offered a lift by the BBC presenter. 'Are you interested in animals?' she enquired as they passed the main offices.

He glanced at the gates embossed with Proto puppies. 'Not especially. I quite like birds.'

'Wild birds?'

'Eating birds.' He flicked open the dashboard and showed her an air pistol. 'I shoot them when I'm driving. Pheasants, that is.'

'In season, you mean.'

'When I see them, I mean.' He sounded his horn as the Proto dogs trooped across the road. 'Where do they come from?'

'Here and there.'

He blew his horn again. 'They're a menace.'

The car in front of them slowed down and stopped. 'What's happening?' he asked.

Charlotte wound down the window and looked out. 'I can't see.'

'Are we nearly there?'

'Not yet.'

They had reached the foot of the hill leading to the executive hamlet and half-way down it a woman was running towards them. Her coat streamed behind her, her mouth was open and scraps of what she was shouting winged over them like birds flying madly from a forest fire. She fell down, rolled over several times and crawled back on to her feet. One shoe was left behind, its heel skewered into the turf and she kicked off the other to preserve her balance.

The presenter leaned across to Charlotte's window and watched her progress. 'My word,' he said, 'she's in a hurry.'

She ran on, tripped and pitched forward on to her hands and knees. The car engines were switched off, one after the other and Charlotte heard her screams, torn by the wind that raked her bright hair.

The presenter packed his air pistol away. 'I thought it was all going too smoothly,' he said.

When Biddy's train left her at the local station she phoned Linda. There was no reply and when she rang Mark's number the girl on the switchboard reminded her of the press conference.

'They're all at it. Till late afternoon, they said.'

'I see.'

She had not forgotten, not exactly. But she had hoped that Mark would have made provision. The next bus was in an hour's time, too long to wait with James already grizzling.

She waved at the solitary taxi on the rank and scrambled into the back. 'Would you take us to Proto, please?'

He whistled through his teeth. 'It'll cost you a bit.'

'How much?'

'Couple of quid. It's there and back, you see. I'm not likely to pick up a fare out there, am I?'

'All right,' she said.

It was too expensive, more than she could afford. But it was worth it to get home quickly. That morning her mother had stood by the open bedroom door and watched her pack her suitcase. With her back turned, Biddy was still aware of her scrutiny and she could smell the cologne sprinkled on the handkerchief peeping from the sleeve of her cardigan.

'I thought I should be seeing more of you,' said Mrs Antrobus.

'Next time, I promise. I really have to get back.'

A faint sigh. 'I don't see why it should be so much of a rush.'

'I simply felt I should be there.'

'So suddenly?'

Biddy turned to face her. 'Very suddenly.' She could not explain in any more detail. The revelation had come in Regents Park, the moment she had called herself a faithful wife. Faithful to what? she thought. To a concept, or to a person? 'I think he needs me there,' she told her mother.

'A bit late in the day to find out.'

'I hope not.'

She glanced through the taxi window. A red tractor crawled across a ploughed field followed by a train of gulls. The air was soapy, blue like washing-up water. Telegraph poles were bleached on one side, black on the other.

'They've had some rain,' said the driver.

'I can see that.'

She zipped up James's siren suit, and adjusted the hood. 'Home soon,' she said. The taxi drew up outside the gate and she paid the driver.

'Do you want a hand with the case?'

She shook her head. 'I'll manage, thank you.'

The taxi drove away as she walked up the path. The front door was ajar and she pushed it open with her shoulder. 'Linda,' she called. 'I'm back.'

The house was cold and there was mud on the hall floor. Scuff marks led to the living room and she hesitated before going in.

'Linda,' she said, uncertainly. Upstairs she heard Baby cry and she peered through the banisters. 'Are you there?' she called.

There was no reply and she stared at the muddy spoor on the hall floor. It looked as though something, or someone had been dragged or had stumbled repeatedly, their toes stubbing against the polished tiles. She felt panic mount rapidly, like an icy tide, cramping her legs and freezing her stomach. James struggled in her arms and she clasped him tightly, guarding the spark between them. 'Linda,' she said again. 'Linda, where are you?' Above her head Baby grizzled a small fretful protest. A normal sound, she thought; distress was normal. She moved cautiously, walking on the balls of her feet. It was important not to make a noise. James squirmed against her chest, but she did not dare to put him down. She needed something to hold. As a child she had exorcized the dark by spelling prayers into the scruff of a toy Scottie. James was her talisman now. She hoisted him on to her hip and breathed through his hair. 'Be a good boy,' she said. 'Be a good, good boy.' No sound came from the living room. She turned the handle of the door and eased it open to reveal a black fireplace, a tea tray and a magazine on the hearth rug. The cover girl wore a white swimsuit, flecked with dark red. The printing was peculiar, thought Biddy; some of the colour had sprayed across the girl's face. She pushed the door fully open and saw a foot wearing one of her own black silk slippers. She whimpered far back in her throat. 'Oh, God!' she said. There was blood on the carpet, most of it coming from the head of a woman lying against the wall. She was naked and turned on to her side and the extraordinary thing, thought Biddy, was that she recognized not her face but her breasts from a day long ago in the Community Centre showers. 'I'm not trying to inflame you,' Louise had said. Recalling the incident was like remembering ancient history, an isolated act, an incident from a saga which she could no longer explain or put into context. Linda was lying several feet away. Her breath stirred a scrap of wool gummed to her lip, but Biddy could not touch her. She backed out of the room and closed the door. She had been right to be afraid, she thought. She had been right and Mark had been wrong. Chaos had come and she had not escaped it.

Baby cried out again and she looked sharply up at the landing. There was no sanctuary, no place of safety. She had to get outside, away from the blood and into the air. Her legs moved automatically and as she crossed the road she felt them move faster. James tugged at her hair and she jerked her head to one side. 'Stop it,' she said. He was holding her back, endangering them both. She thought of drowning men pulling down life rafts, their hands severed for the common good. 'Let go,' she screamed, 'let go of me.' His fingers clung on desperately, reining her like a horse. She pulled them loose and held him at arm's length, his feet drumming against her chest, snot icing his lips and chin. He was suddenly hateful; not the assassin, but his accomplice. She thought of his birth, the blood and the pain. It was not his fault, she told herself. He was not to blame, but to save herself she had to break loose.

She sat him firmly on the grass, crimson-faced and voiceless, gagged by his rage. No one was following her, she thought. No one was in sight. She put her finger to her lips. 'Be good,' she said. He drew breath and roared his protest. 'No,' said Biddy, 'you mustn't.'

He bellowed again, clenching his fists, raising them slowly to shoulder height as though he was winching up the sound from the pit of his belly. She clapped her hand over his mouth. 'You don't understand,' she said, 'he'll hear us. He'll come after us.' James launched himself forward and she gripped his head – front and back – between her hands, holding him like a salmon while his arms and legs flailed the earth. She saw his face turning dark. 'Be still,' she whispered, 'just be still.' He kicked convulsively and then subsided. She took away her hand from his mouth and propped him against her chest. His eyes were closed, and his head drooped down as though he was asleep. She shook him gently. 'James,' she said. 'Wake up, James.'

Below her on the road leading from the centre she saw a convoy of cars. Sunlight bounced from their bonnets and on one radiator a flag fluttered. She waved at them, but they gave no indication of having seen her. She stretched James out on the grass and pressed one ear to the front of his blue siren suit. Through layers of wool his heart beat sturdily. She tore off her scarf and waved, but still the cars did not stop. She ran towards them, aware that she was shouting, ignorant of the words that tumbled from her lips. When she fell down she picked herself up. The ground shelved steeply away beneath her feet, and as she raced on she felt airborne. The cars stopped and people got out of them. She saw Mark, his arms outstretched, coming to meet her. Something had happened to time, she thought. It was as if she had been smoking grass (in America they kept a bag of Acapulco Gold in a coffee can) and every action, every process was dreamlike and extended. The movie cameras were running at high speed and already she knew the sequence by heart. Death could be beautiful in slow, slow motion. But it was not like that at all. She stopped short of his hands and brushed the hair from her face. 'I was right,' she said. 'I knew he'd come back.'

TWENTY-TWO

Ryman heard the cars when they were half a mile away. They sounded like animals, he thought; their horns yelping like a hunting pack hot on the scent. 'They're coming,' he said and Mrs Deeley bobbed her head in reply.

She sat plumply on her picnic chair, hands folded in her lap, her feet resting side by side. He was irritated by her neatness, her immobility. Something, he felt, should have been resolved by now, but the situation had not changed since he had slipped the bolt on Otto's cage. The ape squatted in the open doorway. An early bumblebee droned across the arena. He felt a dwindling of purpose, a slow leak of energy.

'It's you they're looking for,' she said. 'You've done terrible things.'

'We've all done terrible things.'

He did not want to talk about what he had done. It was too confusing to remember all that had happened. His head ached. He was doing no good where he was. He wished he had not come. But there had been a reason, he told himself, and being unable to put his finger on it was worrying because time was running out.

He took one step towards the cage door and Otto raised his head, and bared his gums. His eyes kindled, and he hooted softly. 'He remembers me,' said Ryman.

'He remembers everyone.'

'Not everyone,' he said. 'But we had an understanding.'

'Did you really?' Her voice was sceptical. 'Based on what, may I ask?'

He frowned and tried to answer precisely. 'Fear,' he said at last. 'Otto was afraid of me.'

'But he attacked you.'

'That makes no difference,' said Ryman. 'The basis of the under-standing is unaltered.' The last word came out broken-backed, but he found it hard to enunciate clearly. The syllables were too big for

8

his mouth. Tacking together vowels and consonants was like building a bridge over rough water. He felt the current pick it apart, but he persevered. If he could say the right thing, the necessary thing, the pattern would be complete, the circle joined. He could make it happen and then he could stop worrying.

Otto clambered down from the cage on to the floor of the arena and Ryman watched him settle on his haunches. It was just as he had said; Otto had been afraid of him. But, at the same time, he had been afraid of Otto. He had protected himself with the snake and the electric prod and they had proved inadequate. And what had it been for? Clumsily he turned to face Mrs Deeley. 'What was the point of it all?' he demanded.

'You know what the point was.'

'I've forgotten.'

'You were getting him to talk.'

'Talk about what?'

'About my husband. Otto killed him. I want to know why.'

Ryman shook his head – carefully, so as not to awake the pain. 'He can't tell you.'

'Can't tell or won't.'

'He can't tell you. He doesn't know.'

Mrs Deeley moistened her lips. 'How can you be certain?'

'Jesus Christ,' said Ryman as his legs buckled. He leaned against the bars of the cage, trying to frame an explanation. It was too late, the current was too strong. He saw the rivets pull loose, and the timbers fall away. Soon they were swept out of sight. He was not sorry to see them go. 'Otto and me,' he said. 'No earthly reason.'

Cinders popped distantly as the fleet of cars drew up outside the arena. Two men with rifles edged through the gate and raised the guns to their shoulders. He heard the snap of their safety catches and knew, as if his mind had been rinsed clear, what he had left to say. Nothing else remained. It was such a simple thing, he thought, but it was why he was there. He had forgotten it for too long. He could not let it slip his memory again.

He heaved himself away from the cage and walked towards Otto. The shaggy arms spread like wings and folded at the base of his skull. The pain flared up, but he forced himself to speak quietly. What he had to say was in confidence, it concerned no one else. The smell of dusty fur was in his nostrils, and level with his eyes he saw flakes of dead skin like fish scales. His breath blew a furrow in the fur. 'I'm sorry,' said Ryman as Otto broke his neck.

It was a nightmare thought Lacey-Jones as he reviewed the situation. Within the arena lay one dead man and one unconscious woman; his employer, no less. Louise Hoover was horribly dead and Hoover himself was in a state of shock. He had seen his wife's body in the spattered room, but he had refused to accompany it to the hospital. Charlotte Bloom had helped him into the Rolls, and he sat there now, sipping brandy from Lacey-Jones's own hip flask. Mark Barrow was holding Biddy's hand in one of the press cars, and the press – whose numbers seemed to multiply each time he dared to look in their direction – were massed outside the arena within whose walls Otto roamed free. It was a prescription for total disaster. But was it complete? Was there another ingredient – however small, however grisly – which he had overlooked?

Guy Afton's voice assured him that there was. 'I must say,' he told a group of reporters. 'I find the security arrangements quite inadequate. As you were. Not inadequate. Appalling.'

Lacey-Jones groaned. Afton was rising to the occasion in his own bastardly way. It was not the moment to engage him in debate, and – in any case – he was not the man to do it. Among the huddle of cars he saw film units unpacking their cameras. There was no stopping them, he thought. With lightweight equipment they could go anywhere, shoot anything.

'One tiny request,' he murmured. 'Don't let Afton hog it all.'

'Can we film the ape?'

'We can't let you inside the arena, I'm afraid.'

'Then Afton's the best we've got.'

'Be reasonable,' Lacey-Jones begged. 'Give me a moment. I'll see what I can arrange.'

He brushed past Alec Bell who smiled sadly. 'Whatever you may have thought, I was not crying wolf,' he said. 'There's a poor dead man in there to prove it.'

'Indeed there is,' said Lacey-Jones. 'And who's to blame for the poor dead woman?'

'Mrs Hoover was not my responsibility.'

'I'll remember you said so.'

If nothing else, he thought, the day was giving him an insight into the nature of calamity. Rapidly he was becoming possessed by a fatal calm. There was nothing he could do. He was being forced into the role of an interested spectator. When the Titanic went down, he recalled, the ship's orchestra played until the waters closed over their heads. It was gallant, but it was also intensely practical. The chances were that they had felt useful to the end. Music had been their business and their last distraction.

He glanced hesitantly into the Rolls, but all he could see of Dr Hoover was the back of his head. He lit a cigarette and examined his cufflinks. Afton was still holding forth, but he was too far away to hear. The BBC presenter appeared at his elbow and he summoned a smile. 'A bit of a shambles,' he said.

'In a word, yes.'

'Who's being hammered now?'

'He's past all that. We're on to instant action.'

'For example?'

'He wants to shoot Otto.'

The nearside window of the Rolls was half open and through it Lacey-Jones saw Dr Hoover jerk to attention. He raised his voice slightly. 'That ape belongs to Proto,' he said. 'They have to get someone's O.K. before they put it down.'

'They've got someone. Dr Bell, I think it is.'

'I don't believe it.' Lacey-Jones leaned towards the open window. 'You mean Alec Bell wants to shoot Otto?'

'Any minute now.'

The door of the Rolls swung open and a tall, tweed-suited figure strode between them. Lacey-Jones wagged a finger beneath the presenter's nose. 'Now look what you've done,' he said.

It was not his finest hour, Guy Afton conceded, but it was his most productive in many a lean year. Notebooks fluttered all around him. Cameras cruised about his face like satellites skimming the contours of the moon. A stick microphone reared in front of him and he aimed into it, delivering short bursts of sincerity in rapid fire.

'Gentlemen,' he said, 'I came here to investigate certain allegations of cruelty against animals in this establishment. I have been unable to ascertain whether or not they were true because of far more grievous happenings. Two people died here today. We must act promptly before tragedy strikes again.'

Ballpoints dipped and he saw his words become the flesh of instant news. Somewhere, he thought, there was an apposite quotation but it was hardly the moment to consult his *Garland of Verse*. Almost certainly there was something in Shakespeare. He resolved to set aside fifteen minutes reading time a day to prepare himself for any future emergency.

A hand poked above the crowd. 'Mrs Deeley has not been harmed?'

'Not so far.'

'She seems to be unconscious.'

'So it appears.'

'Is there any reason to suppose that she is in immediate danger?'

'A dead man is sufficient reason.'

It was better than electioneering, he thought. There were no questions of policy to be examined or justified. A slogan was sufficient answer. Not for the first time he envied the military. No one expected them to temporize or make excuses. Unbidden, the quotation he had sought came to mind: 'Bid the soldiers shoot'. The words were nearly right, thought Afton; but it was the wrong audience.

Another hand shot up. 'Has Dr Hoover been consulted?'

'I'm sure you know of Dr Hoover's circumstances. He can hardly be expected to make decisions at this time.

'What does Dr Bell think?'

'Dr Bell agrees with me that the animal should be destroyed.'

In fact, it had been Bell's idea. He had voiced it almost deferentially, but fully aware of what it entailed. It signified that power had changed hands; by default, but effectively. The king was not quite dead, Afton reminded himself, but after today he was bound to abdicate. That was not his concern. His alliance with Bell was short-term, but its yield in publicity was immense.

He signalled to the guards with rifles. 'Are you ready there?'

'Ready, sir.'

'Then do your duty.'

He saw the cameras pan from his profile to the arena gate and without haste followed them. From now on the television coverage was predictable: hand-held shots of the execution (he persisted in thinking in military terms), close-ups of the dead ape and Mrs Deeley, official pronouncements by himself and Bell. He was not certain, however, what footage would be given to Ryman in the edited film. Five seconds, perhaps, but no more. It was a curious anomaly, he thought. For years the screen had been glutted with corpses from foreign wars, but a single home-killed civilian was still taboo at peak viewing time.

He was aware of a disturbance behind him, but before he could turn a hand gripped the collar of his coat and tossed him to one side. His knees ploughed a double furrow in the cinder track and he yelped with pain. He stared skyward through his tears and saw a head crowned with corkscrew curls looming over him.

'You will leave my animals alone,' said Francis Hoover.

Afton did not dare move. He heard cameras click to his right and to his left, and he knew that once again he had been deceived by frailty. He picked gravel from his palms and breathed a silent prayer: God rot all Grand Old Men.

Through the windscreen of the car Mark saw Dr Hoover march towards the arena. Charlotte beckoned to him and he squeezed Biddy's hand. 'I'm sorry, love. They need me.'

'I need you here.'

'I have to go,' he said. 'I'll get someone to come and sit with you.' He kissed her forehead and then her lips. 'Are you warm enough? You feel like ice.'

'I don't feel anything.' She huddled back in the corner of the car and put her arms around James. 'I came back to be with you,' she said. 'I made a mistake.'

'No, you didn't.'

She bit her lip and nodded violently. 'I nearly killed James.'

'Nonsense,' he said.

'You weren't there. You don't know what happened.'

Charlotte waved again and he spread his hands. 'I must go. I won't be long.' She turned her face away as he backed out of the car and tried to shut the door without slamming it. In the circumstances there was something indecent in making a noise. It was one more cause for complaint, something else for which he would have to take the blame.

'How is she?' asked Charlotte.

'Bloody awful. She thinks it's all my fault.'

'She's had a bad time.'

'So have I,' he said. 'So have you. We've all had a bad time.' He turned down his coat collar and tried to compose himself. 'I see that our leader is on his feet again.'

'They wanted to shoot Otto.'

'I don't blame them,' said Mark. 'Who needs a homicidal ape?'

'It's Afton and Bell who want to shoot him.'

'That's different,' he said.

It was an odd thing about loyalty, he thought. Hoover had brought it up on the day of their first meeting. To a large extent its direction and its strength were determined by the going alternatives. There were no absolutes. Sometimes the choice was between evils or idiocies. One chose for survival, or pity, or continuity, or out of habit. He was following Hoover through the blustery spring afternoon not because he believed he was acting logically but because he was conditioned to do so. To act otherwise was, quite literally, unthinkable. And what of Biddy? Why had she returned?

He saw David Dempsey on the fringe of the crowd. 'Do me a favour,' he said.

'Let me guess.'

'Keep an eye on Biddy for a while.'

'It's not me she wants to hold her hand.'

'Just for five minutes,' said Mark. 'I've got to see what the old man's up to.'

Dempsey took a handful of Proto tablets from his coat pocket and spilled them among the cinders. 'All they do is make crumbs,' he said. 'It drives Peg round the bend.' He dusted his palms together and looked Mark up and down. 'All right,' he said finally, 'but from now on you do your own housekeeping.' They saw Hoover barge into Guy Afton and Dempsey waved him on. 'You'd better hurry,' he said. 'You're missing the action.'

'I'm very grateful,' said Mark.

'I doubt it.'

Over Dempsey's shoulder he saw the blue overalls of girls from the factory, all of them running towards the arena. The word had got around. It was turning into a spectacle, a circus in the old sense with one guaranteed wild animal who had made his kill and would possibly kill again. There were reporters to witness the ceremony, and television cameras (an advance on Rome, he thought). Even the weather was propitious. High winds had swept the clouds to the horizon and sunlight was warm on his face.

Charlotte tugged his sleeve. 'He's waiting for us.'

The crowd had fallen back and Dr Hoover stood facing them. He raised his right arm in what was either a summons or a salute, and Mark felt an extraordinary sense of occasion. The gladiator was ready.

'I will not have firearms pointed in my direction,' said Dr Hoover. 'If you insist on clutching them, do so on this side of the wall. The fewer people who come into the arena the better. I do not wish the ape to be made more nervous than he already is.'

He motioned to Mark and Charlotte. 'You will follow me at thirty paces. If and when Otto is in his cage, Dr Barrow will secure the door and Dr Bloom will attend to Mrs Deeley. Do I make myself clear?'

'Perfectly.'

'Very well. Then open the gate.'

He listened critically to his own voice, pleased to note that it was perfectly level. They were all watching him except for Afton who was scurrying back to the Rolls with Lacey-Jones in attendance. He was a contemptible man, thought Dr Hoover, but it was Afton he had to thank for his revitalization. More than that; his resurrection.

From the moment that he had been shown his wife's body he felt himself imprisoned by shock. It was as though he had turned a corner and stepped into an egg of clear plastic in which he floated, his arms and legs stirring feebly, powerless to break the shell or communicate with the outside world. He had allowed them to lead him to the car. Perhaps, he thought with some irritation, they had carried him. Sitting with Charlotte he had sipped Lacey-Jones's brandy, tasting nothing, unable to tell them that it was not grief that pinioned him. He was in suspension, watching his feelings drift by, trying to identify currents and sensations. He knew that a process was going on. It was like reaching the moment in a programme of research when a thousand separate observations flowed together to form a concept which still had to be formalized. He had tried to grapple with it, to lock it into place. But he was in a vacuum. He had no leverage.

The window of the car had been open, he recalled, and he had heard Lacey-Jones and the presenter talking outside. One sentence had come through loud and clear; 'He wants to kill Otto', and he had felt the shell splinter and part. The fluids had gushed out and he was free. He was on fire. His territory was being invaded, and he had to deal with the trespasser.

He had done that, he thought, and now there was more work to be done. Mrs Deeley lay concertinaed on the ground by her picnic chair. Her hat was tipped over her eyes and her chin bulged like a doughnut on to her chest. Ryman lay to her right, his head twisted at an acute angle, his legs folded beneath him. The chances were, thought Hoover, that when his body was removed from the arena it would be transferred to the hospital. Perhaps, for a while it would share the same room as Louise. No one would tell him that, good taste would prevail. But space was restricted. 'Needs must' was one of the matron's favourite sayings.

It would not trouble him. He did not mourn Louise. He regretted the manner of her death, but as the blanket had been drawn up over her face he had felt a quittance, a sense of release. The concept which had teased him minutes earlier took shape. He had a sudden memory of troops returning from Africa, their khaki bleached by sun: time-expired men. The description fitted him exactly. He fought the impulse to smile, holding his jaw rigid until the muscles ached. But restraint was difficult when he longed to laugh out loud.

He was not bereaved, he was liberated. He squatted down, wincing as one of his calf muscles twanged, and softly hooted a greeting. Otto looked up. His nostrils flared and his upper lip wrinkled like tissue. He was looking well, thought Hoover. There was dust on his pelt, but beneath it the hair was glossy and thick. He hooted again and Otto studied him carefully. For a moment he glanced towards the gate and Hoover knew that Mark or Charlotte had moved. Slowly he waved them back. For the time being he had no need of them. He put his weight on his knuckles and poled himself forward, a foot at a time. A yard closer to Otto he stopped and rested. He had no need, no inclination to hurry. He was enjoying the afternoon.

He felt refreshed, physically and mentally. Touching his lower belly his fingers met whole flesh. The wound his mind had made was gone. He shut his eyes and saw it contracting like an iris, sealing itself and leaving no scar. It was a time of healing and restitution. Afton had been a trespasser and he had been routed.

Otto would appreciate that, thought Hoover. Solitaries had to protect their rights, they had little else to sustain them. It was something which Louise had appeared to understand, but the way they had lived, separately in the same house, had been an artificial division of territory. She had fixed the boundaries to suit herself. She had placed herself out of reach and he would not miss her now. He was eager to be gone. His business here was almost concluded.

Cramp tweaked the undersides of his thighs, but it was a minor discomfort. He heard the scuff of skin on cement and saw Otto straining towards him, angled like the figurehead on a sailing ship. He extended the back of his hand but Otto ignored it and he let it drop. His lips, Hoover noted, were drawn back but the canines were not fully exposed. So far, the threat was minimal. He put out his hand again and Otto slapped it, firmly but not hard.

Mrs Deeley sighed like a sleeper struggling out of a bad dream. Her eyelids fluttered and flicked open. 'Keep still,' said Hoover. 'Stay where you are.'

He hooted reassuringly to Otto and poled himself forward until their faces were almost touching. He felt no fear. He was certain the day would not end badly. He was with his own kind and they had an understanding that was beyond words. He was returning to first principles – before Proto, before Contact – and he would not make the mistakes that Ryman had made. He would not trespass like Afton, or impose restrictions like Louise. He would behave correctly, with proper respect, and he would be given safe conduct.

Otto's hand reached out and with infinite care stripped the glasses from his nose.

Hoover counted to five, then put out his own hand and scratched Otto under his right arm. The ape grunted and pressed against his fingers. He stretched forward and rummaged in Hoover's hair.

Ten yards back, Mark and Charlotte watched the grooming continue. After a while Hoover rose slowly to his feet. His knees remained bent, his head and shoulders drooped as though he carried a heavy weight. 'Submissive posture,' thought Mark and instantly erased the caption from his mind. Hoover had abandoned the textbook; he was doing what came naturally. Once he had walked from a forest in the Cameroons leading a gorilla by the hand and now he was reliving the legend.

The ape and the man shuffled towards the open cage, leaning

against each other like lovers, their hands clasped, their postures identical. Otto clambered up on to the platform and as he was about to follow him Hoover turned and smiled. 'There's no need to wait,' he said. 'I may be some little time. We have the future to plan.'

TWENTY-THREE

Mark and Biddy drove back from Southampton in their new
vintage Rover. It had been given to them a week previously by Dr
Hoover the day he had resigned as Director of Contact. 'I won't
be needing it any more,' he said, 'but I thought you might drive
me to the boat.'

'Which boat?' asked Mark.

'The one that's taking me to Lagos. With Otto.' He waited
hopefully, but there was no reaction. 'I'm taking Otto home,' he
said. 'Mrs Deeley has no more questions to ask him. She's letting
him go.'

'I'm glad.'

'I thought you might be. Mind you, I can't imagine how he'll
fit in out there.'

'Better than here,' said Mark. 'But what about you?'

Dr Hoover took out his snuff box and built two brown pyramids
on the back of his hand. 'The same thing applies. I'm expendable
now, better out of the way.' He sniffed fiercely and the snuff
vanished. 'What are you going to do?'

'God knows. They'll be winding this lot up any day now. Afton
will see to that. I'll find something I suppose.'

'I expect you will.' He watched Linda cross the lawn, a bowl of
napkins lodged on her hip. 'Is the girl all right?'

'It's a bit too soon to say. She thinks she's pregnant.'

The napkins cracked in the breeze. 'She's a pretty girl,' said
Dr Hoover. 'It's a good thing she's fond of children.' He blew his
nose and wiped it reflectively. 'I got you into all this, I'm afraid.
I'm exceedingly sorry.'

'Don't be absurd.'

'If there's anyone you'd like me to write to . . . '

'I'll be sure to let you know.'

But there was no one, thought Mark, as the car passed the
Social Centre. Hoover had asked him again before the ship had

sailed and he had tried desperately to think of a name, any name, to end the conversation. 'We may go back to America,' he said at last.

'Really? You'll let me know where you are . . . ?'

'When we've settled in.'

'And tell Dr Bloom to keep in touch.'

'I'll tell her.'

He would mention it when he wrote to her, he thought. If he wrote. He did not think Charlotte wanted him to write. She had refused his offer to come with her to the station. 'If you cast your mind back,' she said, 'we've already said our goodbyes.'

'A lot's happened since then.'

'Not to us.' In the back of her refrigerator she found half a bottle of vodka, and poured it into two glasses. 'Cheers then.'

'Cheers,' he said. 'Are you going back to your husband?'

'I shouldn't think so.'

'Will you come back here, to England I mean?'

'It isn't likely. Who needs another wandering Jew?'

He flinched and she patted his arm. 'It's all right,' she said. 'It's not as bad as all that.'

'Will it be any better with the tribe?'

'I shall have to find out.'

He drew his finger from the base of her throat to the beginning of her breasts, scoring the skin as if to release her body scent. Not even Lacey-Jones with his deodorants and toilet water had tamed it completely. She stepped back and set down her empty glass. 'I have to finish packing,' said Charlotte. 'Go on home.'

By now she was back in Johannesburg and he had his own arrangements to make. He would have to decide something soon. Already Mrs Antrobus was sending them lists from estate agents with red ink crosses against properties described as 'family dwellings'. Most of them, he noticed, had separate flats or rooms over garages where the benefactor could roost. Biddy had refused to discuss the subject. She had moved back to sleep with James and spoke to him grudgingly at breakfast and the evening meal.

He nudged her as they turned the corner. 'That's Malloy's house,' he said. 'The man who came with me on that lunatic patrol.'

'I remember.'

'He really had it in for this place. You'd have had that in common.'

She stared straight ahead, her lips turned to charcoal by the street lighting. 'It's not just the place.'

'I'm not so sure,' said Mark, 'it has a certain something.' He thought of Ryman's notes, the films of bloody surgery, the uniforms and the guard dogs, the smell of good works turned bad. 'Poor old Deeley,' he said. 'He never meant it to turn out like this.'

'How did you expect it to turn out?'

'Better than it did.'

'Is that all?'

'I thought we had a chance.'

She shivered and dug her hands into the pockets of her coat. 'A chance to do what?'

'Like the man said. To make contact, to communicate.'

'It's not enough,' said Biddy. 'It's not enough to know how to say something. What matters is what you say.'

He stopped the car on the brow of the hill. Below them the Proto offices shone like a bone. Smoke curled from the chimneys and nightlights burned on the warehouses and loading bays. 'Very profound,' he said. 'Profound and stupid.'

She shook her head. 'It's not stupid. Why should they want to talk to you? Why should they want to say anything at all?'

'Is there anything that you want to say?'

'Nothing that would help.'

He switched on the ignition and drove home. In the bedroom he watched Biddy undress and felt his heart turn over as she stroked the stretch marks on her thighs. 'They're fading,' he said. 'They'll be as good as new soon.'

'Never,' she said.

He pulled her gently to him and kissed her breasts, tracing the blue tributaries of her veins with his tongue, fitting his mouth over each nipple in turn. She did not try to prevent him, but she did not respond. He slid his hand beneath the elastic of her pants and squeezed her buttocks. 'Stay with me.'

'I can't.'

'Please stay,' he said.

'I'm sorry.'

He let her go and she pulled her nightdress over her head. He waited until she collected tissues, sleeping tablets and her own pillow, and then he opened the door to let her through.

'I'm going out for a while,' he said. 'I won't be long.'

The roads were empty and as he walked briskly towards the Contact block small clouds of his own breath followed him like puffs of fog. He unlocked the door of the laboratory wing and smelled the pine disinfectant that he had noticed on the first day. Blue fluorescent mushrooms shone at intervals down the walls of the corridor and in Rosie's room there was a nightlight above the sleeping platform. He lifted her up and cradled her in his arms. She opened her eyes and stared into his face. 'Papa,' she said. 'Papa.'